I0671798

Oneia

An original novel by Martin Wolfe
Cover illustration by
Martin Wolfe

Published by Martin Wolfe
Printed by Create Space, an Amazon.com Company
Create Space, Charleston SC

ISBN: 978-0-9937453-0-0

Martin Wolfe

Oneia

For Baby Elf Goddess

Martin Wolfe

Acknowledgements

My biggest thanks go to my amazing wife, Alice Leung, without whose support this novel would not exist. Thank you to my wonderful daughter, Oneia, for letting me use her name. My friend and fellow author, Wayne Arthurson, gets my thanks for encouraging me to finish. And thank you to all my friends and family who suffered through the painfully rough first draft.

Martin Wolfe

Chapter One

Prometheus: *Get this thing away from me!* [request ignored]

Static: *Please begin, my friend.*

Master: *Will do.*

Old Master

I arrived upside down and falling.

Static: *My friend, please include a brief preface explaining how and why we arrived.*

Master: *Oh, okay.*

I stood before six Hosts who wanted me caged forever, and one who plotted something less pleasant. They'd given me an ultimatum. Twelve centuries of self-therapy hadn't improved my opinion of being told what to do.

"Forget it, Cerberus!" I spoke the words, because Hosts are telepathic, and I was feeling obstinate. We were milling about on an unnamed dusty red moon. Above us, the three-quarter face of a bright green planet, also unnamed, floated in a nearly starless black sky. Depending on who was asked, the lifeless galaxy we were in had many names, but Milky Way wasn't one of them.

All seven Hosts had chosen bodies they thought would relax me, and thus, would inspire me to imprison myself. Only Cerberus looked human. The Host to his right, a hairy drooling ball with a toothy maw, could have swallowed me whole. It was one of the nightmarish creatures that Static,

7

mutating to my left, had mimicked while trying to look threatening. The subtleties of human interaction were lost on this group.

"You will allow yourselves to be relocated! Accommodations have been prepared!" Cerberus was confident that we would agree. His confidence was justified – I was outnumbered and had nowhere left to metaphorically run. Fighting would only make a mess. I toed some moon dust and wondered how much galaxy we'd destroy when I fought them anyway. Might as well go out with a bang.

A couple dozen kids of various ages suddenly appeared between us. Most of them started crying when they saw Static. He changed into a pink bunny rabbit, and they felt better.

"Cerberus, it was my understanding that the Host council does not permit the wanton destruction of human subjects." Static was as surprised as I was angry.

Cerberus offered a decent impression of a self-satisfied smile. *"It is the research facilities that are forbidden. We extracted these smaller vermin from interstellar vehicles. You deem them valuable?"*

I didn't bother hiding it. "Cerberus, I've decided I'm going to kill you." I clenched my jaw and kicked more dust.

"My friend, the Hosts are immortal, as you are aware. Please contact your assistant before we depart." Static knew as well as I did that Cerberus wouldn't have left their parents alive. I worked on my boot crater and thought of options.

"Cerberus, we do indeed find value in these juveniles. Please bide a moment while my companion seeks an alternate guardian." Static was telling me to hurry up. I love Static like a brother, or maybe a sister, but I find it irritating when people rush me while I'm busy procrastinating. I tried not to sound cranky with my response.

"Yeah fine." Okay, so maybe I didn't manage complete serenity. "Cerberus, I'll have to kill you later. If you let my butler take the kids, we'll go where you want."

"Agreed!" Again with the smile.

Just to feel better, I walked up to Cerberus and punched in his teeth. Surprisingly, he stayed in a physical body. His teeth spilled out in a bloody drool.

"Pain, a novel sensation – and useful. You do not wish it inflicted on these vermin, I am certain."

I hate Hosts. I walked back to my side of the standoff and plane-shifted Paul, my butler, to us. With a whoosh of displaced air, all two tons of him appeared in mid-terrifying lunge – he must have been hunting. The kids huddled together and wailed. I felt for them. Paul landed silently and assumed his butler mien, deceptively unfazed by the interruption.

"Paul, take care of these kids while we're gone. It could be a while."

"Master? You wish me to care for human cubs? Truly?"

"Yes. No choice. Check the library for references. Be very gentle. And most importantly…" I switched to telepathy due to mixed company, *"don't eat them!"*

He paused for just a second, bowed, and shifted away with some utterly terrified children. Only Paul would do this without argument. He'd never admit to being upset, but if I survived, he'd kill me later – several times.

"You ready, Static?"

"Certainly, my friend, you may proceed at your convenience." Static and I shifted to Oneia, a planet that was rumored to change Hosts into humans. Another rumor suggested that I'd be dead on arrival, which was likely Cerberus's favorite. But I decided the first rumor was the better bet, since dead Hosts can't spread rumors.

I arrived upside down and falling. Not yet dead. Thin clouds drifted below me. I'd envisioned appearing on the ground. Go figure.

I commanded my body to stop falling, but it didn't. That was the point of this place: I was human again – as good as dead to a Host. Gravity was relevant.

I called for backup. *"Hey, Static?"* No response. *"Static!"*

"I am here, my friend. Do not be alarmed." A tiny bird dove past. He must have changed in a rush because his yellow feathers were a very odd hue, almost fluorescent.

"Good. I need a lift. Power failure." I was probably the first Host to arrive who'd brought a shape-changing friend along for the ride. He could easily change into something that could carry me.

"I am sorry, my friend, but I am also experiencing difficulties and will be unable to assist you." Static's thoughts echoed frustration that he couldn't be helpful. He empathized more than usual.

I sighed as well as one can while being buffeted by freezing wind – hadn't felt cold in a long, long time. *"It's okay, Static. Don't worry about it."*

I plummeted through the clouds and toward a village on the outskirts of a walled city. I tried to steer myself toward a narrow river that ran between the huddled huts, but my trajectory didn't budge from straight down. Someone had chosen my landing site – a round building with a pointed roof. Sadly, the aliens that forced me here hadn't included a parachute.

It occurred to me then that Paul would probably keep dinner warm for us. The funniest things run through my head at the oddest times.

"Hey, Static, tell Paul not to wait with supper." I hate days like this.

"Perhaps, my friend, there may be something useful in your supplies."

Good thought. I flipped open a belt pouch that held twelve centuries worth of boyish amusements. Before I could request an item, a flea market of miscellaneous toys came blasting out of the opening: a few dozen broken wristwatches, a happy face mug, an arsenal of pointless weaponry, and so forth. Objects less aerodynamic than me caught the breeze and buffeted my legs on their way up. The streamlined stuff clogged the airspace around my head.

I looked around but didn't see anything that was going to stop me. Profanity seemed appropriate. Static didn't comment on my lack of decorum as the mystery building rushed up to greet my arrival. My last thought before I hit was that I probably wouldn't die on impact. Occasionally, it happens that I'm wrong. This wasn't one of those times.

When I could see again, my fractured self was buried under a mound of building materials that used to be a roof. Said materials were jammed into a medieval stone tube that, until I filled it with shingles, had been a storage bin for sand. Landing on the sand would have been nice. I was lying on my back across the broken rafters above it. My head dangled over an edge.

"Don't come in here, Static. This place is still falling apart."

"As you insist, my friend, I shall enter when the structure settles."

I was still alive because I'd designed my body to be durable, but now I suffered for it. I was used to suffering: I'd been mangled before, and Hosts can't override pain – nobody knows why. The only thing different was that I wouldn't be switching to a new body when I died. I wouldn't be coming back.

The sunlight filtering through the wreckage showed that some of my escaped possessions had followed me. That was almost funny. I hadn't seen most of this stuff for a long time. As I waited to die, I tried to remember what each was made to do.

Sticking out of a rafter, one of my swords mocked me. Ice, she was called, and she would have been the ideal thing to have if I were protecting myself from hordes of attackers. That wasn't what I needed. I panned my view past the junk. A metal armband wedged under some stones looked interesting, but I didn't remember making the thing, let alone what it did.

I let my head swivel back to center, and a glint of gold caught my eye. It was my ring, balanced daintily on a teetering section of shingles. I'd designed it to re-grow me in case my rubies didn't work – cliché, I know, but I was young when I made it. It probably wouldn't work any better than the pouch, but I didn't have a lot of options.

With much ado, I reached for it, but complications arose: My goal was not within arm's reach, and my left leg was impaled on a metal spike attached to a slab of wood. I strained to close the distance, but the grinding sounds from my leg made me shake. That upset the pile, and the shingles threatened to dump my ring into the sand below. I froze.

"Change of plans, Static. I need you to grab...." The mountain of rubble collapsed. Crap.

Violence tore the spike from my leg. I ignored the pain, except for the scream, and twisted to lunge for my ring. I didn't make it. The jagged end of a beam plowed through my chest. I hung as limp as a dead fish. My heart stopped.

But I refused to admit that I had a problem, not when my ring was in the sand just below my arms. I stretched to pick it up, realized that I couldn't reach the bloody thing, and succumbed to the reality of my problem. My thoughts were too muddled to share said problem with Static. The end.

Prometheus: *Finally! Now would you please tell this virus to get off my leg? I have important things to do!*

Master: *Relax, Prometheus. Donating a bit of time to your rescuers isn't going to kill you.*

Prometheus: *I have better things to do than sit about telling childish stories! Now, tell this virus to move! It's been holding me prisoner all day!*

Master: *Stop calling Static a virus. If it weren't for him, you'd still be stuck on Oneia. Besides, how can a mouse hold you prisoner?*

Static: [in mouse form] *I take no offence to such terminology, my friend. It is evidently an accurate assessment.*

Prometheus: *There, you see, the virus confessed! I insist that you tell it to move!*

Master: *Look, Prometheus, Static wants to record our stories. You can tell your parts on your own, or I can make them up for you. No doubt, everyone will want to know all about your love affair with Eldora.*

Prometheus: *My what? That's absurd! You wouldn't dare!* [Master raises eyebrow.] *Oh fine, let's just get this nonsense finished! I went with Tiberius to collect my misbehaving avatar! There, I'm done! Now shoo, get away from me!*

Static: *I would like these stories to be entertaining as well as historically informative, Prometheus. The content of your recitation is inadequate. You have made no mention of the priestess or the Eldorans, who are also key players. Please describe the events fully and in chronological order.*

Prometheus: *Oh, very well then, I suppose I can manage a few elaborations.*

Prometheus

Another of my avatars had finally arrived! I was beginning to think that I'd be stuck on the wretched planet forever!

Master: *I'm not an avatar.*

Prometheus: *You certainly are! Your genome is ninety-eight percent grafted from mine! That makes you my avatar!*

Master: *Nope. Not unless you can interrupt yourself.*

Prometheus: [glowers at Master]

My last AVATAR landed ages ago, not that it did me any good. The silly fool went and missed the sand pit I so kindly arranged for him, stupid avatars! He flattened himself on a big rock used by the peasants to dry seaweed. I could barely distinguish his body from the seaweed. The mess it made was absolutely revolting, I tell you!

I scooted into my study to collect my gilded copy of the *Great Book of Holy Prophecies*, which I used for ceremonial occasions. As I'm going on official record, I'll state quite clearly that only *Volume One* of the *Great Book* had any veracity at all. The other three volumes were a self-serving collection of peasant gibberish scrawled by mad men and endorsed by the imperial irritation herself, namely, the Divine Priestess. The Holy Prophet Tibbald wrote *Volume One* for the great god Prometheus; that would be me on both counts.

Armed with my hefty tome, I was off to get the priestess's permission to collect my avatar. It was gallingly beneath my stature to seek approval from anyone, let alone the priestess. Naturally, I could have done it without her permission, but she would have taken it personally and made my life miserable for weeks. So she would just have to be convinced through judicious use of prophecy. That was, after all, the very reason that I made the *Great Book of Holy Prophecies*. If a god tells you to do something, you have to do it! I say so!

I marched into the throne room and strode toward the priestess. She was draped over the ridiculous egg-shaped bed she called a throne and was having her nails done by one of her handmaids.

"Tibbald, it's so nice to see you! I was just telling Emaranth how much I appreciate the hard work of my priests. I hope you can stay awhile." She smiled and reclined deeper into her over-cushioned egg. As usual, she exuded waves of sensuality that were completely wasted on me, but the guards along the walls took notice.

"Priestess, I am here to announce the arrival of the holy catalyst. The much-anticipated sign from the great god Prometheus has come! The champion has at last arrived! As is written in the *Great Book of Holy Prophecies*, Section Six, paragraph two: 'He who is holiest will deliver an emissary unto his sacred people on Oneia, and they will welcome him.'"

With smug satisfaction, the Priestess smiled at my recitation, how rude! I was unable to ignore completely her childish thoughts, because the woman had never learned to guard them. Anyone with the telepathic sensitivity of a Pikkan wiffle could sense what she was thinking. I was startled to find that she was waiting to contradict me. She never contradicted prophecy; she almost always ignored it, but never contradicted. With an imperious wave, she dismissed my prophecies as trivial. Can you imagine the audacity?

"Tibbald, you should not concern yourself with such important matters, for they are obviously far beyond your limited knowledge as a mere prophet. The great god

Prometheus himself, my divine betrothed, explained to me only moments ago that the false catalyst among us must be destroyed immediately."

By the broken wings of fairy tales, now she was having hallucinations! This was an all-new disaster! I had to try something potentially risky to salvage my plans.

"Priestess, if you don't let me welcome the catalyst, the Eldorans will capture him!" There was nothing that would incite the ire of this woman more than the mention of her descendants. The servant woman, an Eldoran, nearly lost control of the nauseating telepathic chant she was transmitting to hide her true thoughts from the priestess.

These Eldorans were amateurs at deception. I wisely chose to maintain a mental façade of constant prophecy that encouraged the priestess to ignore my thoughts completely, because she couldn't understand them. Isn't that grand? The handmaid's chant lavished the priestess with compliments, which I found tedious, but I suppose the servant woman found necessary. The priestess did, after all, execute her descendants whenever she found them. The priestess was too busy glowering at me to notice the handmaid's slip – oh dear. Given her increased level of agitation, I thought it might be prudent to pay more attention to what she was thinking.

"How dare this insolent priest speak of those ungrateful, wretched children in my presence? How dare he hurt me so by reminding me of their hateful treachery?"

Her thoughts were occupied for a few moments with images of Eldorans bursting into flames and writhing in pain. Just so long as it wasn't me, I was fine with it, not that I had anything against Eldorans. In fact, anyone who suffered needlessly at the hands of this woman had my deepest sympathy.

The trembling handmaid made a terrible mess of the priestess's nails. She spread paint everywhere. I really couldn't blame her. If the priestess discovered her true identity, her death would be excruciating. I was particularly thankful at the moment that the handmaid was drawing attention away from me. The priestess noticed the paint on her fingers, and her former train of thought spilled from her head completely, a process that took very little time indeed.

"What are you doing, you stupid woman? Are you trying to make me ugly? Get away from me this instant! I will deal with your sloppiness later!" The servant woman gathered her things and left in a panic, while the Priestess inwardly lamented the supposedly unfair treatment she received from her subjects. She paused in her silent rant and turned her violent attention back to me.

"Let the Eldorans try to steal the false catalyst if they wish! Let them try to steal a useless corpse! The holy assassin will slaughter them all! It will be a just end to their evil ways!"

Well, that was it then; she had taken the final steps to becoming a complete, raving lunatic. She was babbling about divine visions and holy assassins, of all things. I most certainly did not send any visions instructing this woman to destroy my only way off the planet! The next time I designed a prison, I was going to make certain that the power source wasn't prone to mental instability!

"Perhaps you should get some rest, Priestess, while I attend to the needs of the...." She was instantly furious, and it was too late to save my dignity. She blasted me backward with searing waves of pain, and I rolled end over end down the shallow stairs that led away from the throne. By the ribbons in her overdone curls, may she fall on her own hairpins, I tell you!

"I am not fatigued, Prophet! My fiancé doesn't always have to send his visions through inferiors like you! He came to me directly in a holy vision and told me that the catalyst is false! He said that a holy assassin would destroy the infidel!"

The wretched woman continued to torture me where I lay on the floor. Then she stopped as suddenly as she'd started and, bursting out in tears, bawled like an abandoned child.

Abject misery flooded the throne room. Despite her violent attack, I began to feel pity for the woman. Oh bother, I had to buy some time to think; her abrupt shifts in emotion were fraying my nerves. While using my rod of office to heal my bruises, I valiantly tried to sound compassionate in my response, even though the effort was nearly beyond me. The things I did in the name of science were truly amazing.

"Priestess, I insist that you describe the details of this vision. Your holy prophet can help you understand it better." I brushed myself off and climbed the stairs again to where the priestess was waiting impatiently. She looked at me with suspicion, but she couldn't overcome her need to rub my face in her fantasy. To my great irritation, she once again assumed an air of superiority and righteousness. How I ever managed to tolerate this woman for a thousand years, I'll never know!

"Very well, Prophet, as you say. I was about to have my nails painted, when I felt the increase in the source energy that is supposed to herald my champion's arrival. Then I was about to summon you, Tibbald, to attend to the matter, when my future husband spoke directly into my mind as he did in the beginning of the world."

I remembered explaining a few things to her briefly when I first designed my wondrous prison, but I certainly hadn't done so recently. Her current mental state did not bode at all well for my plans.

"Nonsense, Priestess, you said that the great god sent an assassin after the catalyst. Why would he do such a thing when the catalyst is prophesized to unite you with your future husband in marriage? You were obviously dreaming." I was hoping that with a bit of convoluted reasoning, I would be able to convince her that she was imagining things. She looked around, as if someone might be listening. There obviously wasn't anyone, except for a few temple guards slouching against the walls. When she'd started screaming and crying, the throne room emptied faster than a vintage bottle of Soderbine. The volatility of the divine priestess was legendary among her subjects.

She leaned forward secretively and beckoned me to come closer. In the span of a few breaths, I'd changed in her eyes from someone conspiring against her to someone conspiring with her. I'd seen more stability in active volcanoes, I tell you! When I escaped this place, I was determined to give Cerberus a piece of my mind for subjecting me to such interminable nonsense!

"I, too, thought sending an assassin was odd, Tibbald, but my fiancé assured me that this catalyst was false and must be killed immediately. The strangest thing was that he tried to trick me. Is that not unthinkable, a god trying to deceive his own bride to be?"

I couldn't bring myself to commiserate, since it was obviously a hallucination.

"Indeed, Priestess, how did Prometheus trick you?" I actually asked that, if you can imagine! I asked her how 'I' had tricked her! In a moment of weakness I allowed myself to be drawn into her dream world. She was driving me out of my senses, I tell you!

"He didn't manage to fool me, Tibbald, but he did pretend that he was somebody called Cerberus. I found it very unsettling." At that point, the priestess must have rendered me unconscious, because I don't seem to recall anything more until I was awakened by Tiberius's arrival.

Master: *You fainted.*

Prometheus: *Excuse me?*

Master: *You fainted. You figured out that Cerberus sent a saugael mor to finish me off, and you passed out from the shock.*

Prometheus: *Preposterous! I most certainly did not faint, young man! Gods do not faint!*

Master: *Like I said, you fainted. Static should go next.*

Prometheus: *I'm not finished! You can't just leave me lying there on the floor!*

Master: *Don't worry, Prometheus; we won't step on you. Go ahead, Static.*

Static: *Thank you, my friend. You have both related your portions of the narrative in an entertaining manner. I shall attempt to do so also.*

Static

A saugael mor was approaching. The gathered thoughts of the village residents had warned me of the assassin's presence. It was high still and was drifting gently with the wind, but it would arrive in several seconds. The Host, Cerberus, likely had sent it to ensure that my companion's existence was effectively terminated. A saugael mor would normally be a minor irritation for my friend, but, as matters stood, he was in considerable danger. If the beast located my companion's remains, it would dissolve them completely in its corrosive fluids. There would be nothing left for recovery.

My companion is often wont to describe saugael mor as 'mutant spiders' or 'giant daddy-longlegs with club feet and claws.' Although mor have six legs rather than the eight of arachnids or opilionids, my friend's description, otherwise, is visually accurate. This vaguely spider-like appearance is where the similarities end. Saugael mor are deadly parasites that feed on negative emotions and that kill for pleasure. They are far more dangerous than simple arthropods and are highly resistant to all but the most radical extermination efforts.

Evidently unfamiliar with saugael mor, the human villagers stood gawking. Certainly, some of them were armed, but they could not know that such precautions would provide them little protection. The mor soon would be close enough to manipulate their emotions. At which time, they likely would become paralyzed with terror while the mor destroyed them. If my companion was to be rescued, he would require that the assassin be led away from his remains. I first would need to ensure that his body was cared for until a method to access our respective energy sources could be devised.

My current form had the advantageous ability to maneuver through the rubble. The remains of the structure audibly informed me that they were not finished coming to rest. I ignored the danger signs and chose instead to concentrate on the problem at hand, that being the determination of the damage inflicted on my companion's body. When I found him, he did not appear to be in a favorable condition. Not only was he deceased, but also his physical condition looked little better than that of the building he had destroyed.

I searched my memories for past discussions about what was to be done in such a circumstance. I recalled no discussions of that nature. Since I had known him, I had witnessed many of his various bodies become irreparably damaged. To accommodate such unwanted fatalities, he had created numerous alternates to ensure his survival, but in our present location, there was little chance that he would be able to access them. I had yet to discover what his plans were in the event that his emergency system failed to respond. It was a quandary. In the hope that his unmoving form might suggest an appropriate course of action, I studied it closely. I was surprised when it did.

From the tip of his outstretched hand, a drop of blood fell and spattered into a partially congealed puddle of the same substance. At the pool's edge was a ring. I quickly hypothesized that, at the time of his death, my companion had been in the process of obtaining this object, for I recalled belatedly a reference he had once made to a ring with healing properties. Given his condition, I assumed that it must be a solution to his then current problem. I hoped that it was, in fact, a method of rejuvenating his body. I hoped also that it still functioned after he was deceased and that it worked with contact alone, for I was unfamiliar with any operating procedures it might have. With no better solutions readily evident, I tucked the ring into his open mouth.

That task completed, and with little more to do for my companion's body, I went off to distract the saugael mor. I would need to convince the assassin to follow me if my friend's body was to receive the necessary opportunity to repair itself.

Taunting a saugael mor was not a course of action that I was eager to undertake, as I value my freedom and quality of life. I was uncertain as to precisely what would occur should my body become irreparably damaged within the current environment. Even if my substance dissipated from lack of energy, perishing was unlikely in the extreme. I suspected, rather, that I would become a sentient particle of the atmosphere until it dissipated through the planet's geological evolution. That would be substantially longer than my imprisonment within the cube, and I had no wish for it to occur.

I flew several times within striking range of the mor and transmitted mental impressions of my companion. In essence, I raised a signpost that read, "You will not find your given target while I live." I hoped that the assassin would see killing me as necessary to locate my companion's neural signal, which, in truth, was absent only because he was currently deceased. Sadly, the mor was enjoying the slaughter of the terrified humans and was reluctant to leave off its game. The villagers fought to no avail.

I flew faster, recklessly diving and flitting between the mor's slender limbs. I goaded it to attack me, rather than the villagers. Terror reigned as the assassin toyed with its victims before slashing them asunder; memories of my past haunted me. I was once much like the mor, a heartless, thoughtless killer. I yearned to stop its senseless murders, and thus, redeem another part of my character. But the mor was relentless, and my efforts failed. The villagers died.

With its amusement ended, the assassin struck in my direction. The tip of one claw swiped my underside, and I lost a layer of down and several feathers. I pumped my wings and bolted from beneath the mor's bulbous black core. The killer leapt forward in pursuit.

Eluding my pursuer required all the speed and agility of my small avian form, for there are few natural predators as adept at hunting as a saugael mor. In truth, I harbored sizable doubts as to whether the mor were, in fact, natural entities; it was difficult to imagine an evolutionary process that could create such single-minded assassins.

The countryside's changing geography did little to restrict its pace. The mor flowed insect-like around solid obstacles as if gravity's direction were optional. It sped through copses of trees and over uneven ground at speeds equal to a small bird flying. This fact was disconcerting, as I was the small bird providing the verification.

At one point during the chase, I made a poor directional decision and accidentally led the mor into another occupied settlement. Once again, I was helpless to curb the assassin's interest in terror and mayhem. This failure shames my sense of personal competence, but more than that, I am chagrined to admit that I found the slaughter useful. The distraction of murdering the local inhabitants worked to keep the assassin's attention occupied and was beneficial to my goal. I stayed alert to any renewed thought patterns from my companion.

When the assassin stopped its killing games and sped back toward our arrival point, I suspected that my companion was once again alive. I realized that, on this planet, the telepathic range of the mor was greater than my own, for I could not sense my friend's thoughts. A race ensued to determine which of us would reach my companion first.

Chapter Two

Master: *I'll go next.*

Prometheus: *How could you possibly have anything to say? You're dead!*

Master: *Exactly. I'm an expert on the subject. And so, I have things to say about it.*

Young Master

Returning to life is often painful. Sometimes, it's more painful than dying, particularly when the cause of death has been left in the body.

For instance, I was nineteen years old and pushing a broom in an almost empty office building. My new job title was security guard, not custodial engineer, so it can be assumed that I wasn't pleased about sweeping. My boss, who had nothing better to do than torment starving college students, found me pseudo-studying and decided to keep me active. Hunger, combined with lack of sleep and too many petty-little-man encounters, had me in an irritable mood.

As I pushed the broom to no visible effect – the cleaning staff had already cleaned the floors – I silently bemoaned the ache in my empty stomach. My student loan money had run out two weeks ago, and my last complete meal had arrived shortly thereafter. The resulting void in my gut had the straw on the end of the broom looking like a potential food item. I thought of my near-empty cupboards and wondered how many different recipes I could develop with water, flour, and ketchup. My conscience suggested that maybe I should have eaten out less often and stretched my funds a little farther. I told my conscience to shut up; it hadn't been particularly outspoken while I was spending the money.

Coincidentally, there was a food bank across the street, but I was too stubborn and proud to ask for help. Stupid Teenager Kills Himself with Pride: full story at eleven. On the bright side, I was the thinnest I'd ever been, and my pants were very loose and comfortable.

To get my mind off hunger, I tried to concentrate on my three-week, due-tomorrow project, which I hadn't yet started. But that only reminded me of my instructor, who was even more irritating than my boss. I suspected that he was planning to fail me even if I came up with something brilliant, but I'd never be able to prove it. He'd already organized a jury of instructors to judge my expulsion potential, and my future was hanging on the verdict of their farce trial.

During said trial, I'd argued that my instructor was being vindictive because I'd called him an idiot in front of the class – not the wisest defense. He'd told the jury that I was lazy and that I had a bad attitude. We were both right, but only his opinion mattered. My chances of graduating looked grim. I angrily pushed my broom.

And that summed up my pre-Host life. I was miserable, mostly by my own making, but, all in all, it was better than being dead. A miserable existence was better than no existence; that was my motto. Now, if only I could keep from starving to death, I would have considered my life to be just fine the way it was.

Speaking of death – I listened to the sound of a door open and close down the corridor. It was one of the resident businessmen leaving his office for the night. That was nothing new; many people in the building worked long hours. It reminded me of how ludicrous this job was. There was no system in place to determine who was in the building at any given time. A serial killer could walk past me, and, as long as he acted like he belonged, I would never know about it. The only thing my presence accomplished was to keep the street people from conflicting with the décor – stupid job.

The sharp rap of dress shoes came toward me; the sounds echoed eerily through the empty halls. Content with my surly mood, I pushed my broom without so much as looking up as he approached. Being somewhat reclusive by nature, my social skills were weak. He stopped behind me. The elevator was farther down the hall.

Not feeling very polite, I glanced over my shoulder to see what he wanted. What could he do if I decided to be rude, get me fired? Good, I might thank him for it. I looked a bland inquiry into the face of an equally bland-looking businessman. If he was a criminal, he would have to work a lot harder at looking like one. Even if he was, what could I do about it, scare him with my flashlight? The cops wouldn't show up until the city ran out of donuts, and this job didn't pay me enough to tackle somebody stealing office equipment. As far as I was concerned, he could clean the place out. The guy was beginning to make me nervous, because he hadn't moved, and he was staring at me.

"Yes?" I finally asked.

"I completely understand your frustration, young man. My foolish peers have alienated me, too. They're simply too blinded by their conservative arrogance to see my true genius, I tell you! To be unappreciated and overlooked, it's completely galling, is it not? Well, they will soon see their folly; just you wait! Soon they will be begging to…."

This guy was extremely weird, and how had he known what I was thinking about, anyway? I figured he'd probably made a lucky guess based on my sour mien.

"Is there something you wanted?" I was far too tired, hungry, and cranky to deal with a nutcase when I had a project to fail in the morning.

"Well, that was rude! You should learn to respect your betters, young man! Here I am about to do you a favor, and you act like a spoiled child! I have a mind to leave you the way you are, or perhaps I should simply report you to your supervisor! You're a guard, are you not? Aren't you supposed to ask me what my business is here? You should be grateful I choose not to be insulted! I'm not accustomed to being ignored, young man! I demand that you ask me my business!"

Nut, he was a serious nut. I decided to appease him just in case he might be dangerous.

"Do you feel like telling me what your business is here?"

He frowned and pursed his lips.

"You are an arrogant little creature, aren't you? Very well then, this could have been easy, but it appears you need a lesson in manners!" He pulled out a nasty looking antique letter opener from his briefcase and stuck it into my chest right up to the handle. That is to say, he stuck the letter opener in my chest, not the briefcase.

I wasn't fast enough to defend myself, and I was too dumbfounded to take him with me. My fantasies about coolly defeating my enemies were destroyed. As I tried unsuccessfully to breathe, he continued to talk.

"Just so you know, I could have made it much more painful for you. I didn't have to be so compassionate. My first thought was to burn you alive. You should be thankful, really. It usually isn't my preference to lower myself to using such crude implements. For the others I used...."

Okay, this day sucked. I didn't hear the rest of what he said, because, being otherwise occupied with the pointy thing stuck in my chest, I was falling down. I had about another twenty seconds to think about all the things I was never going to experience, and then the lights went out. That was the first time I died.

Old Master

Twelve hundred thirty-four years later, I revived to intense pain in my chest and to the sound of breaking rafter. Having forgotten, in my befuddled hypothermic fog, that I was in a different time and place, I reached to pull out the letter opener – old nightmares. The feel of wood under my fingers confused me. I opened my eyes to a rubble pile of broken black stones, frost-covered timbers, and a jagged splinter poking out between my ribs.

Taking out the splinter seemed important, so with a bit of drooling and screaming, I attended to it. Then, I flopped on my back in the icy sand and shivered uncontrollably.

The stabbing pain, I suffered like an old habit, but the cold didn't seem right. Temperature control was rarely a problem for us Host-hybrids. Host, right - I finally remembered where I was. Oneia. That explained the ring in my mouth.

"Static?" There was no response. Feeling helpless and pathetic, I clumsily wiped away the stinging tears – probably caused by the dirt in my eyes. I became increasingly frustrated and cranky that the cold wouldn't go away.

"Hello? Anybody? I need help!" Actually, I didn't, but I was too groggy and depressed to understand that. All I needed to do was to lay still, and the ring would eventually do the rest. I rolled it around my tongue and chomped on it a few times.

"We will be there soon, Holy One. Be at peace."

Holy one? Not that again, I changed my mind about being rescued.

"I'm not a god. Who's in my head? Get out; I'm tired. Where's Static?" I could sense this guy's cloying devotion, and I wanted to get away.

"I am Bertrand, Holy One, an Eldoran child of the great god Prometheus, your holy master. We will arrive shortly to aid you."

While listening to Bertrand babble, I ran into a wall that someone had placed in my path. I'd apparently managed to stand and walk, although I didn't remember doing either. The oddity of not recalling how I'd arrived at the wall didn't seem as important as the fact that it was in my way. I pushed at it; whereby, it obligingly fell forward with a scraping rumble. Not having the strength to pull back, I joined the falling stones on their tumble to the ground.

My head hit something harder than it, and the world gyrated. I clawed the ground, threw up a few times, and then collapsed. Peaceful nothingness returned.

Master: *Okay, I'm dead again. Prometheus, it's your turn.*

Prometheus: *Why didn't you just let me finish instead of leaving me lying on the floor?*

Master: *You took too long. Besides, it was funny.*

Prometheus: *I've had enough of this foolishness! I will not remain and allow myself to be the subject of your immature amusement! Good day!* [Prometheus rises, dumps Static off his lap.]

Static: *My friend, I would like to retain Prometheus's perspective for this history. I would prefer if, for the duration of this tale, you could refrain from antagonizing him.*

Master: *Sorry, Static, I'll try harder. Have a seat, Prometheus. Apparently, we need your help.*

Prometheus: *Humph! Very well then, but just you remember that I'm doing this out of my charitable sense of goodness! Servant, make certain it goes on the record that my avatar has officially recognized my importance.*

Scribe: [Scribe glares at Prometheus.] *My name, Host, is Paul, and I accept commands from no one but my master, whom I serve by choice. Be aware that there is but one exit from this palace, and I guard that exit.* [Scribe displays teeth.]

Prometheus: [Prometheus shows discomfort.] *Well yes, of course, Paul, is it? It's a fine name, very fine. I believe I have a story to tell. Shall we be about it then? Now, where was I? Oh yes, I was left on the floor!* [Prometheus glares at Master.]

Prometheus

As I was saying, the priestess, in her emotional volatility, must have rendered me unconscious. I did not faint!

By the time I revived from her sneak attack, she'd already switched moods. She was crying for help and cradling my head to her breast. It was a dreadfully embarrassing situation. Can you imagine? I was mortified, I tell you! She must have sensed that I was awake, because her tears of grief turned instantly to joy, and, as if I were her only child returned from the dead, she began to faun over me.

"Oh Tibbald, I'm so happy you're back! I thought I'd lost you! You were just standing there, and all of a sudden, you fell down! I didn't know what to do, and I couldn't revive you! Are you well? Yes, of course you're well; you're fine! Don't you worry, my loyal prophet; your priestess will take care of you now!" Rocking my head back and forth, she continued to suffocate me and pressed her face to my forehead.

"Priestess, this is undignified! Release me immediately!" As I climbed to my feet, she recoiled in shock and backed away like a frightened rabbit. Such a strong reaction may have been an error on my part – oh dear. The features on her face contorted as her emotions fought to decide which one would take dominance. I tried to pacify her before she did something I would regret.

"I was startled, Priestess! Yes, just startled is all! No slight against you, of course! None whatsoever, I tell you!" She was frozen with indecision. This could become very unpleasant.

She was still undecided when an imperial herald entered and saved me years of torment as he announced the arrival of High Commander Tiberius. When the trumpets blared to celebrate Tiberius's impending entrance, his honor guard filed in, and the priestess's eyes narrowed at me in most disturbing manner. Alas, my supply of wine was going to be cut off for certain.

The priestess marched to her throne, turned with purpose, flared her gown, and seated herself with an air of dignified majesty. Such controlled behavior did not promise good things for my future comfort. She riveted her attention on the herald, who approached the steps leading to the throne. Dear me, this was not good at all!

Ah well, it would all be irrelevant if things worked out with my avatar. Once I collected him, I could finally be away from this planet. I merely needed to concentrate on ridding myself of distractions.

The herald kneeled at the base of the steps and commenced with the formalities, a truly bothersome delay in my plans. Every moment that I was detained here, the Eldorans would get that much closer to stealing my avatar. I was not about to let those misguided zealots run away with my property!

"Priestess, I…."

"Silence, Prophet!" Her tone promised death. I graciously decided to wait until the herald finished. He spread his silver cloak across the floor behind him, touched his forehead once to the lowest step, babbled out a list of Tiberius's titles and accomplishments followed by a stream of inane platitudes to the priestess, and then finally asked permission for Tiberius to address her.

"High commander Tiberius may enter." The priestess kept her gaze fixed on the throne room's grand arch and watched Tiberius make his commanding entrance.

And quite invigorating it was, I must say. As usual, Tiberius was flawless in his delivery. When the golden doors opened, he paced in military dignity to the throne room's center, lowered himself gracefully to one knee, and bowed his lovely head. The man made subservience look almost regal, I tell you!

Tiberius always impressed me with his keen sense of aesthetic design. Like his personal herald's, the commander's cloak was splayed out beautifully across the pale marble of the floor. His was deep green velvet trimmed with glittering woven gold rope; the rich folds shimmered in the light shining through the high-set windows of the throne room. I suspected it wasn't mere chance that Tiberius had stopped right in a patch of sunlight. I would have to remember that effect; it was very eye-catching. The gold from his cloak matched the luminous gold plating of his ceremonial chest piece, which was molded to match his marvelous physique. Yes, it was very impressive, indeed! Why, it nearly took my breath away!

"My Divine Priestess, I have come as you requested. May I approach into your heavenly aura?" His deep, resonant voice filled the throne room and sent pleasant shivers all the way down to my slippers.

Normally, I would find it entertaining to watch the coming performance, but I was in somewhat of a rush. I tried to hurry the proceedings along. "Yes, yes, what is it that you have to say, Tiberius?" The Priestess jerked her hand in my direction and caused me considerable pain; may she wake in the morning with crow's feet! I refused to fall down! I would not be subjected to such humiliation in the commander's presence!

"You would do well to keep your tongue in your mouth, Prophet! The high commander has come at my request and is fully welcome in my presence. Please approach, Commander." Radiating sexual invitation, she forgot all about her recent episode and beckoned him, how disgusting!

I fumed as Tiberius rose with a flourish and strode forward; his honor guards swooped in and created an archway of gold-fringed spears above him. Yes, yes, get on with it! This display was entirely for the benefit of the priestess. When not in her presence, the commander was a no-nonsense military man of few carefully chosen words. He was the true force behind the Oneian empire and was responsible for its rapid growth, but he somehow made it seem like the priestess was in complete control. He was also the undisputed master at dealing with her moodiness. I must admit that I wouldn't be able to stomach such galling acts of subservience, even pretended. They made his act all the more intriguing.

What was I thinking? I had no time to be intrigued! The Eldorans were going to get my avatar! I nearly grabbed my rod and transported myself from the throne room. But then I imagined what the Priestess would do to me if I did, and I decided against it. There was nothing I could do but wait.

I tried to relax. Those bothersome peasants couldn't shift directly, anyway. Even if a few of them picked up my avatar and walked away, the powers they inherited from the Priestess wouldn't be enough to keep me from taking him back. My rod of office would overpower them easily, unless they'd converged in the dozens, which bordered on suicidal for their fugitive race. I had no need to worry unduly, but I still had the nagging feeling that I was forgetting something important. Bah, it would come to me soon enough.

Tiberius spoke. "My Divine Priestess and Imperial Majesty, do you desire to hear of the recent happenings in your holy empire?" With his right hand placed over his heart, he feigned a look of adoring servitude, underpinned by strength and majesty. The Priestess was enthralled just to hear the man speak. I couldn't really blame her. Even I found Tiberius to be rather intoxicating.

"In fact, Commander, I summoned you for a different matter entirely, but it would be lovely to hear a report of my empire. For being a loyal and conscientious servant, you are granted the honor of kissing the hand of your divine priestess." She extended her hand, but leaned back in her throne so that Tiberius would need to stretch over her full length to kiss it, how obnoxious!

The priestess's thoughts followed her eyes over the commander's handsome physique. For more than a thousand years, this woman had tried to seduce Tiberius. It baffled me that she still tried to bed the man, when she must have known that he wasn't nearly foolish enough to do something that lethal. The priestess's lovers, since her early days, had turned up prematurely dead. This began when she discovered that some of her powers were passed on to her Eldoran offspring. She blamed the men for it, if you can imagine!

This was not to say that Tiberius spurned her advances, as that would prove equally deadly. Rather, he walked a dramatic line between desired passion and the tragedy of unattainable love, completely false, but nonetheless effective. Whether or not the priestess was present, his mental façade always alternated between romantic fantasies and military strategy. It seemed a bit paranoid, if you ask me, and it had me convinced that Tiberius was Eldoran.

He leaned over, almost but not quite touching her body. His heavily scented cloak enveloped her on both sides, and his thoughts dripped passion, but he never looked directly into her eyes. As if he were truly touching a goddess, Tiberius reverently lifted the priestess's hand, caressed it once, and placed a single kiss at the tips of her fingers. The kiss was so light and brief that it almost never happened. Then, he released her hand, fed her feelings of loss and sorrow, and smoothly backed away.

Suddenly remembering to breathe, the priestess inhaled sharply.

"High Commander Tiberius, you may kiss me again, perhaps for longer this time." With her hand stretched out, she leaned forward and exuded her deadly feminine charms, but the commander would have nothing to do with it. A consummate professional, he merely hung his head in tragic loss.

"Nay, Divine Priestess, please do not offer again. My heart would die if I were to touch your beauty twice in a day. Your servant is too strong in his love for his goddess and cannot endure her radiance. Please forgive my weakness." When he raised his head, his eyes were glistening, and a single tear rolled over his powerful jaw, bravo! Well done, I say! The Priestess took a moment to recompose, since she was radiating enough lust to fill the temple.

"Yes, of course, Commander, I understand completely; only, I wish sometimes that I wasn't quite so beautiful. Such beauty becomes lonely at times. I'm not a goddess yet, you know. I don't think your heart would be damaged permanently with just a few more kisses."

"In truth, my goddess – for to me, you are already so – even from this distance, I fear your beauty could spell my end. Your mere closeness is all it might take."

I just couldn't do it, I tell you! If I never saw the man away from the Priestess, I would swear that he was completely infatuated with her!

"This beauty is a curse, my loyal Tiberius. Do not be ashamed. It is not a weakness in your character that you love me so, but merely a demonstration of devotion to your divine priestess. We will set the matter aside and carry on with other business. I believe you mentioned a report on the state of my empire?"

So long as her fruit was fresh and her gems were plenty, the woman couldn't care less about the state of her empire. While Tiberius made his tiresome reports, she reclined in her throne and entertained herself with romantic fantasies. Being Eldoran, Tiberius would have sensed the priestess's thoughts as well, but to his credit, he didn't even blink when she mentally undressed him. He droned on at length about provincial takeovers, barbarian encroachments, cavalry training, and other military minutia. But only when he mentioned that fresh tapa fruit would be available along a new supply line did the priestess's attention perk up.

"Tapas? Oh, I love tapas! This is wonderful news, High Commander!"

"I am pleased that my divine priestess approves." He said with a warm smile that dimmed quickly. "But there is one more matter that is somewhat closer to our hearts. I have been informed of a small group of rebels that are gathering in the nearby village of Honn. Forgive me for mentioning this, my Divine Priestess, but the rebels are Eldoran." The priestess's brow clouded, but she said nothing, and Tiberius continued. "Their magic leaves my troops at a disadvantage. Might you permit me to use the good Prophet's magical services for a short reconnaissance mission?"

"You may. Take him, and quell this rebellion. All of the Eldorans are to be burned in a retribution ceremony."

Of all the injustice! Why was his silly request for company more important than my much greater need? This was so unfair! I had an avatar to find, and had no time to be a playmate for Tiberius, however entertaining that might be.

"I will do no such thing! I must leave at once to greet my avatar... I mean my... the holy catalyst!" I stood my ground. With a cold glare, she turned her head to me, and I prepared myself for another attack. It thankfully didn't come. Instead, her frown turned into a conniving smirk, how rude!

"That works out well then, Tibbald. Isn't the village of Honn in the same area that the false catalyst arrived?"

"How should I know?" I didn't make a habit of remembering the arbitrary names that these humans kept to define their borders. That is, not unless they had good wines.

"Good Prophet, the village of Honn lies on the outskirts of our capital city, in that direction." Tiberius pointed toward where my avatar landed.

Eek! There were Eldorans near my avatar! I knew it!

"How many are there?" I had to know. If there were more than two dozen, I was in trouble.

"Do you refer to Eldorans, good Prophet? My reports suggest from thirty to forty." Tiberius looked bemused. It was so unlike him.

"What? No! Quickly, we must gather my brother priests immediately and confront them! Call out the imperial guard! The Holy Catalyst must not be taken!" There were far too many to overpower with just one rod.

"Tibbald, control yourself in my presence! Have you forgotten my vision so quickly? The holy assassin will destroy the false catalyst! I'm certain that the assassin will recognize the Eldorans as traitors and will bring retribution to them as well. High Commander Tiberius, I would like you to assist the holy assassin in destroying the infidels."

Oh dear, that's what I'd forgotten! Cerberus had sent an assassin to kill my avatar! Tiberius, I noted, was still looking bemused, and somewhat blurry, too.

"Good Prophet, you are listing precariously to one side. Are you feeling well? You look disturbingly pale." Tiberius was obviously concerned for my welfare, but there was nothing he could do. As punishment for my independence, the priestess rendered me unconscious again.

Prometheus: *I did not faint! You wipe that smirk off your face this instant, young man, or my charitable donation to this nonsense is finished!*

Master: [Master expresses contrived innocence.] *I didn't say a word.*

Static: *I will now resume narration of my encounter with the saugael mor.*

Martin Wolfe

Chapter Three

Static

I had been deceived. My strategy to lead the saugael mor away from our landing site had succeeded, but not for the reason that I assumed. I had imagined that I possessed sufficient speed to elude my pursuer, and that it chased my erratic flight path out of frustration. But as the assassin raced back toward my companion, all illusions of my superior speed dissipated; it was faster than I. It had merely been feeding on my anxiety.

The mor's trajectory was invariant. It passed over and under obstacles, rather than around them; it refused to deviate from a straight line. This suggested to me that it could no longer detect my companion's life signs, and that it continued to focus on the original signal received. I would have gladly attempted to disrupt its concentration had I possessed the ability to close the distance between us, but it easily maintained a substantial lead. The mor's decision to climb over trees, rather than around them, was the sole reason I was able to keep it in sight. I longed for an energy source that I could use to mutate into something faster and more predatorily useful.

A reprieve came when we arrived at a lake that we had unknowingly avoided in our original route. The mor evidently had an aversion to crossing bodies of water, for it stopped at the water's edge. I do not know how the assassin navigated this obstacle because I sped past and continued onward. My companion needed to be warned of the impending danger, or if he was still immobile, he would require a suitable means of protection.

When I arrived at the site of my companion's demise, I was surprised to discover a group of human telepaths, of varying shapes and sizes, gathered at the base of the ruined structure. They were new arrivals – the villagers had been killed by the mor. Seemingly unconcerned about the recent carnage, the gathered telepaths debated their respective rights to a piece of property.

I surmised this from their spoken words, for their private thoughts were guarded, and their telepathic transmissions were inconsistent with either their actions or their surroundings. Their mental chants consisted of trite accolades to a being they referred to as the divine priestess. I wondered why they bothered masking their true thoughts with irrelevant material, when it would be more effective to block their minds from intrusion until they had something useful to communicate.

As their conversation was not of interest to me, I flew around them. The remains of the building appeared undisturbed, but upon closer inspection, I discovered that my companion's body was no longer present. The humans then became relevant, because his departing trail led in their direction.

I followed the footprints in the sand until I arrived at the structure's edge. From the lowest point in the damaged wall, a drop of three human body lengths stretched to the ground below, where the collapsed masonry had spread outward in a circular formation. From this angle, I could see that the gathering of humans was thinner. My companion's body lay at their feet. I hypothesized that my friend had jumped or fallen from the edge and had died again on impact. The signal the mor followed had indeed been too short.

I now found the heated conversation of the humans to be of greater interest, although it still lacked basis in reality. The property over which they continued to argue their right of ownership was my companion himself, except that they referred to him as a known cultural representative. If my friend were alive, he would have disapproved of the designation provided to him. Many civilizations have attempted to recruit him as an icon for their respective political and revolutionary causes, but his natural desire is to be left in relative solitude.

It occurred to me that their passionate arguments might be beneficial to my friend's safety. Judging by their desperate pleas of ownership, I suspected that these people would be willing to offer their assistance in defending my friend against the saugael mor.

His safety in this situation was unfortunately not a certainty. I was concerned that the rival factions might segment his body and use the parts as revolutionary symbols. This disturbing circumstance had, in fact, occurred on previous occasions. I would need to follow their present conversation more closely if I was to determine whether or not my friend would be safe in their company.

I flew to the ground, hopped through a forest of legs, and arrived at my companion's body; whereupon, I immediately identified one of the gathered participants as a Host. It was Prometheus.

Encountering Prometheus was not entirely unexpected, for I knew that he was the Host responsible for creating this planet. I intended to question him on his methods for departing, but in politeness, I chose to wait until he finished conversing. I did not wish to damage his assumed identity among these people – they were addressing him by a different name and title.

With a false sense of security, I settled onto my friend's arm. I imagined that Prometheus, on his own planet, would have ample means of dealing with a single saugael mor. It shames me that I continued to make such dangerously inaccurate assumptions.

"And then the holy catalyst will return from the plane of gray and will restore upon her children their own fate." Bertrand, the spokesman for the Eldorans, as Prometheus called them, patiently but firmly cited his latest argument. I listened with only mild interest; both debating platforms derived from similar literary works.

"Her? Don't be absurd! The Catalyst is male! I've already explained to you people that only *Volume One* of the *Great Book* has any relevance! Now go back to your hiding holes before I lose my patience completely! You should consider yourselves fortunate that I'm more understanding than the Priestess, or the whole lot of you would already be roasted alive for building a roof over my sand pit! What in the name of broken catalysts did you peasants think you were doing?"

On one side of the argument were thirty-four mixed Eldorans of varying age, race, gender, size, health, and social prosperity. Prometheus, the sole opposing debater, appeared agitated; impatience and agitation were character traits that I had witnessed in him before. His only supporter appeared to be a man dressed in military uniform. This individual seemed disinclined to join in the debate, but showed interest in my presence. He stood slightly apart from the others and stared at me.

"Our humble covering was created to protect the sacred sands from the elements, Holy Prophet. As to the prophecy, we are quoting from *Volume One*. Your own holy words speak of the catalyst rising from the dead and ridding the Eldoran people of their ancestral mother. In this way, we, the Eldoran children of the Priestess, will be given control over our own fate."

"It means no such thing! It certainly says nothing about someone stealing my catalyst! How do you people come up with this nonsense? Sacred sands, of all things, just look at what you've done to the catalyst!"

I noted curiously that the false thoughts of the Eldorans did not match the false thoughts of Prometheus, which were, in turn, dissimilar from the false thoughts of his military companion. My own thoughts were blocked from intrusion until I chose to share them.

"As it is written in *Volume Four*, Section…."

"I didn't write that part! Desist with this nonsense immediately, and stand away from the catalyst!"

"Holy Prophet, we respect your divine wisdom, but the holy catalyst is our only salvation. He must not be allowed to fall into the hands of the divine priestess, our ancient mother, for then, our time on this world may end. Sadly, to protect our future, we must use our small powers against you."

"Don't be ridiculous! None of you has a chance of standing against me! I could easily roast the lot of you! Now stand aside!"

"And yet, Holy Prophet, you have not done so. It is true that our separate powers cannot withstand the might of the rods, but, together, we are formidable. We must protect the holy catalyst."

The verbal battle for ownership of my companion's body continued, while the military individual continued to watch me intently. An immature Eldoran female also showed interest in my presence, but rather than observing, she approached and initiated contact.

"Hello, birdie."

"Greetings, I am called Static."

The child was startled by my response, which, in politeness to the debaters, I transmitted to her alone. I noted that her façade of devotions dropped during telepathic converse. I sensed her excitement.

"You can talk?"

45

"My avian vocal cords are not currently adapted for verbal communication, but I am willing to converse telepathically, if that is acceptable to you."

"I don't understand. Your words are too big."

"Telepathy does not, in fact, consist of verbal words, but rather the concepts from which the words derive. If you wish, I shall attempt to choose simpler concepts."

I was largely unpracticed at conversing with juveniles, who had underdeveloped mental capacity. Not having a childhood of my own had left me at a disadvantage. Nonetheless, I tried to adapt, for I intended to request her assistance.

"My name is Alenna. You're awfully smart for a bird."

"I am not a normal bird, Alenna. Would you please perform a task for me? My dead friend has a ring in his mouth. I would like you to put it on his finger."

I detected her squeamishness over handling a corpse. It was an understandable precaution in an underdeveloped civilization; a dead body could conceivably be diseased and affect her health.

"Do not be concerned for your welfare. My companion did not expire from a viral illness and harbors no contagion."

She was confused again; I had forgotten to simplify my concepts. But she did not ask for clarification. Alenna rapidly developed an accepting comfort with my thought patterns.

"It's gross!"

Most of my companion's lacerations and contusions had been repaired, but his body remained coated with frozen, dried, and congealed blood. His apparel had been reduced to a collection of red-stained rags that had stiffened in the cold. With only a cursory inspection, Alenna might assume that he was horribly injured, yet her reaction seemed more emotional than intellectual.

"It is true that my companion requires cleansing, but this should not prove to be a deterrent. Do you agree to perform this task, or shall I ask another?"

"I can do it, Static."

With obvious distaste and reluctance, Alenna approached my friend's corpse. She squatted and peered into his open mouth.

"It isn't there.

"A visual inspection is inadequate, Alenna. You must use your fingers and thumbs to probe the interior of his mouth and throat. If the ring has not traversed into his interior, it will be unstable and may fall out."

Her apprehension returned.

"Maybe it fell out already. It could be in the snow. Why don't I check there first?"

I was impressed with her thought process. It was a more reasonable hypothesis that the ring had dislodged when my companion fell. This would also explain why he was still deceased.

"That is an excellent suggestion, Alenna. You have a keen mind for a juvenile. I will search, also."

Her relief returned and mingled with pride. We began to examine the trampled snow around my friend's body. Prometheus's martial companion stepped forward to assist us in our search. He assumed a crouched position.

"Greetings, I am called Static." My salutation was greeted with neither response, nor recognition. I found this curious. His dichotomic thoughts of love and war proved that he was an accomplished telepath. Perhaps, as with Alenna's mental chant, his could not be maintained during telepathic communication. It seemed an intellectually wasteful expenditure.

I continued my search, as did Alenna. Our military volunteer discovered the ring first. He extracted it from a bloodied patch of snow and rolled it between his fingers. I worried that he might try to claim the valuable item as salvage. In my current form, I did not possess the ability to apprehend him. Alenna had not yet noticed that the ring had been found.

"Are you looking for this, little one?" The man spoke to her. He displayed the ring on the tip of his finger.

"Yes, thank you." Alenna was excited by the discovery. She extended her hand to receive it. The man examined it once more before placing it into her small palm.

"It's very pretty. Is it yours?" He smiled. Alenna shook her head and moved to place the ring on my companion's finger. She completed the task successfully, albeit with evident squeamishness.

"It's Static's. He wanted me to put it on his friend's finger." Alenna had smeared blood on her hands. She grimaced and wiped her soiled hands on her garments.

"Static. That's an interesting name for your pet. Have you had him for long?" His question remained unanswered.

"Tiberius, did you just say Static? Where did you hear that name?" Prometheus's eyes were wide. His outburst had interrupted the debate.

"Alenna, get away from there!" Bertrand joined the new conversation.

"I was just talking to Static, Father."

"Where did you hear the name Static? Speak up, I tell you!" This time, Prometheus directed his angry question at Alenna.

Before I could address Prometheus, and thereby, defend Alenna's behavior, one of the Eldorans at the gathering's perimeter cried out in alarm. The saugael mor had arrived.

It leapt from a nearby roof and attacked. Several Eldorans died amidst the chaos as the assassin fought to reach my companion's body. A head flew above us and bounced across the rubble. Tiberius half drew his sword, reconsidered, and sheathed it.

The Eldorans had responded by repelling the creature with an energy shield, evidently sustained in a group effort. Bertrand moved to the forefront and guided the defense.

"Holy Prophet, help us defeat the evil that seeks to destroy the catalyst!" He bellowed to Prometheus.

"Nonsense, young man, you're doing fine! You people fend it off, and I'll stay back to protect the catalyst! He must be saved at all costs, you know!" Prometheus dismissed Alenna and questioned Tiberius again. "Out with it, where did you hear the name Static?"

"It is the bird's name, good Prophet." Tiberius gestured in my direction. He seemed amused by Prometheus's excited demand and unconcerned about the battle.

Prometheus looked at me and gasped.

"You, thing, get away from my avatar this instant!"

He grabbed a carved rod that hung at his waist and pointed it at me. Alenna, who was standing next to my companion's body, assumed that Prometheus was referring to her, a reasonable mistake. Fear temporarily seized control over her motor functions.

"Prometheus, you are frightening this child with your aggressive actions. Please endeavor to be rational."

"It is you! Get away from him! Go, shoo!"

His actions were even more bizarre than those I had witnessed from him in the past. His rod flared brightly; Alenna stood in harm's way. I shot forward to intercept his attack.

Crackling white power blazed from his rod and swarmed around me. My small body was transfixed in the air, but only until I absorbed the energy and mutated into a large hunting feline. I landed, catlike, and roared. Had Prometheus been thinking clearly, he likely would not have assisted my transformation. His energy attack was useful.

"Father!" Terrified anew, Alenna cried to her guardian. Bertrand assumed his daughter was in jeopardy and turned from the battle. He turned his back on the assassin.

He was killed an instant later when the tips of three long claws extruded from his chest, came together, and withdrew. His startled features displayed the evidence of his demise.

"Father!" Alenna screamed in distress and attempted to approach her deceased parent. I placed my predatory musculature in her path and arrested her progress, lest she be killed. She struggled against me and cried.

"Tiberius, we're leaving!"

Prometheus suddenly shifted, disappearing with Tiberius and with my companion's body. I would have preferred that he also transport the Eldorans, who were struggling to maintain their defense. Without their leader, they were demoralized, and the mor approached ever closer. Their strength and resolve weakened with each death.

"Alenna, climb onto my back. We shall flee."

I intended to repay this small female. She did not immediately respond, for she had succumbed to grief over the loss of her father.

"You have my sincere condolences on your loss, but if you do not accept my offer, you will perish along with your people. Please, mount my back, and hold on tightly, for I have no arms with which to carry you."

Alenna chose to live and mounted. My feline body would be considerably slower than my previous form, but it would provide a small degree of defense against any brief conflicts with the mor. In the event of a prolonged conflict, I would likely be dismembered, and Alenna would perish soon after.

"Alenna, please hypothesize: Where would Prometheus most likely have taken my companion?"

She pointed weakly to the distant city at the end of a nearby watercourse. Alenna confirmed my suspicion; the city would have been my chosen destination.

We stayed close to the river. I conserved my energy and maintained a smooth, brisk pace. The sounds of dying Eldorans followed us over the gently rolling countryside. With each scream heard, Alenna's grip on my hide tightened. I shared her anxiety, but mine was not as sharp, and it did not increase until the dying cries of the defenders ended. With no other victims to terrorize, the mor would consider us its next amusement.

Martin Wolfe

Chapter Four

Master: *Okay, it's my turn.*

Young Master

Late one night during my nineteenth year, a psychopathic businessman stabbed me. He drove a letter opener straight through my heart. I died – or so I assumed while dying.

The next thing I knew, I was screaming. The fires of a raging inferno washed down my throat and scoured my flesh. My eyes were fused shut. Being the stubborn type, I refused to believe I was dead: I hurt; therefore, I was, and all that philosophical stuff.

"Would you please stop this ridiculous screaming? The noise is beginning to fray my nerves!"

I gently probed my chest. The letter opener and the hole it made were gone, but my skin was crispy and slid away when I touched it. I choked on my screams and gagged. I should have been dead.

"Ah, blissful silence, that's much better! Now, heal yourself. I want to conduct a few more experiments on you before I leave."

Either I was having a horribly realistic nightmare, or I needed to check myself into a psychiatric facility as soon as possible. What kind of real life circumstance, I wondered, could have created a nightmare like this? My screwy teenage life could have easily inspired the imagery, but the pain wasn't possible unless I'd fallen asleep in a furnace.

"Hurry up, and heal yourself, would you? I have important things to do!"

I tried very hard to wake up, but it wasn't working. The concept of a bad nightmare was giving way to the unpleasant idea of mental instability. Maybe I was under too much stress.

"I certainly hope you're not always this hopeless! I'm placing a great deal of emphasis on your human ability to survive, you know. Just this once, I'll help you, but you really must learn to adapt, or you'll be no use to me at all."

The pain suddenly went away, and I could see again. What I saw inspired me to scream a bit more, just for good measure.

My body was healed, albeit naked, and lying on the floor of the building where I worked. Scattered around me was charred material that looked like it once belonged to something living. The psycho office worker, looking disgusted, was standing over me.

It was a nightmare, and that was my final answer. I must have been so tired from my many late nights that, during a crazy dream about work, I'd accidentally rolled over onto the radiator next to my bed. Yep, that was it, had to be.

Now that I understood the situation, I wasn't nearly as frightened. I climbed to my feet and tried to look casual, which wasn't easy. Even in a dream, I was uncomfortable being naked at work. I folded my arms and leaned back against a cold marble wall. My manhood shriveled in the chill breeze wafting down the hallway. Only one thing could have made the situation more embarrassing: The elevator dinged to announce a new arrival.

I closed my eyes; please, don't let it be a woman. I opened my eyes. It was a woman. She unwound her scarf, took off her gloves, saw me standing naked over a pile of smoking flesh, and froze. The psycho office worker, still holding his briefcase, waved her away with his bloody letter opener.

"We're using this floor right now. You'll just have to find another one."

The elevator door began to close behind her. She turned and slammed herself through the opening. I could hear the close-door button clicking rapidly, but as usual, the door took the regular amount of time to close. I think they put those buttons in there just so people could feel like they had control.

The woman left her scarf and one glove lying on the floor. My instinct was to run after her and give them back, but I wisely ignored the urge and turned to confront my nightmare.

"In the first part of this dream, you said you weren't going to set me on fire. How am I going to trust my nightmares, if they can't even keep their word?"

I tried to show a front of confidence, but my chattering teeth ruined the effect. My apartment window must have been open when I went to sleep, or maybe I'd collapsed from exhaustion on the way home and was now going through the various stages of hypothermia.

"Well, I see you've finally decided to acknowledge my presence! You humans and your inflated sense of self-importance, you're truly arrogant creatures sometimes! It's a wonder I choose to help your primitive species at all! If I didn't need test subjects, I would leave you just where I found you! Imagine, it's been only …." He waved his arms to emphasize his rambling statements, but his lips weren't moving.

"Hey, Mr. Psycho, I asked you a question."

When I was a kid and dreamed of scary monsters, I used to give them stupid names and boss them around. It made me feel better. He stopped waving his arms, frowned, and pursed his lips. The letter opener came at me again, but this time, I was ready for it. Unfortunately, it still ended up in my chest. He was a very fast monster. I silently mouthed some words that fit the occasion and slid to the floor. My bare back squeaked against the marble.

"Now, heal yourself. I'm not going to help you this time." He grimaced at the blood on his hand, and the blood disappeared, just like that.

Well if he could do it, then so could I. It was my nightmare, after all. But first things first, I grabbed the handle of the letter opener and pulled. My chest burned like white fire, my eyes rolled back in my head, and my lips quivered as the bloody shaft came out. I let it tumble from my shaking hands, and it clinked against the stone floor. Blood spilled from the corner of my mouth as I coughed up the last of my air.

"You see, this kind of primitive thinking is precisely what I was talking about! Next time, just eliminate the silly thing. You're not a human anymore, you know. Stop acting like one! Now, heal yourself, and stand up. We have some work to do before I go."

Fine, I imagined myself as healed. And by golly, it worked. This nightmare was getting better. I decided to stay where I was and think my words. It was working okay for him.

"You never mentioned your name."

"Do you really not know who I am?" He looked hurt that I didn't recognize him.

To me, he looked like an average Middle Eastern man, or maybe Mediterranean, with dark hair and dark eyes. He was a bit short, and his nose was a touch big for his face. He kind of looked like Napoleon, but his skin was too dark to be French.

"I'm certainly not this person you refer to as Napoleon. Do you recognize me if I do this?" He cradled his briefcase like a book, and defiantly thrust his arm into the air. His fist looked like it should be holding something.

"You were the guy that designed the Statue of Liberty?" It was as good a guess as any.

"I am the great god Prometheus! Your ancestors worshipped my divine greatness and made beautiful monuments in my image. Does that refresh your simple memory?" He looked disgusted again.

"The god who was punished for giving fire to man, ancient Greek mythology, I've heard the story." One of us needed some serious medication.

"I am not insane, young man, nor am I a myth! I am the great god Prometheus, and you should have more respect and appreciation for the gift I have given you!"

Whether I was dreaming or crazy, I felt that my subconscious could have come up with a better image of what a god should look like.

"You are insufferably arrogant! Bromes would turn in his grave if he knew that the descendants of his people would turn out so disrespectful!"

Who was Bromes, I wondered? I didn't recall his name from my high school mythology class. My nightmare was becoming stranger by the minute. Maybe it was the kind caused by starvation.

"You're not dreaming, you imbecile! Do you mean to tell me that you don't even know who Bromes is? How can you not know who Bromes is? He was the man responsible for founding your entire civilization! I leave you people alone for a few millennia, and you forget your own heritage! It's a wonder that you manage to survive at all! Here I am giving the gift of immortal life to a...."

My nightmare was getting on my nerves. I imagined him bursting into flames, and he did – cool. He stopped yakking for a few seconds; that was nice. The flames suddenly fizzled out and left behind the charred and blackened god who was set on fire by man. I thought it was funny, but he took it amiss.

"Childish!" He blew me to pieces. *"I have no time to deal with this juvenile behavior! You'll just have to teach yourself."* He disappeared.

As my mind exploded in all directions, I examined the surreal mess that used to be me. I very badly wanted to sit up in bed and realize that it was all just a bad dream.

Master: *By the way, Prometheus, I couldn't have known about Bromes because he was from another one of your planets. You have so many now that you can't keep them all straight in your head.*

Prometheus: *You're one to talk! You've changed your name so often, I doubt you even remember who you are!*

Master: *At least I adapt, unlike you. Case in point…*

Old Master

Sometime after falling out of the sand bin and cracking my head on some rocks, I revived to Prometheus's face, which hadn't changed in twelve centuries, except for the addition of a long beard. His preference to keep the same features wherever he relocated made him stand out like ragweed in a rose garden. When he first made his body, it was probably considered attractive. Prometheus was unaware that the standards of beauty had changed around him.

Prometheus: *Just what are you implying?*

Master: *Nothing.*

Whatever I was lying on was too hard to be considered comfortable. My body felt miserable, but the misery was receding. I decided not to get up until it went away.

"*Static?*" No response. He must have been busy.

Prometheus waved a glowing stick over me. That struck me as hypocritical. He'd always claimed that using simple tools was primitive, and here he was using a tool. I couldn't resist pointing it out.

"*That's a nice stick you have there, Prometheus. Did you make it yourself?*"

"*Don't be childish, and don't call me Prometheus! On Oneia, I'm the holy prophet Tibbald, the chosen messenger of the great god Prometheus, and you're the holy catalyst, champion of the great god*

Prometheus. Remember that, and stay still, so I can finish healing you."

This wasn't the first time he'd involved me in one of his schemes. As usual, I wanted nothing to do with it, but I wouldn't be able to leave his planet without his help. There were several questions I wanted to ask. I started with the two I wanted answered most.

"Who's your soldier friend, and why is he pretending to be in love with somebody?"

A telepathic guy in fancy armor was staring at me. He was projecting sappy romantic fantasies mixed with rote battle strategies. I wondered who could be naïve enough to believe that those fake thoughts were real.

"That is High Commander Tiberius. He is of no concern, as long as you play your role."

Notwithstanding the loving diatribe coming from his head, he didn't appear to be a man of no concern. His armor and grooming were as vain as a strutting peacock, but his sword pommel was worn, and he stood balanced and ready – a warrior's stance. Most notably, his body was young, but his eyes screamed of age, just like mine. I pegged him as competent and socially cunning, with a subtle edge of the ruthless hunter.

"Why is he staring at me?" People stare at me often for various reasons, but Tiberius was sizing me up like a prize pig: Did I have any show potential left in me, or I would be better with a honey mustard glaze and an apple in my mouth? He made me uncomfortable, and that's hard to do. I decided to stare back and to see if I could make him look away first.

"I have no idea why he's staring at you. It probably has something to do with the priestess telling him to kill you for being a false catalyst. That woman is constantly trying to ruin my plans, I tell you! It's a wonder that I've made any progress in the past millennium! There, I'm finished; you're good as new! I'll just collect my things, and we can

be on our way." Prometheus switched abruptly to regular speech, which I couldn't understand in the slightest because he reflexively projected a bunch of neural gibberish when he started talking.

"Not that I'm interested in playing your game, but sharing the local lingo might be helpful." I usually pay people for the privilege of copying their language. Static's even luckier; he automatically understands languages, even through a mind block. We don't know why.

Prometheus paused, distractedly waved his stick, and ta da!

"You see, Tiberius, I told you I could revive the holy catalyst. You may leave now. Your presence is no longer required. I must speak in private with the great god's champion."

Tiberius didn't look like he was planning to leave anytime soon. He broke off our staring match. Good, I was too old to play kids' games – even when I won them. I got up and wandered around the room.

"Good Prophet, the divine priestess commanded me to destroy the false catalyst, yet you have claimed that this is the true catalyst and must not be destroyed. I would be remiss in my duties if I were to leave before this confusing dilemma is resolved."

Their conversation reeked of politics. I dislike politics because I think it's akin to lying, which goes against my philosophical framework, and I suck at it. I wanted as little to do with either as possible. Besides, there were far more important things to deal with, like eating something before I starved to death. I found a platter of food on a nearby table.

"Hey, Prometheus, do you mind if I eat some of this cheese?"

Prometheus looked at me blankly and then waved me out of his head. I took that as permission.

"Tiberius, I'm fully capable of defending myself should this prove to be a false catalyst, although I assure you, he is most certainly not. There's no need for you to be here."

I sat on the table and looked about the room as I wolfed down a chunk of mild-tasting white cheese. The room we were in boasted hundreds of dusty books on heavy wooden bookshelves; two massive brick fireplaces, complete with fire; and two sets of enormous wooden doors decorated with gold trim and relief carvings. I assumed that the room also had four walls, a floor, and a ceiling, but I couldn't see them with all the overlapping tapestries, rugs, paintings, sculptures, and chandeliers. There were also various tables that were unanimously overflowing – except for the one cleared to hold me – with expensive-looking knickknacks.

Of all the chairs and sofas, only one, a red velvet recliner with gold tassels and buttons, looked like it was designed to be comfortably used. An open bottle of red wine sat on a small table next to the chair. By way of these various observations, I came to the conclusion that the cheese was quite good. Tiberius, meanwhile, was holding his ground in the debate.

"Nonetheless, good Prophet, I must attend to the duty assigned to me. You may rest assured that any information gained from your questioning of the holy catalyst, should he be true or false, will not pass beyond this room."

"Prometheus, do you mind if I have some of these grapes, too?"

He scowled at me.

"Eat the tray if you wish! Just stop interrupting me! I'm trying to…."

"Holy One, allow me to introduce myself. I am High Commander Tiberius of the Holy Imperial Army and servant to her Majesty, the Divine Priestess." Tiberius words interrupted Prometheus's thoughts. Apparently, we all were supposed to pretend like he wasn't really a telepath.

I truly hate dishonesty. It makes me not want to trust anyone, not that I do, anyway.

"Who am I supposed to be again?" I asked Prometheus.

The grapes weren't quenching my thirst very well. There was plenty of wine around, but I've never liked either the taste or the effect of alcohol. I wished I had some hot chocolate.

Tiberius answered, "You are supposed to be the holy catalyst, the champion of the great god Prometheus. As the good Prophet has written, you are to receive the power and glory of our divine priestess, who will then rise to the heavens and become one with the great god. Or, you are a false catalyst, and thus, by order of the priestess, you must be killed immediately."

Translation: He knew I wasn't the catalyst, but if I didn't play the part, he was going to kill me. I wasn't terribly worried. I'm not that easy to kill.

To translate my role in Prometheus's phony prophesy, one needed to be familiar with Prometheus: He'd apparently set me up to be some kind conduit for this priestess, whose body would dematerialize during a power transfer. That would mean her death unless she happened to be a Host. My departure from Oneia via human sacrifice wasn't what I had in mind.

"What happens to the catalyst after he receives the power and the glory? Does he get to rise to the heavens, too?" I asked Prometheus.

"Yes, well, the prophecies are rather unclear on that point." He looked uncomfortable; he either didn't know, or what he knew wasn't good, probably both.

Tiberius explained, "There is a passage in the *Great Book of Holy Prophecies* that clearly suggests the catalyst will remain to care for the people of Oneia. Yet in the same volume, there is another passage that makes this unclear: '...and the champion of the holiest, for his loyal service, shall be consumed in the ecstasy of divine fire and share his triumph with the world.'" During his recitation, Tiberius looked at Prometheus; he laid the blame where it belonged.

So, Prometheus figured that I would either get left behind or blow myself up along with the planet; that was my take on it. I might not die if my power returned while Oneia exploded, but everyone else would. Someday, I was going to learn not to trust Prometheus, not that I do anyway.

"Do the prophecies mention how Prometheus and the catalyst are going to deal with the other gods? Divine rumor has it that they're in a bad mood these days, and they're in the neighborhood."

"The good prophet has made no mention of other gods in the first volume of the prophecies. There are other volumes with such references, but the good prophet was responsible only for the first."

Now, that was interesting, not that there were no other gods mentioned – Prometheus was just avoiding his problems – but that Tiberius knew I would be interested only in the parts that Prometheus wrote. Tiberius was obviously more than Prometheus thought he was. I was done playing mind games. It was time to get some straight answers.

"Who are you? Or more to the point, what are you, and what can you tell me about Prometheus's plans?" Tiberius's brow furrowed. My prize pig status took a hard turn toward pork chops.

"Holy Catalyst!" Prometheus tried to keep his secret identity from Tiberius, who already knew it. "You are delirious from your fall! I will heal the damage to your memory! You must rest... Tiberius, what in the name of wounded catalysts are you doing? Put that thing away!"

Tiberius had drawn his sword, which looked functional, despite its decorations. "Good Prophet, it appears as though the catalyst is false. Please stand aside while this humble soldier does as his divine priestess commands." He pointed the sword at my chest and waited to attack; he was offering me one last chance to play by the rules. Too bad for him, I make my own rules.

"This is foolishness!" Prometheus voiced his opinion, "High Commander Tiberius, I will be most upset if you damage the holy catalyst...."

He ranted, but nobody listened. Tiberius and I were entrenched in a psychological battle. I sat next to the cheese platter and casually popped grapes into my mouth. Tiberius waited, his sword hovering in line with my heart. We were testing each other, and the person who lost the test might become dead.

I suspected Tiberius was one of me. That is, he was once mortal, probably human, and had been turned into a Host. If it weren't for the odd effects on Oneia, I could have sensed his Hostly heritage by now, but it wasn't that hard to tell, anyway. Immortals have a certain fearless confidence about them that's difficult to hide from one of their own. I don't know how he managed to fool Prometheus for so long, but there you have it.

I casually tossed a grape at his forehead. A young, skilled swordsman, like Tiberius looked to be, should be able to move aside or to knock the grape away, and thus, demonstrate superior skill to his opponent. An aged, experienced swordsman would ignore the grape for the obvious ploy it was. It bounced off his forehead; he didn't even blink. That's what I thought would happen.

If Prometheus arrived on Oneia ten centuries ago, he would've had to modify Tiberius before that. Tiberius could be even older than I was. One can master almost any skill when one has a millennium or so to practice. A weapon would have been a good thing to have right about then.

"You would be wise not to do that twice." Tiberius didn't seem pleased with my grape attack.

"Please excuse the interruption, my friend, but could you lend your assistance in exterminating a saugael mor? I am defending a young female human, yet my current form is insufficient to the task."

I must have started slightly when Static contacted me, because Tiberius tensed. I still wasn't worried; he probably wouldn't attack until I actually did something. I heard the echo of a horn call from somewhere in the building. Tiberius heard it, too. He frowned, probably trying to decide what to do with me. I could tell that he wanted to see what the alarm was about, or maybe he'd already guessed and wanted to see if he was right. He would have to kill me, or let me go. Life was full of tough choices.

"Static, where are you?" I sensed his direction, but that was about it.

"We are in what appears to be an audience chamber."

'I have to go now, Tiberius. There's a saugael mor in your building. You might want to help me get rid of it – nasty things, big spiders with claws." I did a deadpan pantomime of claws. My eyes said, 'Get out of my way.'

"You will most certainly not be going anywhere near one of those horrid assassins, young man! I need you alive!"

Prometheus seemed adamant, but Tiberius and I ignored him. I sometimes feel bad for Prometheus that no one takes him seriously, but he causes it himself.

"We will resume this discussion in private after the creature is destroyed." I was tempted to ask if the creature he meant was Prometheus, but Static needed my help. I nodded. Tiberius lowered his sword.

"It's in your audience chamber," I told him, and he sprinted out the door. I followed.

"Return here this instant! This is undignified! Desist I tell you!" Prometheus scolded as he ran after us. His robes flapped behind him, and his beard billowed around his neck. He looked out of place, but he kept up.

We sprinted past some people, who cringed in shock against the walls. I couldn't blame them. We were probably an odd sight, their sword-wielding High Commander racing by like an armed juggernaut, chased by a big man in bloody rags, and followed by their Prophet waving a stick.

At the end of a long hallway, a door barred our path. Tiberius shouldered into it, but it didn't budge.

"This door has been sealed by one of your priests, good Prophet. Please use your rod to open it." Tiberius didn't look like he was in the mood to argue.

"I most certainly will not!" Prometheus crossed his arms. "The joining ceremony won't work if the holy catalyst is chopped into little bits! I need him intact and breathing!"

Muffled battle sounds filtered through the door. Static was in trouble. I kicked the door hard, but it barely moved, demonstrating that it wasn't a normal door. I glowered at Prometheus and considered using his head as a battering ram, but I decided against it. Prometheus wasn't keeping me from helping Static; the door was. He was just being a selfish idiot, and that wasn't a problem I should solve with violence. On the other side of the door was a problem I could solve with violence.

"Prometheus, if you open the door, I'll help you with your ceremony. Otherwise, you can forget it."

Prometheus was startled by the deal I'd offered. He'd never suspected that I might refuse to help. "If I let you through that door, you're just going to get yourself killed! What good is that going to do me?"

"Good Prophet, if you assist in the battle, the holy catalyst might not be harmed," Tiberius suggested.

"Oh very well then, stand aside!" Prometheus's stick glowed in his hand, and the door opened to chaos.

Master: *Back to you, Static.*

Prometheus: *Oh, just continue, why don't you? You're going to be dead in a few moments, anyway! I told you that would happen, you know! If you had listened to me, none of this would have happened!*

Master: *If I hadn't listened to you, I wouldn't have been trapped on Oneia in the first place.*

Static: *That is correct, my friend. And yet, if that were the case, we may not have discovered a possible solution to our difficulties, nor would we have met Alenna. It is an inefficient use of time to ruminate on past decisions unless something can be learned from them.*

Master: *Too true.*

Static: *I will now relate my efforts to rescue Alenna from the mor.*

Martin Wolfe

Chapter Five

Static

"Are we there yet, Static? I'm really scared." Alenna clung to my sodden hide and shivered.

"We are now approaching the entrance to the city, Alenna. I will seek permission to enter."

"You're going to ask? Can't we just go in? It's going to get us."

We had just completed our latest crossing of the river, which I had kept between us and the assassin. Alenna's hands were mottled red and white from dips into the freezing current; her leggings and boots were soaked. Behind us, the mor found a narrow span, leapt across, and devoured our lead as it had before. But we had left the relative safety of the river and were vulnerable.

"I aim to encourage the gatekeeper to raise the bridge. The moat will then become a barrier to the saugael mor." I noted that the sentries along the city wall were not emitting telepathic chants. *"Alenna, are all individuals on this planet capable of telepathic communication?"*

"No, just us," she paused and then added, *"and I guess the priestess, too."* Alenna referred to Eldorans.

The men guarding the moat wall were not Eldoran; I would be unable to convey the real danger. They would react with antagonism to my presence and would not see the mor as the greater threat. The only alternative was a simple vocal warning. I roared. Alenna flinched. The men began raising the bridge. My success in achieving my goal was premature. I had intended to cross the drawbridge before it was raised.

"Alenna, please maintain a firm grip on my hide. We will be airborne for a moment."

Although I leapt as smoothly as possible, my large mass catapulted Alenna beyond the apex of the half-raised drawbridge. She lost her grip and sailed above the courtyard. I paused on the bridge's lip, estimated Alenna's trajectory, and leapt mightily to intercept her. Gathering Alenna against my chest, I twisted to shield her from the greater impact, and landed with jarring force on my back. We struggled to breathe.

I recovered first and waited for Alenna. She rose to her feet as exclamations of surprise echoed down from the watch stations. The mor's efforts to cross the moat were frightening the guards. We had little time to waste. The assassin would not be detained for long by the moat, and the wall would pose no difficulties to it whatsoever, nor would the sentries, who were uneducated in defending against such a creature. Alenna dutifully climbed onto my back.

"I require direction, Alenna."

"The holy prophet lives in the priestess's temple." She pointed to a megalithic edifice at the end of the street we faced. I waited until she regained her grip, roared in warning, and accelerated, causing pandemonium on the busy street. Bystanders stumbled into each other as we rushed past.

When I reached a wide staircase leading to the temple entrance, I paused. Two guards at the top of the stairs moved to arrest our progress. I heard the first agonized scream echo from behind us. The saugael mor was within the city walls. Unless it was distracted by the wanton desire to kill humans, it would soon close the distance between us.

I identified one of the temple guards as a telepath. *"The child I carry is of your Eldoran heritage. Please allow us to pass. We are pursued by a deadly beast."*

The man stepped back, startled, but he did not stand aside. In the market street behind us, the cacophony inspired by the mor drew nearer.

"It's coming really fast, Static!"

The guards' faces turned ashen.

"You and your associate are not equipped to deter a saugael mor. I suggest that you call for reinforcements. Several dozen men with nets and bludgeoning weapons should be sufficient. Strike its feet only."

I batted the spear from the Eldoran and stepped around his fellow, who seemed disinclined to approach. The Eldoran sentry instructed his comrade-in-arms to seek help. He did not, however, request specific weaponry, and he chose to remain and defend the temple entrance. His gesture was futile. The man's skills had been insufficient to detain a large cat and would be no use at all against the mor. He would be murdered shortly.

I took the most direct approach into the temple and charged to the large double doors at the far end of the foyer's hallway. Another pair of sentries, standing at the doors, panicked and threw their spears at us as we approached. I knocked their projectiles aside and roared so loudly that one man nearly lost his footing. Their disregard for the unprotected child on my back had raised my ire, and I wished to maul them. I struggled to contain my anger and refrained from using excessive force.

The men pressed themselves against the doors that barred our path. I stalked forward, bared my fangs, and growled my displeasure. They struggled to draw their swords. With more enthusiasm than required, I swatted the guards aside.

The doors were neither locked nor barred. I hooked a claw between the edges and forced them open. Alenna's grip on my hide tightened. I turned to see the saugael mor flow spider-like through the sunlit entrance. The Eldoran sentry dangled on the end of its outstretched claws; his dead face was cast in horror. The assassin tossed the corpse aside and crept forward. It still tried to draw uninhibited terror from us, but we refused to abandon our mental barricades, and thus, it was moderately thwarted. But the downed sentries curled into heaps and whimpered. I slipped through the doorway and hoped for a more defensible location beyond.

Unfortunately, the adjoining room, which appeared to be a type of audience chamber, was grandiosely spacious and more appropriate for full-scale battle than solitary defense. The occupants of the room were roused and reacted with hostility to my presence. Several guards organized to subdue me, but I skirted the chamber's perimeter before we could be surrounded. We arrived at a small alcove, which contained a single door that did not open to my prodding. The gathered sentries cornered us.

Twenty-three of the temple's defenders crept toward my position. I welcomed their presence; several armed obstacles now stood in the path of the saugael mor. They turned to the sound of a screaming man who sailed through the air of the audience chamber. The dead sentry skidded and flopped to a landing. His blood streaked and spattered across the white tiles.

Balanced on the tips of its long, slender claws, the mor entered through the open doors. Its excited hissing clicks mingled with the panicked cries of women and the frightened shouts of men; the unnatural fear it induced intensified. It prepared to kill its chosen prey.

"Alenna, please dismount and stand in the corner. I shall attempt to defend us."

The mor disemboweled three soldiers in its first round of strikes. It punctured and peeled them open as if their bronze breastplates were made of leather. Unused spears fell from lifeless hands and clattered to the floor. The remaining twenty guardsmen turned to defend against the real threat. They ignored me, surrounded the mor, and pressed forward with their spears and swords.

The assassin braced itself on two tripod legs, long jointed spindles ending in bulbous feet that splayed three claws each. Its remaining four limbs jerked and flailed from its body; men died. The spastic attacks were deceptive. All twelve claws parried, pierced, or severed their targets; the mor wasted few efforts.

Four guards rushed between the mor's limbs and lanced its body, which hung above their heads. Three spears and one sword penetrated the spongy black ball. Caustic acid gushed over the arms, head, and chest of the unknowing victims. A hissing sheet of blackened blood washed over the stumps of their bones, and clumps of half-dissolved flesh splattered to their feet. Plumes of sour gray smoke rose from the carnage as the guards' corpses tumbled and writhed in a reddish-brown pool. The assassin's wounds closed. Its body was a decoy; the mor's brains and vital organs were housed in its feet.

The remaining defenders were demoralized. They swiped at the mor's limbs and missed. I silently applauded their failure. Beheading a saugael mor's eyeless feet would only compound the problem.

My own attacks fared little better, but I was nonetheless persistent. With each lunge and retreat, I scratched a foot of the mor at least once. The mor returned my wounds cut for cut, and my fur was matted with blood, but my vital organs had not been breached. I continued. My claws dulled in its acid, which was less virulent in its feet, but still burned. The mor's injuries healed; whereas, mine did not. I had no surplus energy to mend wounds, and thus, my attacks only delayed the inevitable. My body would soon be inoperable; Alenna would die.

Then, I realized my failure to contact my companion. If he were once again alive, he would be a valuable addition to the defending force. He did not have access to his Host powers, but his manufactured physique exceeded normal human parameters in terms of strength, stamina, and dexterity.

He responded when I called to him; I requested assistance.

Shortly thereafter, additional human reinforcements arrived through the double doors. These new defenders wore different uniforms than their counterparts and conducted themselves with greater skill and martial discipline. I held out hope that Alenna and I might remain intact until my companion arrived.

I was not disappointed. Two collisions sounded from the door next to Alenna. Moments later, the door opened, and my friend entered. He paused to collect two swords from the hands of two equally deceased sentries and then leapt into the fray. Tiberius joined the melee also. Prometheus skirted the perimeter.

The assassin went berserk. It lunged at my friend, its attacks doubled, and I knew that I had been duped again. I had led the mor directly to my companion so that I could protect the girl I had recruited to save him. The mor had used my fear of failure against me and had goaded me into a conflict of interest. Now, both Alenna and my friend were in jeopardy. I felt foolish.

My companion was nonetheless equipped to deal with the mor's frenzied rush, for he had long ago honed his martial skills against Paul, his personal assistant, who is one of the few clawed beings deadlier than a saugael mor.

Amid rapid parries, he speared one of the assassin's foot-housed brains. The leg convulsed, died, and swung to dangle from the mor's body. A few moments later, the assassin shed the useless limb, which dropped into the carnage. Its empty joint slowly sprouted a new leg, complete with a clawed foot, which grew and stiffened as though filling with air. But when the expansion stopped, the tips of the claws reached no farther than the length of a man's forearm; the limb was miniature. The tiny appendage struggled to kill but reached nothing.

I had witnessed a mor's spontaneous regeneration in the past, but then, its new limbs had grown to full size. The planet's energy-restricting environment must have stunted its growth. If this phenomenon continued, we would likely survive the encounter.

Tiberius attacked the mor on its opposite side. He showed himself to be an outstanding martial combatant with skills and abilities similar to those of my companion; I suspected that he was a Host-hybrid like my companion. With a deft cut, he severed one of the assassin's limbs.

"No! No! No! Tiberius, don't cut off the legs! Kill the feet! Kill the feet!" Prometheus yelled. His assessment mirrored my own. If Tiberius was indeed a Host, he had evidently not come in previous contact with a saugael mor.

The detached foot skittered about on its three claws; its leg-stump fell away. Six new limbs sprouted, each sporting a clawed foot. Then the old claws were shed from its body. The liberated black ball had transformed itself into another saugael mor, and it was ready to kill. But like the new legs that grew from the stumps of the first mor, the results were miniature. The new assassin grew no taller than the knee of the shortest guard.

I pounced on the smaller beast, held down its thrashing legs, and crushed its brains with my teeth. My mouth was scorched, but the small creature did not have enough acid to prevent me from killing it.

Prometheus attacked the larger mor with energy he summoned from his rod. White-hot power crackled in jagged bands around the assassin's limbs. The mor was unharmed, but the blast pushed it forward, and my friend suffered for its unexpected movement. Claws destined for a parry changed trajectory and sheared off three of his fingers. One of his salvaged weapons tumbled after his severed digits.

Just then, a woman's authoritative shriek cut through the battle sounds. "What is the meaning of this? Why are you people making a mess in my temple? Someone is keeping thoughts from me! Who is it? I demand to know this instant! Stop this immediately! I command you to stop!" She was assumedly the priestess.

The central portion of the saugael mor, and its two stunted limbs, detonated. Acid sprayed in all directions. Being the closest to the creature, my companion received the largest dose. He fell. Four new assassins formed from the feet that rolled across the chamber. Guards chased after them.

"Alenna, please mount."

Alenna climbed aboard and resumed her mental chant. I developed a telepathic façade of my own, lest the priestess detonate me also.

"Static, aren't we going to help your friend?"

A single mor escaped the notice of the remaining defenders and approached us. I slapped the beast aside, and it scrambled off in search of more fearful victims.

"My companion is dead, Alenna. His body is no longer suitable for rejuvenation."

I did not point out the charred human detritus – my friend's remains – where it laid like a cluster of islands within a lake of blood. I searched the lake and found the tiny island with a band of gold; my companion's severed finger still wore his ring. I collected the digit with my teeth and held it out to Alenna.

"Please store this, Alenna."

She shook her head; her jaw hung slack. I suspected that I looked unpleasant; the fur around my snout had been burned by the mor's acid, and my jaws dripped blood. I held my position. She whined but surrendered, picking the finger from between my fangs and dropping it into a pocket of her winter apparel.

Prometheus, shoulders slumped, stood over my companion's remains. Nearby, Tiberius stood sporting a blistered face and leg. He glared at the Priestess, who was calling for the guards to collect the miniature assassins for her appraisal. She evidently found some aesthetic value in their existence.

Ignored, I padded across the audience chamber and through the double doorway. My companion's body would take time to regenerate from only a finger. I needed to procure a defensible shelter away from the city, so I could await his recovery. But first, I needed to locate Alenna's alternate guardians and return her to safety.

Static: *Prometheus, please relate your activities following the battle.*

Prometheus: [sighs] *Oh, if I must.*

Prometheus

I looked down at my ninth avatar. He was completely ruined! And if that weren't depressing enough, my favorite slippers were drenched, as was the bottom half of my beautiful white robe. Revolting bits dripped from the beadwork along the hem and splattered into a sea of red.

That was the straw that broke the prophet's back, I tell you! I lifted my foot and turned to vent my fury at the priestess, but the wet hem of my robe slapped against my leg and stuck. My stomach roiled, and I nearly lost my balance. I put my slippered sole back into the blood. Stone-chilled ooze squished between my toes – what a hideously revolting sensation! I stoically slogged through the gore.

When I reached dry land, I peeled off my slippers and tossed them away. Venting could wait. I stalked toward one of Tiberius's guardsmen. He was dragging a corpse out of the throne room.

"You there, soldier, tell my servants to prepare my bathing chamber! Have them put out the blue towels, not the red! I'll have no more red today, none of it, I tell you!"

The simpleton just stood there blinking at me. He looked to Tiberius, whose stony gaze was transfixed on the priestess. Without turning, Tiberius nodded his permission. The soldier laid down the body and left to follow my instructions.

My feet made red prints on the marble as I turned and marched by Tiberius. Horror! Half of his face had been blackened and cauterized by the beastie's acid. His right leg, too, from mid-thigh downward, looked the same. My colleagues should have destroyed those nasty vermin long ago. Using them as assassins was entirely unethical.

"I must say, Tiberius, you look absolutely ghastly! You really should see your face! It's quite the mess! It must be terribly painful! Your...." I'd been about to tell him that some of his hair had melted off, when he turned and glared at me. Tiberius can be quite intimidating at times.

"Yes, well, that is, I should probably heal you. Your appearance is most disturbing!"

Tiberius nodded and turned back to glare at the priestess, who was being entertained by her new pets – assassins for pets, of all things! She was having the four little beasts dance for her amusement while dead and dying soldiers were carried from the throne room. Tiberius must have been rather perturbed by that. His mental devotions to the Priestess had stopped.

He stood motionless while I healed him. The residual acid interfered with the rod and made the healing incomplete. He wasn't going to die, but he wasn't going to be handsome, anymore. A mass of rippling scars bubbled outward from his nose and reached past his ear. His leg hadn't healed properly either, but that could be covered. The loss of his face was truly a shame. He'd been such a lovely man.

"Very well then, I suppose that will have to do. Maybe you could have a mask made to cover that, so you don't frighten the servants." He glared at me again. I really wished he wouldn't do that. Now that he was half hideous, his penetrating stare was even more unnerving. I followed as he turned and walked toward the priestess. He had a noticeable limp. This was entirely the priestess's fault; may assassins shave her bald!

The little beasts performed acrobatics for their new mistress. They piled onto one another and formed a tower. She clapped her hands in approval. I wished that her new pets would escape her control and dice her into tiny bits! I inhaled to vent, but Tiberius was faster.

"Divine Priestess, the good prophet and I ask to be excused from your presence, so that we may restore order and heal the wounded." Tiberius spoke with a lisp – oh, how horrible! The former richness of his voice was made tragic by the slurring.

The priestess hadn't noticed what she'd done to Tiberius. His appearance startled her. She radiated disgust and then resentment that Tiberius had abandoned her. The miniature assassins hissed, mimicking her mood. Time in the universe could wrap around and start over before I ever understood this woman!

Tiberius resumed his loving chant, but it was different than before. He now projected the role of a trusted and respected advisor, rather than a charismatic and infatuated warrior; his scars were not tragic; they were badges of honor for serving his priestess. He stood straight and proud, but with his head lowered in respect. By the blood of soggy slippers, his ruse actually worked! The priestess's puny mind wrapped around the idea like a piece of flotsam from a shipwreck!

"High Commander Tiberius, your suggestion is most wise. Please attend to these matters." She turned and looked at me. "See if you can do something about the commander's face!"

Stupid woman, did she think that his scars formed by themselves? "I already tried! The blasted rod of office didn't work! You'll just have to do it yourself!"

"So, you seek to blame me, Prophet? I'm at fault because I made the rods, is that it? Insolence! It is you that didn't work! Fix your own failure! Get out!"

Tiberius glared at me. Of all the nerve! What did I do? I turned and stormed out of the throne room. Little beasties came skittering after me. The wicked woman had sent her evil pets to get me; may assassins ransack her wardrobe! I dashed through the servants' entrance and slammed the door behind me. Tiberius knocked a moment or so later.

"Have they gone, Tiberius?" How I detest those creatures, especially the little ones that look like fat spiders!

"They have left with the priestess, good Prophet. You are safe," he replied through the door. If I didn't know better, I would have sworn he was mocking me. I tossed opened the door.

"Naturally, I'm safe! I merely wished to keep my robe from further damage. Their claws are quite sharp, you know."

He drew his sword, and for a moment, I thought he was going to attack me. "They are sharp indeed, good Prophet! You may see for yourself the nicks they make in good steel. I would appreciate any intelligence you have on the priestess's new pets." He put his sword away and motioned for me to walk with him. "My quarters are those of a humble soldier. Let us adjourn to your chambers. We will be more comfortable." He hooked his arm in mine.

This was unprecedented! I'd propositioned Tiberius often, but sadly, he'd never accepted. I was delighted by his change of heart, although his ruined face dampened my enthusiasm somewhat.

Arm in arm, we strolled the route to my rooms. Along the way, I spotted one of my personal servants, who stood and gawked as Tiberius and I passed. He must have been shocked by Tiberius's wounds. I gave stern orders that my bathing chamber had best be prepared for our arrival. The simpleton shook off his stupor and ran to do my bidding.

When we arrived, Tiberius opened my sitting room doors for me and called for one of my personal attendants. A boy appeared from the servants' quarters and bowed.

"The good Prophet and I are not to be disturbed this evening. Inform everyone, not just the prophet's retainers."

My next avatar could take his time arriving. If things went as I hoped, I'd be suitably entertained in the interim. The servants left, and Tiberius closed the doors. Oh, I could hardly wait!

"Good Prophet, I will wait for you in your sitting room. We can talk when you finish your bath." He walked to a bookshelf and fingered through the titles.

Oh, blast, that wasn't what I had in mind at all! Two disasters in one day were more than I could take! I stormed into my bathing chamber. A warm bath and clean robes helped sooth my nerves. I was somewhat calmer when I returned to find Tiberius sitting in my favorite chair.

"You will just have to move, young man! I haven't given you permission to sit in my chair! I don't care how charming you think you are! Get up! Get up!"

He rose slowly and carried the book he was reading to a spindle-backed wooden chair next to the wine cupboard.

"Good Prophet, you forget that I am the immortal high commander, chosen, as legend tells it, by the priestess herself and kept alive these past eleven centuries by her magic. I was old before you arrived on Oneia. Perhaps I should consider you to be a young man."

Such impertinence! I was tired of the lack of respect I received around here! I made a decision.

"It is time that you learn who I truly am!" I stood, spread my arms, and assumed my godly persona. "I have existed for longer than your tiny mind can fathom! I have created stars and watched them age! Hear my holy words, and tremble, for I am he who created the world! I am the great god Prometheus!" My rod of office made my voice echo, which I always thought was a nice effect.

Tiberius tilted his head and raised his remaining eyebrow. He must have been overawed by my divine presence.

"Good Prophet, I have always known you were Prometheus. You created this prison and then learned that it was meant for you. So you created the catalysts as a means of escape, a means that your compatriots would find threatening, and thus, unknowingly send after you into confinement. You are creative, good Prophet, unique from your fellows. So I ask this: Why did you not flee, rather than condemning others to share your fate?"

I was flabbergasted! "Who sent you? Was it the Eldorans? Don't think for a blink that you're going to keep me from my avatars! Who are you? Speak up!"

He poured my wine from my decanter and drank from my glass! I'm a god! Nobody drinks a god's wine without asking! The man had absolutely no respect for divinity!

"Good Prophet, I have reached my limit of patience for your prison, and I find that I am willing to take greater risks to escape it. If we are to assist one another, we will need to share intelligence. To that end, I will confess that my name is, in fact, Tiberius, as it has always been. The vanity of keeping my name is the simple reason that your compatriots discovered my existence. The history of a name can be traced. And my history is longer than most. I was a boy of eight summers when you transformed me."

"You're obviously mistaken, young man. Except for the priestess, I've never made any avatars from children.

You all had to be so dangerously adaptive that this was the only prison ingenious enough to hold you."

"Indeed, perhaps I am mistaken. Still, I wonder how someone so creative as yourself could be found so easily?"

"Obviously, you haven't met those Neo-Genesis boors I enhanced! I'm not the only god with emotions, you know! I generously endowed several of my fellow gods with human genes, and it just so happens that humans are naturally creative."

Tiberius nodded. "The one called Cerberus – you knew he would find you."

"He still refuses to recognize that my research made us safer! We were too genetically similar! Something had to be done!"

"Safe from what, good Prophet? It was my understanding that your species could not be killed? Could you mean the bird named Static, whom you helped turn into a lion? Your reaction to it intrigues me."

That volatile virus was none of his concern!

Chapter Six

Master: *That sounds like a good lead-in for you, Static.*

Static: *I agree, my friend. I will relate our flight from the city.*

Static

"We should leave, Static!"

"There is an Eldoran in this building, Alenna." I sought an alternate guardian for Alenna. She had informed me that she had no surviving family.

"Static!" Alenna feared that the city's enraged denizens, who wrongly pursued us for assaulting their Priestess, would discover our presence.

"Alenna, we are in no more danger now than we were moments ago. The danger is less, in fact, as our pursuers will need to find us."

The building we had entered was an establishment for conducting trade. It housed supplies and implements for preparing and manipulating animal skins. There were numerous items of leather apparel, some tools, and many leather accessories displayed about the shop. The scent of protective oils was intense.

"I would have discourse with you," I addressed the Eldoran, likely the shop's proprietor, who hid on the floor above. Concealing his physical presence was an ineffective means of avoiding discovery. I could easily detect his mental chanting.

"Get out of my shop!" The ladder leading to the upper level jostled from contact.

"I have in my care an orphaned Eldoran child. Would you consent to be her guardian?" He was unlikely to assist us when

he disdained our presence, but I would be remiss in my chosen duty if I forsook the effort.

"Get out! To the pits with you, get out! Priests will find you here and burn my shop while I'm still in it!"

"Could you perhaps descend and entertain a more rational conversation? I will not harm you unless you attack."

A moment passed before he climbed down, awkwardly holding a woodcutting axe against the outer edge of the ladder. He laid his weapon across the countertop that separated him from us, but he kept one hand on the shaft.

"Don't want anything to do with raising a kid. Too dangerous in the city. Try out in the woods."

That made little sense. In the wilderness, a child would be easy prey, but in the city, there would be no indigenous wildlife to defend against.

"May I inquire as to why age is an impediment? Humans generally have more favorable reactions toward juveniles."

"Kids can't fake it good enough. Priestess finds them quick and burns them with everybody they know." His brow furrowed deeper. "What are you, anyhow? Never met an Eldoran that could change shape."

"I am unaware of my origins or of any species related to me."

Outside, the mob that had passed us by when we entered the shop returned for a dwelling-to-dwelling search. The proprietor moved to the oilskin-paned window and cracked it open. He bared his teeth and hissed his disapproval. "To the pits, you've led them right to me! Get in with the drying racks, and stay quiet!" He gestured toward a narrow doorway draped with a sheet of tanned leather.

I carried Alenna toward the curtain and passed through. The darkened room, which was cramped with wooden racks and animal hides, had only the single egress. I turned and peered through an opening where the draped skin met the wall.

"Static, you're still bleeding."

"I will be fine, Alenna. Please do not distract me at this juncture."

"But we have to get your cuts cleaned and bandaged, or you'll get feverish. My father told me so."

"I thank you for your concern, Alenna, but I cannot be killed, nor do I succumb to poison or infection. When I have a suitable supply of energy, I will regenerate my torn flesh."

Someone pounded on the door of the building. The proprietor moved to admit the unwelcome guest.

"Does it hurt?"

"Yes, Alenna, my wounds cause me discomfort. Please refrain from transmitting thoughts at this time." I am not an entity that is easily frustrated, but Alenna's mental chatter was distracting me from maintaining vigilance.

When the shop's door opened, city guards filed in. I could see behind them the mob of discontented citizenry carrying impromptu weaponry. A man wearing robes and carrying a rod similar to Prometheus's followed the guards. His manner of dress identified him as a priest of the local religious order. An under-grown saugael mor perched on his forearm. He seemed confident that his artifact offered him the same level of assassin-control that his Priestess enjoyed. I did not share his confidence. The beast currently suppressed its fear-inspiring tactics, but I suspected that its game would soon change.

"Static, if you think to yourself that it doesn't hurt then…."

"Alenna, be silent! Block your thoughts and hold on tightly. There is a saugael mor present." She offered no more thoughts that the assassin could interpret. This would not stop the mor from controlling our feelings, but we did not need to offer it exploitable details, such as the knowledge that I suffered from blood loss.

I felt responsible for endangering the storeowner. *"Stay away from the invertebrate creature. It is extremely deadly and unpredictable."* He gave no indication that he had received my message, but I was reasonably certain that he had.

He prostrated himself on the wooden floor. "Your Holiness, I am honored by your visit. May the divine priestess live forever," he said.

The guards surveyed the room while the priest said, "Where are the Eldoran girl and her beast? Speak the truth, tanner; the power of the divine priestess will tell me if you lie." With the tips of his fingers, the priest stroked the saugael mor's body; he would likely not live out the day.

"I have seen no one enter, but you and your escort, Holiness." The tanner offered a cleverly misleading version of the truth, for he had not, in fact, witnessed our entry.

Sadly, his deception would fool only the humans. The mor already knew we were present. Had it realized that we carried the remains of my companion, it would have been exceptionally pleased with its good fortune. Segmented saugael mor possess the knowledge of their predecessor and retain its need to destroy their given target.

Then the assassin spat forth the characteristic hisses and clicks indicative of its kind. Unnatural fear coursed through me. Alenna clenched my hide in her fists, but she otherwise remained still.

The guards and the priest stiffened, while the storeowner covered his head. I chose the distraction as our moment to escape and leapt from concealment. Only the mor responded. It sprang from the priest's arm and sailed toward us, but in its reduced size, it was overconfident. I swatted the tiny beast aside as a housecat would swat a rodent. Its needle-sharp claws sliced my paw, and I trailed fresh blood as I bolted through the open doorway.

The priest turned and ejected from his rod a column of energy at my haunches. I absorbed the power and healed my wounds. The power flow ended abruptly, but not because the priest had recognized his error. He screamed.

"Static, the saggelmore cut his neck! It killed a priest!"

"That is to be expected, Alenna. Saugael mor are not pets and should not be treated as such. Please face forward and concentrate on maintaining your purchase."

The gathered citizens acted as shocked by the priest's death as Alenna. They offered no resistance as I sped between them and raced toward the city gate, which was presently clogged with cavalry headed toward the temple. Horses rumbled three abreast across the now lowered drawbridge. The soldiers looked upon Alenna and I as a curiosity as we approached; they were likely late arrivals, called upon to deal with a giant spider, not a girl and her peculiar pet. Their mounts panicked and reared at my presence. Unhorsed riders tumbled onto the bridge and into the moat. I bounded harmlessly through the chaos and sprinted into the distance. When I could no longer sense the thoughts of the city's residents, I slowed and caught my breath.

"Static, can I talk now?"

"Yes, Alenna, you may. I apologize for my abruptness."

"That's okay, Static. My father always says that I talk too much. He says…" Alenna paused sadly with remembered grief that her father was now deceased. "He used to say that I drove him crazy."

"Do not be concerned for the loss of your guardian, Alenna. We should find a replacement shortly."

She did not respond, and I realized that my condolence might have been too practical to soothe her emotional trauma. Moments passed in silence as I loped toward the village where my companion landed.

"Static, I'm cold."

"I am chagrinned that I have been remiss in your proper care, Alenna. I shall seek a shelter for the evening immediately."

I reached the village and found an abandoned dwelling that did not have dismembered bodies in its vicinity. The humble interior contained a straw-filled linen mattress, a thresh-covered dirt floor, a wooden table, a stone fire pit, and a pantry shelf with one of each: pot, mug, knife, bag of barley flour, urn of water, and head of cabbage. A circular hearth ringed the fire pit, and a pile of wood sat at the hearth's edge, as did a flint stone and hammer.

Alenna sat on the bedding and hugged herself for warmth, while I stacked logs into the fire pit and pondered my dilemma: I had no thumbs with which to strike flint against steel, nor did I have the energy to adapt my paws. I felt helpless to raise the temperature above freezing.

"Alenna, please assist me in starting a fire."

She frowned at the stack of wood, and it burst into flames. Surprised but pleased, I added more fuel to the happy conflagration and singed my whiskers while doing so.

"That is a very useful skill, Alenna. Do all Eldorans have these abilities?"

Alenna shrugged, unimpressed with her accomplishment. "Everybody does different things mostly."

"Can you perform other tasks?"

"I can throw rocks this big," she weakly mimed the size of a large cabbage, "but I shouldn't do too much here. The priests might find me." Her shoulders slumped, and she began to cry.

I padded toward the Alenna and attempted to hug her, but my body was not human, and I was largely unpracticed at comforting emotionally distressed children. I flattened her onto the bedding, and she was nearly smothered in my mane. I nonetheless achieved the desired result. Alenna giggled through my fur and returned my awkward embrace.

"I don't want to be alone, Static."

"As I have mentioned, Alenna, I will locate a guardian for you. You will not be alone for long."

"I don't want a guardian. I want to stay with you."

I moved back slightly and replied with all seriousness. *I am an inappropriate parent for a human child, Alenna. My total experience in a human body is less than one hundred eighty-seven years, which is insufficient practice, and I have no childhood memories to use as a frame of reference.*

"You'll do okay, Static, and I can help, too. Besides, my father had only fifteen summers of practice before he had me. You have way more."

I would be a liability to your safety. Traveling with a predatory cat would not be conducive to a life of secrecy.

"You can change into a bird, again."

I require energy to effect a change, Alenna. On Oneia, I have none, nor do I have ready access to a priest's rod.

"I can give you energy." Alenna briefly infused me with her power, which would be enough for me to mutate into a smaller form.

Were I to transform into a bird, I would be unable to regain my larger mass, and thus, I would be unable to protect you.

"You can still protect me against the priests and the priestess. And if anybody else bothers me, I can just set them on fire, or throw things at them. I'll get stronger, too. My father said so."

I had run out of arguments, and Alenna's reasons were sound; she would likely fare better under my limited protection, which would eliminate the threat of energy attacks. Still, I was reluctant, for I feared unfamiliar emotional territory.

We will first search for a more serviceable guardian. If we are unsuccessful, I shall accept the responsibility of your care and education.

Alenna frowned, at first unhappy with my conditional acceptance, but then she brightened and agreed. "Okay, Static, nobody will want me, anyway. My father taught me all about that, too."

Had her father been alive, I would have questioned him about the appropriateness of offering such a peculiar lesson.

Alenna offered her energy, again, and I transformed into a large hunting bird. I then flew out of the shelter and searched for supplements to our evening meal of bannock and cabbage.

Unless I could find another caretaker for Alenna, I would become her permanent provider. I comforted myself by ruminating on ways that Alenna's power could rejuvenate my companion's body more quickly. He would undoubtedly be a more appropriate role model for Alenna than I.

Prometheus: *You know, I think Tiberius was looking for that girl. What ever happened to her?*

Master: *You have a mind like a sieve, Prometheus. You just met her.*

Prometheus: *Nonsense! I haven't laid eyes on a human girl in years! They weren't permitted in the temple, you know. They always told the priestess exactly what they were thinking. Can you imagine?*

Static: *Prometheus, Alenna should return from her bath shortly. You will meet her again.* [addresses Master] *My friend, would you please continue your tale of youthful tribulations. They offer valuable insights.*

Master: *Yeah sure.*

Young Master

Near the end of a wacky nightmare, I floated through the window of my darkened apartment and entered a new body, which hadn't existed until I wished for it. I awoke to sunlight cooking my brain. The clock showed eleven thirty; I'd missed my presentation. I groaned, rubbed my face, and rolled out of bed, or mattress rather.

As I stumbled toward the washroom, I noted that my neighbors were unusually loud. Their voices echoed inside my head – weird.

I conducted my ritual inspection in the mirror, which was lower than it should have been. I slapped myself a couple times, shook my head, and checked the mirror again. Nope, it was still too low, or I was too tall. And my face looked prettier than it should. Not that I was complaining, but it looked too good to slough off as having a decent hair day. That was enough looking in the mirror. It was causing me disturbing thoughts.

I shuffled to the couch and picked up my jeans. My security guard uniform should have been on the couch, too, but it wasn't. I pretended that I left the cheap blue outfit at work last night. But my subconscious pointed out that I'd worn my uniform to work and asked if I remembered walking home naked. I told my subconscious to shut up and threw on my shirt, which was too tight. I tried to kick into my jeans, which didn't fit either – you've grown, you idiot; the new body you made in your dream is bigger than the old one, and a deranged businessman burned your uniform off you.

So, that was it then; I was definitely insane.

Admitting it was a relief. I now had an excuse for my laziness. My problems were officially someone else's. Maybe they could put me in a support group for people with severe hallucinations. Did I really walk home from work naked? Hopefully, I hadn't set any businessmen on fire. Thinking about that, I realized that I could be dangerous and that I should probably get to the hospital. The doctors would need to examine my brain.

But first, I needed to get to class and explain that I was mentally ill. A medical emergency was a valid excuse for failing to complete an assignment, and it would make me happy to frustrate my instructor.

My neighbors' voices reminded me that I was starving. I empathized with a lady enjoying her bagel and cream cheese. My mouth chewed food that wasn't there. I seriously needed a psychiatrist. Make that a psychiatrist, an MRI, and a turkey sandwich. My forced fast had been bearable up until then because I'd been avoiding thinking about food. Now my hallucinations were torturing me. I desperately wished for my hunger to go away. I nearly choked on air when it did.

Go with the flow. I wished that my clothes fit, and they did. While trying not to think about that, I grabbed my pack of unopened books, and headed out the door and down the hall.

A neighbor came out of his rented abode and stood next to me as I waited for the elevator. I kept my head down because I didn't like talking to people. The guy was mumbling to himself. Great, here was another lunatic. Now I wouldn't be lonely on my elevator ride. He was in a bad mood about having to deal with his boss. Well, I couldn't blame him for that. He kept repeating the same obscenities, which branded him as somewhat uncreative. I made a mental note not to babble out loud, no matter how crazy I became.

Before stepping forward to push the elevator button, he called me an idiot for not pushing the button. Startled, I looked up at him. He calmly waited for the elevator, as if he hadn't just insulted his neighbor. His lips weren't moving, but I could still hear him talking – so to speak. I reminded myself that I was nuts and probably just imagining things.

He noticed me staring, which made him nervous. I gathered what was left of my courage and decided to find out, once and for all, whether or not my marbles had rolled away.

"Excuse me; do you work for a Mr. Peterson?" How he answered would tell me if I was hallucinating, or if I could actually understand his thoughts. Which answer I would find more unsettling was open to debate.

The man had a sudden fear that his boss had sent me to fire him, but he shook it off. "Yes, do I know you?"

I'd been afraid he would answer like that, mostly because I knew that he would. "Not really, I just heard you thinking about a bastard named Peterson and wanted to see if I was crazy." I don't excel at lying.

The elevator doors opened, and I boarded. Dubious of my mental status, my neighbor changed his mind and walked back to his apartment. I rode down alone, left the building, and headed toward the train station. Three blocks away, I could still sense him thinking about how much of a freak I was. The city crowd washed him out.

The train arrived at the platform when I did. Following the rest of the cattle, I squeezed in. A young babe was thinking nice things about me. I sat down next to her.

"You think I'm attractive." My statement was a curious announcement of the obvious. Her thoughts and feelings already told me what I wanted to know.

Let me explain: when I was a kid, my father left, my mother worked, and I had few friends to mimic. I'd turned out somewhat different than those around me; my social skills were weak. And so, I'd had little luck with girls. I figured that my new mind-reading trick might get me a date.

"What?" Her mouth dropped open, and she frowned.

I was confused by her reaction, which was just like the other girls'. "I've never met anyone who thought I was attractive. Would you like to go out with me?"

After I said that, she radiated so many conflicting emotions that I couldn't pick one from the batch. Her thoughts were scattered until she came to a decision, which wouldn't have been my choice among the available options.

She smiled the nauseating smile I received so often. "No, thank you. That's very sweet, but I have a boyfriend," she lied.

Great, I could sense people's thoughts, and I still couldn't get a date. Keeping my anger from showing wasn't one of my main concerns, because others' opinions of my character weren't important to me, or so I told myself. I sat back and brooded.

Three blocks before arriving at my stop, I sensed the thoughts of two transit cops waiting to fine some deadbeats like me. Oops, I forgot about them. Being broke as I was, I'd already received two fines for failing to pay the train fare, and the fine had just gone up. Avoiding these two gentlemen would be wise.

I judged their moods. One planned to ride to the next stop because he liked to capture people who had nowhere to run. The other intended to wait at the station doors until the perpetrators came to him. If I knew what they planned to do, I could do the opposite and avoid them, but that wouldn't be possible until they made up their collective minds. For crap's sake people, let's have some coordination here!

The train stopped. The doors opened and were about to close, but they still hadn't reached a consensus. I didn't have the same option. Holding the doors open and waiting would have been like holding up a sign that read, *I'm guilty*.

The first transit man was determined to enter the train, so the second would have to follow. I threw my dice and stepped off. But the first realized that the second wasn't cooperating and backed up. The train clicked away without any of us on it. It was just my luck to get a couple of transit cops undergoing power struggle - ticket number three coming up.

"May I see your proof of fare please, sir?"

"I don't have one."

"Why is that, sir?" He took his ticket book out from where it was shoved down the back of his pants, or so it looked to me.

This was the part I didn't like. The guy didn't give a rat's butt why I hadn't paid the fare, and he was going to fine me anyway. I wanted to tell him just to give me the bloody ticket and get out of my way. "I don't have any money."

"There are social programs that can provide you with a monthly pass, sir."

Said programs didn't apply to me. I had a student loan and a part-time income, which I'd spent to busted and beyond. Making stupid decisions didn't count as being poor. I ground my teeth, avoided eye contact, and said nothing.

"May I see a piece of photo identification, sir?"

"I left it at home." It was true.

"Why would you do that, sir?"

"So I could say 'I left it at home' to someone like you." Also true.

At nineteen, I thought I was mature. That worries me, because I still think I'm mature.

"Please purchase a fare next time, sir." I offered my actual name and address so he could write me a proper ticket. The inability to lie well is a definite handicap in a species of born liars.

I wanted to say something memorable and cutting as I left, but nothing came to mind. My thoughts soured further when I realized I'd left my backpack on the train.

All the way up the staircase to the campus, I lashed my anger at the undeserving transit cop. I envisioned him burning like the psycho in my nightmare. Uh oh. I sped back down the stairs; my feet touched only the top and bottom landings.

I expected to find the charred remains of the transit cop on the station floor. He was giving a ticket to the next deadbeat in line. I breathed easier; my subconscious could tell a serious wish from a bad mood - phew. The old maxim to be careful what you wished for had added meaning where I was concerned. I climbed toward campus.

It was lunchtime when I cut through the cafeteria, which was full of my peers stuffing their faces. I would need to wait until classes started again before I could tell my instructor…. Tell him what? I was pretty sure by then that I wasn't nuts, a freak for sure, but not nuts. My medical excuse for tardiness was no longer relevant. Hanging out on campus was a bad idea; I was probably considered a fugitive.

The police would likely be at my workplace by now. They'd be examining the burned human flesh in the hallway and inquiring about the missing security guard. Everyone would soon think I was chopping up bodies and burning them in office buildings.

My options were thus: (1) confess and explain how the Greek god Prometheus burned me to crispy bits but gave me mind powers so that I could make a new body; (2) make up a story that was more believable and dazzle everyone with my skill at lying; or (3) run and hide.

Option three it was. But first, since I was already on campus, I decided to ask out my college crush – standard fugitive business.

She was, as usual, hanging out with a flock of ogling jocks. I interrupted. "What time on Friday night should I pick you up for dinner?" I was still angry at being rejected, and it showed as false confidence. Had any of the jocks tried to stop me, I probably would have set them on fire.

She looked shocked at first and then smiled. "Seven?" Apparently, she responded well to aggression. That explained her interest in jerks – I mean jocks.

Not wanting to screw up my good fortune, I nodded, turned, and walked away. She realized that she hadn't given me her address. Her thoughts were all I needed. I kept walking and rounded the corner.

I'd almost made my escape when the voice of my least favorite instructor stopped me. "These gentlemen have some questions to ask you."

Oh, frig it all! I turned for the showdown at high noon. We faced off in an aisle between rows of crowded tables. The air stilled in a hushed silence that ended with the loud ping of a microwave's timer. Two cops – real ones - stood with my enemy. Wow, they got here fast. And wow, how stupid was I for not paying attention to their thoughts? I should have known they were in the building.

My instructor was disappointed over losing the chance to fail me; those were his thoughts of the moment. I suddenly wanted to delve deeper and see why he hated me. Acting on impulses I didn't have the day before, I dove into his memories and took a copy. In two blinks, I'd lived my instructor's life; I now felt his feelings and knew his knowledge. In essence, I became my instructor, except I was still myself – a truly mind-warping experience.

I was thus forced to see my character through the eyes of a man who judged me poorly, and I had to care because I was the judge as much as he. My instructor – whose name, in all irony, I can't remember – sank to the floor and cried in front of his students.

The cops, assuming that I'd somehow injured the man, went for their holsters and yelled at me to lay face down on the floor. They had no intention of shooting me, not in a room full of students, and not unless they wanted to shuffle paper for the rest of their lives.

I ran. They followed. Or rather, they tried to follow; I was way too fast. More cops waited at the main doors, so I found one of the lesser-known exits and bolted into a blizzard and obscurity – free and clear. Well, I was free from capture. No matter how fast my legs carried me, I couldn't escape my instructor's judgment, which followed me forever.

Martin Wolfe

Chapter Seven

Prometheus: *You make it sound like sharing memories is bad! How does it possibly hurt anyone?*

Master: *How would you like someone to 'share' your memories without asking?*

Static: *My friend, we are, at present, coercing Prometheus to share his memories.*

Prometheus: *Quite right! Now be quiet; it's my turn to share!*

Prometheus

It was a lovely late-winter day. Happy birds flitted across a clear blue sky, and snowy hills sparkled where the sun shone though the trees. I breathed deeply of the fresh, clean air and admired the scenery as I floated aloft in my comfortable shield bubble.

Tiberius crunched through the drifts ahead of me. I didn't care if we ever got to wherever he was taking us. I hadn't been out of the temple this long in ages. The sunshine alone was enough to please me for hours. I basked in its light. Oh, what my fellow gods were missing by refusing the pleasures a physical body could bring.

Then, my rod of office hummed, and the bane of gentle gods everywhere shattered my serenity; may the planet fall on her head!

"Tibbald, what do you think you're doing? I didn't give you permission to drain my power! My pets won't do their tricks while you're using up my holy gift!"

"You told me to go with Tiberius! I'm merely trying to make the best of an unpleasant situation."

"I told the high commander that he could use you for transportation! That doesn't include draining my power because you don't want to get your feet wet! Don't use the rod again until commander Tiberius is ready to return!"

She cut off the power stream, my bubble popped, and I fell into a sharply crusted drift. The hateful environment attacked at once. Vicious ice scraped my palms, and snow billowed under my robe. If I had my power back, I would have tried to obliterate the entire wretched planet, I tell you!

"Tiberius, blast you, help me out of this vile pit!"

He stopped and peered back at me. "Are you well, good Prophet?"

"No, I'm not well! I'm freezing to death! We have to get back to the temple!" Snow melted against my legs, and frigid wind knifed painfully through the wet silk of my robe.

"Good Prophet, it is a mild winter day. You will survive until we find Hogarth's cabin. It should be near." Without turning, he stepped back through his snowshoe prints, grasped my upper arm, and righted me. He started walking again.

"Find? Do you mean to tell me that you don't even know where you're taking us?" I brushed off my robe and followed as best I could in my slippers.

Tiberius shrugged. "When I came here last, good Prophet, it was summer. The landscape is different enough in winter to obscure identifying marks."

The snow's crust ravaged my shins as I stumbled through it. Every step brought fresh agony to my aching toes, and every tree dumped its powdered load on me. This planet hated me. My one solace was that Tiberius still had a limp.

"My name is Prometheus, young man! Stop calling me 'Good Prophet', and desist with that drivel for the priestess, why don't you! We're in the middle of oblivion! She couldn't possibly sense your thoughts from here!"

"Good Prophet, I have remained alive thus far because I take risks only when there is something to gain from them. Please do the same, lest I regret taking a risk with you." His voice sounded ever so threatening – how rude!

"Why the blazes are we out here, anyway? I thought you wanted to find that girl from the throne room. She couldn't possibly have come this far."

"To find an Eldoran, we must ask another Eldoran. Hogarth's hereditary talent allows him to know things that his brethren do not. He will know of the girl's whereabouts, and she will lead us to the shape-shifter."

"I won't let you join with that virus, young man. You're my last avatar!"

"I wish to leave Oneia, good Prophet. The shape-shifter provides the best chance."

"Tiberius, those viruses don't help gods! They kill us! You don't know if a merger with that thing will even work!"

"Death is a risk I am willing to take. It is a risk I take regularly as high commander."

"Well I'm not willing to risk it! I need you for the joining ceremony with the priestess! By the frozen toes in my slippers, I'm not going to let you join with that virus!"

"You will assist me in my search, and I will assist you in your ceremony. Then we will have two opportunities to escape." He marched onward, insensitive to my suffering.

My teeth chattered. I tried to draw heat from my rod, but none came out – rotten priestess. The trek was interminable. Eventually, my extremities went numb, leaving only a heavy weariness behind. A long nap was well overdue. We finally stopped. I laid down to rest in the soft, warm snow.

"Hogarth's cabin," Tiberius announced.

I looked up blearily. Cabin? This thing wasn't a cabin. It was more like a pile of mismatched deadwood; I could barely tell it apart from the forest! A door opened, and a truly enormous and ugly man stepped out. His teeth were dirty, crooked, and rotting; his face was pocked and misshapen; and his hair and scraggly beard were matted into a revolting, tangled mess. Even his tattered furs were filthy. Only the monstrous axe at his waist was clean and well kept.

The brute spoke in a voice as gruff as its face, "Hogarth sees that he has uninvited guests. There is the pretty half-man, who now has half a face and is not so pretty. And there is the hated half-man, who imprisoned Oneia and is now more than half frozen. If the other half-man were here, then Hogarth would have one whole uninvited guest, plus a finger. Hah! Hogarth laughs at this!" He did, in fact, laugh at his own nonsense, and quite loudly at that, the imbecile!

"A pleasant day to you, good Hogarth. We need to know the whereabouts of an Eldoran girl and her shape-shifting pet. What do you want for the boon I ask?"

"Hah! Hogarth laughs at this word, 'ask'! The pretty half-man makes threats with pretty words. He will try to kill Hogarth one day, and that day will come when Hogarth believes he is 'asking' for Hogarth's help. Tell Hogarth what you want with the child and her ancient pet, pretty half-man. Hogarth will give only what is worth less than Hogarth's life. If it is worth more, then Hogarth will be worms and dirt and be happy that he lived."

"Good Hogarth, you misjudge my abilities. You have great Eldoran powers where I have none."

"Hah! Truth and yet not truth! Deception is the strength of the pretty half-man, for he has no true honor in his pretty words."

Tiberius's jaw clenched, his eyes narrowed, and his hand drifted to his sword. Hogarth's hand fell to his axe. I tried to keep my eyes open so I didn't miss anything.

"Will the pretty half-man lose his temper today? This would amuse Hogarth, for then the pretty half-man might lose the only pretty half of his pretty head."

I was absolutely enthralled to hear someone speak this way to Tiberius. I would have given my favorite chair to see the expression on Tiberius's face, but my lids were too heavy to lift just then.

"I would be foolish to attack you, good Hogarth. Your magic powers would overwhelm me. I seek only a companionable meeting with the Eldoran child and her pet. I have no quarrel with you and your mighty magic."

"Hah! The pretty half-man thinks to trick Hogarth. He mentions Hogarth's great magic many times so Hogarth will think that he fears magic. Hah! Hogarth will trust his mighty axe, which does not heal the wounds it causes."

How the blazes did this lout know that Tiberius was automatically healed by Oneian energy? Even I hadn't known that until Tiberius told me. Someone would be held responsible for giving a lowly peasant more information than the holy prophet!

"The child and her pet, Hogarth, where are they?" Tiberius's voice had lost its usual charm.

"Cannot the pretty half-man satisfy his foul tastes with other pets and children?"

Tiberius's sword hissed from its sheath. "Where are they?"

"Someday, the pretty half-man will find the other half he seeks and remember what it means to be whole – worms and dirt, half-man, for you and yours. Hogarth will tell his foolish kin that gold has been offered for the child and the pretend pet. This is all that Hogarth will sell for his life."

"I do not want them harmed."

"Hah! Hogarth has no sway over his kin, pretty half-man. They will try to use the girl and cage her pretend pet. But the pet is old and will teach the girl to survive as

Hogarth survives: by knowing which guests to un-invite. The half-men will leave now before Hogarth forgets his good heart and halves them. Then there would be four halves of two half-men and the mathematicians would go mad. Hah! Hogarth laughs at this!"

"Taberii…," I tried to say that we should go before this maniacal brute killed us, but I was too tired to form the words.

"Pretty half-man, your foolish half-man priest will soon be worms and dirt. He wears bedclothes outside in winter and allows Oneia the chance to kill him, as is her right."

Bedclothes? Of all the nerve! "Howdaryooo…."

"Our mother world desires this half-man dead, but she would be filled with sorrow for the deed. Hogarth will save her that sorrow."

Huge, calloused hands suddenly rapped around my neck and lifted me off the ground. Eek, the beast was going to kill me! Of all the sorrowful injustice, a great god was about to die at the hands of a lowly, malodorous peasant! May the universe remember my greatness!

Fire blossomed from his hands and scalded my flesh from nose to toes! My very existence was a torrent of agony, I tell you! It wasn't enough for him to just to kill me! He had to torture me first! Oh, I was so woefully undeserving of such cruel treatment!

"Should that not be done gradually?" Tiberius asked indifferently.

Slower? Tiberius wanted me tortured to death slower? What had I ever done to the man?

"Hogarth says aye, but the hated half-man is worth less than half the patience. Hogarth will save Oneia from grief, but offers no comfort for her enemy."

I was roasted alive over and over again, but the pain cleared my head. Hogarth dumped me back into the snow. Waves of fire throbbed through my fingers and toes. My face, hands, and feet burned, but my body shivered uncontrollably. I was freezing and burning at the same time. Experiences like this were why I rarely left the temple.

"Send Hogarth six crates of salt pork, two rolls of soft leather, and a sturdy grinding wheel to sharpen his axe. That should appease the pretty half-man's sense of the game, or shall Hogarth pretend to demand more?"

Tiberius sheathed his sword. "Thank you for your help, good Hogarth. I insist, an extra two crates of your favorite salted pork for helping the holy prophet."

"Hah! Well enough, pretty half-man! To ease the insult given to the pork, Hogarth will enjoy the meat enough for three men!" He stepped back into his hovel and slammed the door.

I staggered to my feet and confronted Tiberius. "Two measly crates of salted pork, is that all my life is worth to you?"

"Take us back to the temple," Tiberius replied curtly. He was obviously still upset.

"Don't get snappy with me! Why didn't you just make him tell you where the girl is? He obviously knows!"

Tiberius glowered at me – oh dear. He was quite frightening. I took us back.

Master: *I'll go next. Thinking of Hogarth gave me a good way to start.*

Young Master

Happiness is hot chocolate.

Prometheus: *How could you possibly get that from Hogarth?*

Master: *He seems to enjoy the simple things in life. Please, shut up now.* [Prometheus scowls.]

I entered a coffee shop and ordered happiness. The counter girl readied a mug and pressed the magic button. Happiness dispensed. She added whipped cream and sprinkles. I slid fake dimes across the counter. She examined them suspiciously. The original dime had grown with my pants that morning; I'd wished for copies of an oversized dime. She accepted them anyway. I collected my mug, meandered to a table by the window, and enjoyed my hot chocolate.

Happiness dwindled as I watched the storm outside and sorted through two lifetime's worth of memories, which swirled within me like eddies of drifting snow. My instructor's character fought with mine for dominance. His half of my conscience said that I shouldn't counterfeit money and told me to get a job. He also wanted to order coffee, which tasted to me like burned dirt and water.

I tried to ignore him and wished my mug full again. By golly, it worked. Happiness returned with whipped cream and chocolate sprinkles, which I quietly vacuumed up. Creating hot chocolate was much more impressive than copying dimes. Then it hit me. Why did I need money if I could just wish for whatever I wanted? I wished for a piece of pecan pie. It appeared, sans plate, on my table. So I requested a plate to appear beneath it. And that's when I noticed that I was freaking out one of the shop's other patrons. Lest he consider himself nuts, he assumed I must be some kind of street magician.

"Just practicing," I shrugged for him.

"Amazing!" He ogled.

The counter girl had something to say too.

"I'm sorry, sir, but we don't allow any outside food or beverages."

Sigh. I turned the pie into a hollow piece of plastic and tapped it on the table. She nodded, smiled, and went back to work. Wishing stuff into existence drew too much attention. My instructor's memories offered a suggestion that messed with my adrenaline – there was a casino nearby. The thought of it gave me a rush I'd never experienced. One of my selves was in denial about his gambling addiction. He'd just criticized my counterfeiting, and now he was having me think about cheating at poker – hypocrite. I reminded both of my selves that, legally, it takes money to make money. Any suggestions?

A job was out. I was a fugitive. Besides, a god, or superhero, or whatever I was shouldn't have to work for a living. One self didn't think I was superhero material – too self-absorbed for altruism. The other thought that gods were myths to control the masses. So I was a broke, unemployable, fugitive, freak with an identity crisis.

Two cops came in just then and ordered coffee. I lowered my head and stared intently at my happiness. The counter girl wondered whether she should ask them about my strange dimes. Forget it; I wasn't leaving my hot chocolate behind. They could take me to jail as long as I got to finish my good-mood-in-a-mug. She decided against snitching on me. The cops left with their burned dirt and water.

So those cops weren't after me, and there were no others in the area. Why then did I feel like somebody was watching me? Creepy. I drained my chocolate, zipped up my jacket, and headed back into the blizzard. I walked with my head down and my hood up, but ice and snow still blew into my face and snuck behind my ears. The streets and businesses were dead from the storm, which grew worse by the minute. I was alone but for the random thoughts of diehard storeowners, who still hoped that customers might brave the weather.

The coffee shop was four blocks behind; the casino was eight blocks ahead. I glanced up to get my bearings and spotted a man heading toward me. I looked down and kept walking – hey, his thoughts were missing. When I looked up again, he was gone. My fear of insanity resurfaced, but I shook it off. Somebody inhuman had an interest in me. I shrugged and trudged onward – nothing I could do about it.

Passing through the grand entrance to the Money Palace was like stepping into a different world. Outside was a land of cold grays and blinding whites, where the street people were at home and where the real transients had places to go. Inside was a world of sunless warmth, crazy color, and noisy, disposable income, where throngs of busy gamblers whiled away their leisure time. Loud bells, lights, and a churning sea of thoughts jarred my hyper senses. I stood dazed at the entrance and earned the attention of a big man in a tuxedo.

"Can I help you, sir?" His thoughts matched his words – that was nice.

"I need some money."

"Down the center aisle to your left, sir." He thought I was asking directions to the cashier.

I thanked him and strolled between the rows of clanging, chirping boxes that looked to me like old-fashioned cash registers on digital steroids. What to do? I shrugged and wished to know the next winning machine. Forty-three slot machines seized: Lights flashed, sirens wailed, buzzers buzzed, bells clanged, and digital wheels spun. Then they died, and the aisle went dark – oops.

Thirty-seven irate gamblers replaced the missing racket with noise of their own. I slipped away, hoping no one would notice. No one did, of course. I hadn't done anything but stand and watch. My instructor persona felt that I should turn myself in and offer to pay damages – oh, shut up.

I walked to another aisle and stopped to think of a different approach. A lady pulled a lever. I watched the symbols loop and made a guess: SEVEN/CLUB/HEART. The digital tumblers stopped: SEVEN/CLUB/HEART –

well, I'll be. I strolled down the aisle and watched the dials spin. Each had algorithms that determined how often and how much it was going to put out. I kept walking, did some math, and stopped behind a pretty woman, who, by my calculations, would win in four turns. She pushed the button and lost once. She noticed me watching and got up to leave.

"Don't go now. You're about to win."

She smiled politely, thinking that I was flirting with her. "You can have it. I've spent enough already, and my husband will have a fit if I don't get home soon." She wasn't married. This sensing of thoughts gave me more info than I needed.

"No, I'm serious. You should keep playing."

"Thank you, but I have to go." She left, thinking that I was cute but scary – way more than I needed.

I looked around for a partner in crime.

Three machines away, an elderly couple was wasting some of their retirement money. The woman played. The man was bored. I waved to get his attention. Curious, he ambled toward me.

"This one's going to win in three tries," I screamed in his face because his thoughts said he was hard of hearing. "I don't have any money!" I told him.

He didn't care which game he played, and decided to enable me, despite my obvious gambling problem. His big leathery hands inserted a card and pushed the appropriate buttons. He lost two times. I hoped my new math powers worked more than once.

The symbols dinged to a stop, alarms went off, and a colorful counter added a bunch of money to his card. The old guy guffawed and hammered me on the back. I nodded my satisfaction. He let me have half.

Exhilarated, I set off merrily down the aisles and looked for the next winning box. After an hour, I'd found only one pending winner with nobody playing it. I won. Then half of me thought we had enough, but my other half convinced me that we should try other games. Poker first. I lost – the other players could read my face better than I could read their thoughts. Then I tried blackjack. Reading thoughts wasn't useful, but the order of cards let me figure out the automatic shuffler. The chips piled up.

Pretending to lose occasionally would have been a good idea. The casino bigwigs were thinking about having me turfed. I headed toward the cashier before they came to get me. But my new gambling addiction made me stop by the craps table on the way. I rolled the dice and wished for sevens. Sevens they were – all sevens. One die had all fours, and one had all threes. That did it. Security rushed in from everywhere. But I hadn't cashed in yet – stupid instructor!

I ran. The thoughts of various casino workers led me toward one of the receiving bays, but a clever ox of a bouncer beat me to the people door next the big locked one for trucks. No way around. I tried to shove him aside, which worked way better than expected. Drywall snapped and buckled. Thin steel studs twisted aside as he slumped through a gaping hole into the next room. He coughed and moaned. I left.

Only when I stepped into the alley did I remember leaving my jacket on a chair. I clenched my teeth, balled my fists, and huffed vapor. Wind gusted in whorls and piled sharp snowdrifts against trash bags. I hopped down the stairs and boot-skated along the alley. Yeah, I know, I could have made a new jacket – didn't think of it.

En route to freedom, I was stopped by five shadowy figures that appeared out of nowhere and corked the alley's single exit. Trapped. They weren't thieves, or cops, and they didn't work for the casino. Despite not knowing each other, or me, or even how they got there, they all wanted to kill me.

Chapter Eight

Prometheus: *Entirely, understandable.*

Master: *Funny.*

Prometheus: *I'm quite serious! You're that annoying!*

Master: *If it didn't happen so often, I'd disagree.*

Static: *I will now resume our Oneian timeline.*

Prometheus: *But he's about to die again! It's becoming entertaining.*

Master: *Static found Tiberius naked in the woods.*

Prometheus: *Really?*

Master: *No. I'm just living down to your expectations. Go, Static.*

Static

Soldiers surrounded our location, but only one, an Eldoran, had detected our presence. Alenna, huddling beneath a rock overhang, was safe from visual inspection unless approached directly. The man's Eldoran heritage would be uncovered if he claimed success without proof of her presence. Coincidentally, he had, several times, studied my owl form where I perched in a nearby tree. But I did not fit the description of his quarry – a girl and a large cat. To find Alenna, he would need to traverse into the deep snow of the ravine, which had a steep, uninviting perimeter.

I resumed the lesson that his arrival had interrupted. *"Alenna, please describe to me what you see."*

"Static, shouldn't we be quiet?"

"The Eldoran will not call for assistance until he makes a visual identification. Please begin."

The soldier used his sword to probe for an easy descent. His boots were not suited to deep snow.

"We're in a forest in the middle of two big hills." Alenna paused to think, having learned by then that I would want her to make conclusions from her findings. She was eager to gain my approval. Our search for alternate guardians had, thus far, been unsuccessful, and she strove to gain my commitment to her permanent care.

"Do you see any trees that are different from the rest?" I offered a hint.

"Static, that tree has two marks! We've been this way before!" Alenna had burned small circles in the bark of trees along our path. It was a survival technique she had learned from her father.

"Well done, Alenna, I have led us across our path. The soldiers do not have tracking animals, and I had hoped multiple trails might confuse them. What new deductions can you glean from this?"

"They haven't caught us?"

"Yes, but what should we see in addition to your trail markers?"

"Footprints! The footprints in the snow are gone!" She paused, confused. *"But it isn't snowing!"*

"Very good, Alenna, your powers of observation are improving. What other inconsistencies do you see?"

"Static, did we...?" She was conflicted by the available evidence, as was I.

"No, Alenna, we have not previously passed through a ravine. The landscape has since changed."

It had changed in our favor. To reach her hiding place, Alenna had walked down a gentle grade covered with shallow snow. I had watched her tracks fill in and vanish behind her. The Eldoran soldier followed the same route, but he tumbled down a rocky embankment into waist-deep snow. Someone with the power to alter topography was assisting us.

The man inexorably achieved his goal, despite several spills along the way. He discovered Alenna and paused, likely pondering a moral conundrum: She was Eldoran and a child, but he was charged with her capture, which would likely lead to her execution.

"I can set his pants on fire, Static."

"Please direct your energy at me instead, Alenna." I dove from my perch. Alenna's power streamed past the soldier's head. I accepted the energy, transformed into a small venomous snake, and slithered under his breastplate. He flailed and pulled at his armor. I felt the vibrations of his screams.

"Be still. My poison is virulent, and I will not hesitate to bite you."

"Don't! I'm not moving!"

"Reassure your companions that all is well. Convince them to search elsewhere."

His fellows had responded to his panic and now gathered at the ravine's edge. From their thoughts I extrapolated our prisoner's offered ruse: A hibernating bear had startled him. They expressed jovial derision and likened his cries to that of their frenzied priestess. They gladly granted him the ravine to search on his own and dispersed.

After they left, I detected the vibrations of a verbal conversation between Alenna and our captured soldier.

"Please communicate telepathically. Snakes do not have ears."

"Let me go," he demanded meekly.

"We will release you when we are safely past your comrades." I instructed him to carry Alenna on his shoulders. She needed rest. I peered above his breastplate's neckpiece and directed our progress. The snow was once again shallow, and the ravine, which had not existed hours before, extended onward. We stayed within its walls.

Sometime after we left the searchers behind, our prisoner complained of fatigue. I instructed him to lower Alenna to the ground. I then maneuvered down the sleeve of his chain mail and bit his hand. He jerked and flung me into the snow.

"Alenna, please assist me." She offered her energy. I mutated into my owl body and alighted to her shoulder.

"You said you'd let me go!" He shouted his rage and gripped the wrist of his envenomed hand.

"I have. If you move slowly, the cold will reduce your fever and will keep you alive until the venom exits your bloodstream. Removing your armor may help also."

He cursed us bitterly and stalked away. Alenna and I left to find a suitable shelter for the evening, our third since my companion's near destruction.

By the time darkness fell, we had built a temporary pine bough shelter against a deadwood frame. Under my guidance, Alenna used her power to snap branches from trees and to assemble them. She now sat upon a mat of woven evergreen boughs and roasted the pheasant that I hunted. I perched upon her knee and remarked that we made a good working team.

"Does that mean I can stay with you, Static?" She beamed with delight.

"I remain hopeful that we will find a more appropriate guardian, one who can teach you the proper survival techniques of your society."

She fell silent. Our fowl finished roasting. Alenna ate her fill and then placed the scraps in a pocket. I did not require food as long as Alenna periodically recharged me.

"Static, when was the last time you saw your parents?"

"I have no memory of parents, Alenna. My existence has been largely solitary."

"That's sad." Inspired by her loss, Alenna hugged me. I could not return her embrace, for she pressed my wings against me.

"Yes, Alenna, I was once lonely, but my loneliness was due to isolation that I caused myself."

"Why?" She asked.

"If you wish, I will share an abbreviated tale of my life."

"Okay." She sighed and stared into the fire.

"I have survived nearly one hundred million years."

"How much is a million?"

"You require schooling, Alenna." I thought of a simple comparison. *"I am older than a mountain."*

"Wow, that's really old."

"Age is relative. To a Host, like Prometheus, I am young."

She struggled to imagine lifetimes that were beyond her comprehension.

"For most of my existence, I wandered without purpose. I killed innocents randomly and without provocation. My imagined superiority allowed me to slay beings that I felt were inferior. I was, in effect, no better than a saugael mor."

Alenna's back stiffened, and I could sense her sudden anxiety.

"Do not worry, Alenna. I have learned to control my destructive impulses. You are safe in my presence."

"I'm not worried, Static." She nervously stroked my feathers and calmed.

"At length, I realized that I was jealous of mortals, for they had innate purpose, while I did not. Like all living things, their purpose was to survive. Their lives required maintenance. Mine did not. I could not die."

"You can't die?" Alenna was suddenly hopeful; her parents had perished, and thus, had abandoned her.

"That is correct Alenna. To my knowledge, I cannot die."

She hugged me so tightly that my breathing became labored. I mused that she wished to test the theory. She loosened her hold and possessively stroked my feathers.

"As my life needed no effort, and thus, had no purpose, I endeavored to die."

"No! I don't want you to die, Static!" Alenna crushed me to her again. She verged on tears.

"I no longer have that purpose, Alenna. Please refrain from squeezing me too tightly, lest I need repair."

She loosened her grip and cradled me to her chest. I allowed Alenna her comfort.

"To achieve my goal, I attacked beings far more powerful than I. They would, I hoped, end my life while defending themselves. I had not thought to ask for assistance. The entities I harassed could not kill me, so I continued for ages until I encountered the Hosts, who imprisoned me. Then, I learned my first purpose: freedom."

Alenna glumly put me down. I had not intended to imply that she had taken my freedom, but she was growing sensitive from fatigue.

"Perhaps you should retire for the evening, Alenna. I will finish my tale tomorrow."

"No, I'm not tired," she whined.

"Very well, I shall continue."

"Prison allowed me ample time to ponder my actions, and I vowed to change my character. But endless isolation took its toll on my resolve, and I once again wished to die.

"When my companion came to be imprisoned with me, I saw him only as a means to an end. I threatened to torture him if he did not destroy me. He refused and suggested another purpose that I could pursue: happiness. I was intrigued and accepted his challenge. He offered suggestions on how to begin. Soon after, I learned to pursue happiness on my own."

"How?" She absently poked the leather satchel that held my companion's remains. His finger was now in a small bag that hung from a braided-hair necklace Alenna had crafted.

"That is not an easily answerable question, Alenna. Most individuals pursue happiness in their own ways. I have found that setting goals and achieving them brings fulfillment to my life. Temporary deprivation and delayed gratification are also useful."

"I don't understand."

"Consider our shelter. Building it was a necessary chore that brought satisfaction when completed. Do you agree?"

Alenna nodded and then shrugged to show her lack of commitment.

"Now, consider your coniferous bedding. Weaving it together was not necessary for survival, yet you labored extensively. Does it bring you happiness?"

"It's nicer than sleeping on old sticks," Alenna answered defensively. She would soon need rest.

"Yes, Alenna, you pursued a goal of comfort, a type of happiness, and achieved it. You will undoubtedly pursue other rewarding goals in the future. It is now time for you to sleep."

She sighed, toppled onto her bedding, and curled into a fetal position. I searched the nearby forest for combustible material, lest the fire extinguish prematurely.

"Static, I've heard people say that raising children is rewarding." Her persistence was admirable.

"I have heard that also, Alenna. Please close your eyes."

Moments later, she succumbed to fatigue. After stoking the fire, I commenced vigil and pondered. Training a child while my companion regenerated would indeed be productive, but it would also be irresponsible. Alenna should be raised by one of her own species.

I examined the constellations, as was my wont during a nightly watch. Few stars shone within the expanse. Fresh memories of drifting alone for ages resurfaced. Melancholy encroached. I gazed toward Alenna, who lay dreaming by the fire. She breathed slowly and deeply – peaceful and content. I would miss her. Regrettably, owls do not weep.

Master: *I think I need a hug.*

Static: *Are you in earnest, my friend? I can transform, if you wish.*

Master: *That's okay, Static. Maybe later. Prometheus, your turn.*

Prometheus: *The virus was too depressing! You go! Having you die will cheer me up.*

Master: [indecipherable mumble]

Young Master

Five random people – one guy in a suit, two in coveralls, one in jeans, and one chick in a skirt – all wanted me dead, but they didn't know why.

Movie action heroes knew what to do in situations like this. I didn't. Action heroes rarely needed to pee when cornered. Wetting myself while getting beaten to death would be very un-cool. I wished my bladder empty – hopefully it was still there.

My attackers rushed me and knocked me to the ground. The hurting began. I tried to guard against the steel toes of the coveralls and the stabbing stilettos of the skirt, but the suit's dress shoes turned out to be the most dangerous. He kicked me in the head. My innards wanted to crawl up my neck and escape. I changed what was left of my mind and guarded against works of Italian craftsmanship, but they kept finding places to strike. Defending myself wasn't working; I didn't know how.

I attacked instead. My foot found a coverall, who fell and skidded away. I scrambled to my feet, reeled, and puked all in the same motion. I spun and backhanded a chest, which snapped. A dress shoe cracked me in the head again. I wished myself well before I blacked out. A dress shoe nailed me in the head, and I was unwell, again. I assessed to the best of my ability. One coverall was dead against a brick wall. The other climbed to his feet as the jeans and the suit continued to beat the snot out of me. The skirt was just irritating now that I was upright.

I shoved the skirt into some trash bags, backed away from the suit and the jeans, and bumped into the coverall, who wrapped his leg-sized arm around my neck. He squeezed as the suit drove his foot toward my sternum. I aimed a kick of my own. Both kicks landed. The suit's heel cracked my ribs on the left side. My boot, which he blocked but couldn't stop, crushed his arm, throat, and jaw. With his good arm, he hugged my leg and slumped to the ground.

For a second, I half-dangled between the two of them. The coverall had my neck and the suit had my calf. The jeans pummeled my kidney, while the skirt still tried to breathe.

The suit's thoughts suddenly cleared as if waking from a nightmare. With the last of his strength, he atoned by punching in the jeans' face, and delivering a roundhouse kick to the side of the coverall's head. My strangler let me go, and I fell on top of James Stuart Loren, the suit – my hero. He'd been working late at the office before he'd decided to kill me. Now he was dying. We stared at each other. His thoughts said he wanted his son to have his watch. He choked on blood. A stiletto gouged my back. A heavy boot landed on my shoulder. I dove into James's memories and took a copy as he faded. Blows rained as I watched my third self die.

I rolled and caught the next foot that headed my way. It belonged to the coverall. I used his leg as leverage, spun, and tripped the jeans. The skirt aimed a four-inch shoe-dagger at my face. I slapped it aside and flipped from my back to standing – just like that. The coverall swung at me. I punched him in the fist, and his hand went limp. The T-shirt lurched up and tried to tackle me. I grabbed his wrist, twisted, and flipped him back onto the asphalt. James had three black belts – handy.

Guns materialized in my attackers' hands. That complicated things, and it proved that this encounter was alien-guided. With James's skills, I might still win, but his part of my character couldn't tolerate more innocents dying. Time to run.

The alley's exit wasn't close enough. I jumped, reaching for a dangling fire-escape ladder. The remaining conscripts fired, trailing bullets after me.

I'd estimated my jump with James's memory of rock climbing, but he'd never had my freakish legs. With enough momentum to reach the third floor, I plowed headfirst into the second-floor fire escape. I was dead before I hit the ground.

Just like last night, I drifted apart. I resisted. The tendrils of my gaseous self reached various points in the alley. Wherever I touched, the world came alive in ways I couldn't understand. All three of my selves were terrified beyond reason. Sensory information flooded in, as did emotions too powerful to handle. It was wrong – unhealthy; I shouldn't be here.

I surveyed the macabre scene as if it were part of me, which it was. Two zombie-like men and one woman stood around my corpse and toed me; they were inside me and beside me at the same time. For some reason, I found this funny.

Silent laughter rolled in waves through my invisible mind. The terror fled; I was euphoric. This was nuts. If it didn't stop soon, I'd be nuts, too. I willed my corpse repaired and stuffed myself back inside.

I opened my eyes. Three statues stared down at me. They reanimated and filled me full of holes. Rats. I was dead again.

This time, I was ready to be gaseous. But my emotions were still too intense. I stayed cool long enough to squeeze back into a newly healed body.

I played dead for a few seconds. Then I flipped to my feet and leapt for the roof. The building was four stories; I covered three. I clung to cracks between bricks and climbed. Two bullets tore through my back; one ricocheted off the wall and buzzed my ear. My breath left, and I cringed, but I stayed put. I threw my arm over the roof's ledge and struggled to follow. Bullets whizzed past and spattered around me. Another caught my ankle before I rolled to safety. I collapsed onto the roof and bled. Then I healed myself before I died again.

The shooting stopped. I put my back against the roof's concrete lip and waited. If they followed, they'd have to come up the fire escape. I could disarm them one at a time.

Two minutes passed. Nobody came. I knelt and peeked down into the alley. They were gone – even the corpses. James's watch was gone too. Crap! His/my Grandfather had worn that watch during the First World War. Its glass face had stopped a bayonet aimed at Grandpa Loren's heart. The watch hadn't worked since, but Grandpa lived to pass it down his line. James/I was supposed to give it to his/my eldest son. But now it was gone.

Or was it? I concentrated, and a copy of the watch appeared on my wrist. It was perfect, which was problematic. I wished for the face to be broken and for the watch to stop at one twenty-three, like it had been for nearly a century.

Sparks jumped around my wrist. Complex equations with no solutions spiraled through my head. That was new. I considered the equations and made conclusions. The sparks stopped and Grandpa's watch was just as it should be.

My adrenalin ebbed as I exhaled a cloud of relief. Winter reintroduced itself. I sat on a roof in a blizzard. Frozen blood stiffened my thin shirt, and icy wind whipped through the bullet holes. My jaws ached from clenching my teeth against the cold. I wished myself warm, and I was. That was almost as good as hot chocolate.

I peeled off my shirt and washed myself with snow, which felt as warm as I did – nifty. I didn't think to make myself a new shirt. There were countless things I should have done better, but didn't. Such was the confusion caused by multiple lives inhabiting a single head. Three personalities were two more than any one person should have. I took a character break and organized my selves into a unified front, before we did something stupid.

My strongest instinct was to lead with my original personality, but my other selves disagreed. They marked me as a lazy, whiny kid with a bad attitude. I still held the reins of control, but I realized that I wasn't the strongest link in the character chain. This admission was made possible by the fact that I was now a better person. The original me wouldn't have admitted anything.

As a new man, I reexamined my day's performance. I'd made a tactical error: The cops at college hadn't been looking *for* me; they'd been looking for information *about* me, the dead guy whose remains had been found. They hadn't expected my corpse to answer questions, until I showed up alive on campus. Only then did I become a murder suspect. I'd created my own fugitive status – so much for not doing stupid things.

I needed to get some sleep, so I could work with a fresh head. My inner voice suggested that fatigue could be wished away, but I shook off the urge. I wanted something familiar in my life, which was getting way too weird.

The trip to the ground was more nerve-wracking than the trip to the roof. James was a rock-climber, but my instructor and I were afraid of heights. That made two votes to three against scaling more buildings, unless absolutely necessary. I eased myself onto the fire escape and used the stairs.

Once down, I trudged off to a nearby hotel. The desk clerk looked me over when I walked into his lobby. He wrinkled his nose and planned to phone the police as soon as I left. I glanced down to see the problem. I was naked from the waist up and slick with diluted blood, which I hadn't cleaned well in the dark. Hey, my muscles were bigger – cool. I flexed my chest.

"I got attacked," I told him.

He wondered how I'd lost my shirt. "Should I call an ambulance, sir?"

"No, I just need a shower and a bed. I don't suppose you take casino credit?"

"We require a major credit card for the deposit, sir."

"I don't have one." I didn't have to read minds to know that he wasn't going to let me stay in his hotel. "Okay then, can you suggest a place that might take casino credit?"

He shrugged. His thoughts suggested a homeless shelter.

I wanted to slap him. "Can you call a cab at least?"

He clicked his teeth, and wondered how I was going to pay. Then he decided that it wasn't his problem – at least I'd be gone. He speed-dialed.

"Name?" He asked.

Three identities popped into my head. I gave the original. Important note: Fugitives should not give out their real names - oops. He dropped the phone. His thoughts offered a summary of current events as reported by Channel 10 News: Police had me surrounded inside my apartment, and I wasn't taking hostages. I'd already butchered seven innocent bystanders and most of a tactical response team. The clerk added his own update, which included the murder of an innocent hotel employee.

A massacre in my own home – my mystery tormentor had invited me to a showdown. I accept. Sleep would have to wait.

The clerk blinked, terrified. I plucked the receiver off the counter and talked to the dispatcher. When I left to wait for the cab, the clerk recovered and phoned the cops.

I was curious to see if their efforts to draw the fake me out of my building would work to keep the real me from entering.

Chapter Nine

Master: *Okay, I'm done. You can go now, Prometheus.*

Prometheus: *It's about time. You two took so long, I can't remember where I was.*

Master: *You'd just met Hogarth.*

Prometheus: *Oh yes, now I remember. Tiberius was surly for days afterward.*

Prometheus

"Get out of my way, blast you!"

"I'm sorry, Holiness, but the high commander has asked that he not be disturbed today." Two of Tiberius's soldiers had crossed spears in front of me. They wouldn't let me into the military wing. No one stops the holy prophet in his own temple!

I flicked my rod of office. Blue funnels of light picked them up and tossed them out of my way. They yelled for help. A dozen more confronted me by the time I reached Tiberius's waiting room. I flicked bodies aside, but they kept bouncing back. I wasn't getting anywhere, so I set a few of them on fire. The screams brought Tiberius from his office.

He looked around, clenched his jaw, and gave orders to a subordinate, "Have these men healed by a priest." They looked at me and then back to him. "Another priest," he said. They saluted and carried away the wounded. Tiberius turned and glowered at me. "Good Prophet, please come in."

127

I followed him into his office and vented. "That's it, I tell you! I'm not going to take it anymore! First, that lunatic woman refuses to cooperate, and now you're trying to hide from me! What's the matter with you people?"

"Lieutenant." Tiberius said. There was a soldier in the room with us. I hadn't noticed.

"Yes, High Commander?"

"The good prophet has honored you by speaking candidly of his mistress. You will not share this information with anyone. Is that understood?"

Mistress? What in the name of stuffy offices was Tiberius plotting now? He'd already started a rumor about us having an affair – sadly unfulfilled – and now he was starting another about me having a mistress! A mistress, of all things, not in this lifetime, I tell you!

"Yes, High Commander." The lieutenant saluted.

"Dismissed."

When the door closed, Tiberius paced across his office and twisted a cloak hook on the wall. He pushed, and a door-sized section of brickwork swung into his secret room.

He motioned for me to follow, and we walked into a gray brick cube large enough to hold two chairs, a desk, and a set of shelves. In the past few days, I'd come here to update Tiberius on the wedding preparations. I would need to give him some decorating tips; the room was distressingly plain.

Tiberius pushed on a steel latch, and the heavy door whispered shut behind us. I poised to vent again, but he slapped me in the face – eek! He grabbed my throat and slammed me against the wall. By the whites of his angry green eyes, Tiberius was moody lately!

"Good Prophet, if you ever again speak words of treason in front of my staff, I will personally end you!"

Well, I'm sorry, but…."

He slapped me again! What did I do?

He let go of my throat. "Speak your words! Have you forgotten how paranoid the priestess is? If she has sensed you, good Prophet, I will declare you an Eldoran myself."

I needed to rest before my rotten day overwhelmed me. Tiberius must have guessed, because he gestured for me to sit. I lowered myself into one of his stiff wooden chairs. He poured a glass of wine from an open bottle and handed it to me.

"The empire requires maintenance, good Prophet. So I shall ask you again: Please do not interrupt my days with the Priestess's wedding plans."

"The joining ceremony is ready!"

He shrugged with his open hand. "I have little time to waste on a ceremony that will not work. Your pretend wedding can happen without me."

"You said you'd help me if I helped you find that virus!"

He nodded. "When our quarry is located, I will have a member of my staff notify you."

"Tiberius, this is going to work! I've already factored in your reaction to the Priestess's power."

He leaned against his desk, rubbed his temples, and sighed. "Very well, good Prophet, tell me what you need."

I gulped down my wine and hopped up, excited. "That can wait for now. Just get ready and meet me in the ceremonial chamber." I paused, remembering an important detail. "Oh, and talk some sense into the Priestess, will you? She's refusing to get married unless her husband stands with her at the altar. Impossible!"

Tiberius sighed again and massaged the back of his neck. He pulled back the heavy door. "We will arrive within the hour, good Prophet."

I left his office and scurried off to get dressed for the wedding.

One hour later, Tiberius limped into the ceremonial chamber and found me adding last minute touches to my floral arrangements. I straightened and smoothed my lovely outfit: a white silk robe with a translucent blue-green scarf draped over the shoulders.

Tiberius nodded in greeting. "The priestess will arrive shortly, good Prophet." He wore his formal military uniform, the white one with black epaulettes and gold buttons. In the flickering candlelight, his scars weren't quite as repulsive; he almost looked handsome.

He glanced only briefly at my inspired wedding decorations before he noticed the unsightly scribbling on the walls. Oh drat!

Tiberius's eyes widened. "Good Prophet, there must be thousands of equations here."

"There are only three, actually. I was hoping no one would notice."

He hadn't said anything about my flower arrangements. White lilies against green lianth petals should have drawn far more attention than blue writing on a dark wall.

"You completed all of these calculations in three days?"

"Are you trying to insult me, young man? The calculations took only a few hours! Writing them down is what took three days!"

He wandered around the chamber and studied my figures. Maybe the Priestess would appreciate my decorations.

"I once killed mathematicians," he said. "I thought them wizards."

I grabbed my rod of office.

He smiled and shook his head. "You have no need to worry, good Prophet. I too am now a mathematician."

That didn't mean a thing; maybe he didn't like competition. I held my rod and eyed him suspiciously.

He explained, "When I conquered my birth world, I killed all who dared count higher than eight; I burned books that taught math and science. But one night, I read a book I planned to burn. My starved mind devoured its simple equations. I solved its problems easily and hungered for more. I thereafter led the revolt that overthrew me, so math and science could flourish. I discovered that I was the greatest mathematician my world had ever known."

"Later, I travelled to other worlds and sought mathematicians who might challenge my talents. But none ever have. On all the worlds I have traveled, I have always been the best at mathematics." He smiled ruefully at my scribbles.

Well, they may have been simple, but I've always considered myself as more of a creative genius, anyway. "That's very nice, Tiberius. After the ceremony is finished, maybe you can offer suggestions."

"I wish I were able, good Prophet, but I do not understand more than half of this. You are a genius among geniuses."

"Well, of course I am! I've told you that before!" Why was everyone always so surprised about that?

He looked at my decorations. "Your floral arrangements are quite fetching, good Prophet!"

"Oh, do you think so? They're nothing really; I just tossed them together at the last moment." Ah, it was so nice to be appreciated for my true talent!

Tiberius smiled benignly. "As to the ceremony, what do you need me to do?"

"Just stand outside the pentagram until my priests and I link to the priestess. Then I need you to jump her and tear off her clothes. We need skin to skin contact, so you'll have to be naked, too."

Tiberius scowled enough to look ugly again. "Unlike you, good Prophet, my sanity is still intact. I will not be 'jumping' the priestess."

"There's no need to be insulting! Oh very well, I suppose you can just hold her hand if you're going to be squeamish about it! Really, Tiberius, she's not that repulsive!"

He continued to glare at me as the first of my priests strode solemnly into the chamber. Three more followed, and then came the priestess herself, clad in a translucent white gown, which would have been beautiful if the flickering candlelight didn't reveal parts of her body beneath. Bringing up the rear, four assassin bugs carried her bridal train.

"What in the name of wilting lilies are those putrid little beasts doing in the ceremonial chamber?"

The processional halted.

The priestess spoke without turning her head. "If you ruin my wedding, Prophet, I'll have my pets skin you alive!"

She was serious!

"But Priestess, I don't have any mutant insects figured into my equations! Those things are energy resistant! They'll ruin everything!"

"Silence!" She screamed. Then she moved to take her place at the pentagram's center.

My underlings took their positions on four points of the star while I stood on the fifth. To my absolute dismay, the four assassins moved to stand behind me and three of my priests. What a catastrophe, my pentagram was unbalanced! If that wasn't bad enough, I could barely read my notes. Oh blast it all, I should have used white chalk!

"Tiberius, go stand behind Homer," I told him. Maybe that would balance things better; Tiberius was energy-resistant, too.

"Begin the ceremony," the priestess ordered.

I recited a few passages from the *Great Book of Holy Prophecies*. Then I signaled my priests to raise their rods.

"Prophet Tibbald, you have forgotten the wedding psalm.

"There's no such thing as a wedding psalm."

"You dare to contradict the word of your Divine priestess?"

"I wrote the bloody prophecies! There's no wedding psalm!"

"You wrote only *Volume One*! The wedding psalm is in *Volume Three*! It's beautiful and touching, and I demand that you read it!"

"And how do you suggest I do that? I don't keep a library of banned books under my robe!"

Pieto cleared his throat. I looked at him, and he handed me a copy of *Volume Three*. My subordinate was harboring subversive materials – the heretic! I'd deal with him later.

The wedding psalm, I was aghast to learn, was used quite often. The book fell open to the page, which was marked with a red ribbon – blasted insubordinate priests! I read the passage as quickly as possible.

"Read slower!" The Priestess snapped.

Who wrote this nonsense, anyway? It went on forever! I finally read to the point where a groom was needed. Then, I lifted my rod of office and created the first circuit. It arched prettily in blue from the tip of the rod to the center of the Priestess's bodice. My priests added their own arcs until she glowed. Then the bolts split to include the vermin. Wait, no, not them! In seconds, the assassins grew to full size. Their spindle legs created a forest around us.

Tiberius stepped up to the priestess and took her hand. She smiled, surprised. His scars had been healed by her power; he was beautiful again. She stroked his face.

Suddenly, the dancing trails of light coalesced and shot from the Priestess's head. They tore through the ceiling. Mosaic tiles rained everywhere. Oh blast, what had that woman done now? The Priestess was exultant, thinking that everything was working as it should. Well, it wasn't, I tell you, not even close!

Just then, an assassin sunk its claws into my back and probed my sacred flesh for nerve endings – eek! The beasties were out of control!

The tornado of power settled into a tower of white light, and the assassins stopped, but my priests and I were stuck like pincushions. I couldn't move. Only the priestess could break the link, or we'd all be charred to cinders.

"Are you there, beloved?" The priestess spoke to the ceiling. The column of light around her grew wider and a hazy figure appeared next to her. By the hearts of skewered prophets, now she was bringing her fantasies to life! Tiberius released the priestess's hand and backed out of the spotlight.

The hazy figure solidified. It was Cerberus – eek! I tried to run for my life, but the claws in my back held me in place. Cerberus saw me and grinned wickedly.

"You will come with me, traitor. I have made you a new cage: a lightless well of endless pain."

"Tiberius, save me!" I groaned.

Cerberus's eyes narrowed when he saw Tiberius. The grin left his face. *"You! Why have you come to this place?"*

Tiberius ignored him and bowed to the Priestess. "The great god Prometheus has come to wed you, my divine priestess."

She wrung her hands. "But I can't! He's ugly!"

Cerberus scowled at me. *"You will come with me now, or I will destroy you!"*

"Tiberius?" I looked to him imploringly.

"If he could harm you, good Prophet, he would have done so already. He is confined to the light."

"This circle is expanding," Cerberus replied.

I peered down and saw that Cerberus was right. The column was growing. I tried to back away, but that only pushed the assassin's claws deeper.

"Make yourself beautiful, or I won't marry you!" The Priestess ordered.

Cerberus glanced at her and sneered. *"Your test subject is bothersome, traitor. It should be terminated."* That wasn't a wise thing to say.

The priestess's face turned as red as I'd ever seen it. She clawed the air and screamed. Then Cerberus's body exploded. Chunks of him splattered everywhere.

He immediately started to form another body, but the priestess swiped the air, and the light column vanished; the conduit closed. Still screaming, she stormed out of the ceremonial chamber. The vermin left, too, yanking their claws from the backs of priests and creeping after their mistress. I groaned and collapsed with my underlings.

One by one, my priests picked themselves from the rubble and repaired their bodies. They weren't certain whether they should heal me. I lay on my back and stared through the smoke at the cinders of my beautiful decorations. I waved my priests away, so I could die in peace.

Tiberius stayed behind. He stood over me and wiped blood from his face. "I tried to exit through your conduit, good Prophet. I could not, but I nonetheless thank you for healing me." His uniform was just as plastered with gore as my robe. I felt better about that.

"Go away," I croaked.

"Heal yourself, good Prophet," he said. "I will require your services later."

Irritating man – I drew healing power through my rod. Satisfied, Tiberius left. I stayed and moped – what a horrible day!

Prometheus: *Telling this story is like living through the misery all over again!*

Master: *Consider it therapy, Prometheus.*

Prometheus: *I don't need therapy, young man!*

Master: *Are you sure?*

Prometheus: *Absolutely!*

Master: *Then you probably need therapy.*

Prometheus: *Oh, shut up!*

Static: *I shall continue.*

Chapter Ten

Static

"Do we have to, Static?" Alenna inquired, as she had many times in the past few days, if we must continue our search for an alternate guardian.

"Yes, Alenna."

"But why?"

"I suspect that you have understood my previous explanations."

"But I promise to be really good."

"Your repetitive questioning does not support your claim to good behavior, Alenna." My patience, which normally extended to thousands of years, had diminished to only a few more seconds. *"Please turn to your left. I have spied a dwelling."*

I soared above a tight copse of trees surrounding a shelter. Due to its impressive camouflage and remote location, I suspected that it belonged to an Eldoran. I tucked into a dive and returned to perch on Alenna's shoulder. From that height, the cabin, formed of upright logs, was nearly indistinguishable from the surrounding forest. A thin trail of smoke issuing from a depression in the snowy roof had given away its location.

"Are you sure we should go this way, Static? There are trees in the way."

"I am certain, Alenna. The timber you see is part of the shelter." I realized then that the birdsong, which had led me to this area, was in fact a flawless telepathic projection emanating from the cabin itself. The Eldoran resident was evidently skilled at mimicking avian sounds. Only the unlikelihood of small birds vocalizing in the presence of their natural predator had foiled the illusion. The projection itself was perfect.

137

"I don't want to go in," Alenna whined. *"This one's just going to be scary, like the last one."*

Alenna referred to the Eldoran we had propositioned the previous day. He had lived in an equally camouflaged dwelling, and when asked to care for Alenna, he had expressed keen interest, although not for the reasons we had hoped. His preoccupation with Alenna's body was distinctly non-parental. I declined his overtures politely, but he did not easily accept defeat. He attacked Alenna; whereupon, I clawed his eyes while Alenna ignited his clothing. The cumulative damage was not fatal, but he would unable to pursue us.

With that encounter in mind, I hoped that this next candidate proved more appropriate. We stood before the wall of trees and awaited acknowledgement, but no one came to greet us. I found this peculiar. The Eldoran within could have easily detected our telepathic converse as we approached. *"Perhaps we are expected to perform some form of ritual announcement. Alenna, how do Eldorans introduce themselves?"*

"We just knock, like everybody else."

"Please knock on our behalf." I wondered where the entrance might be located, as there was no obvious sign of an aperture. Most of the logs were lashed together with animal sinew, but others were grasped by the roots and limbs of living trees. I suspected that the helpful geography had assisted in construction.

"Static, do I have...."

"Yes, Alenna, you do." My impatience surprised me. Interrupting someone in the midst of discourse had not previously been one of my habits. I reminded myself that Alenna was a juvenile of her species, and I resolved to be more accepting of her limitations until I could train her properly.

With that thought, I realized that I had already subconsciously accepted the responsibility of her care, despite my pretense of searching for an alternate. This revelation distracted me enough that I failed to react when a door swung outward revealing a mature human female, who immediately cast a net over us. We toppled, and she bound us deftly with woven strips of rawhide. Her small hands were nearly as corded as the ropes that held us.

"Get up, girl."

With the rough assistance of our captor, Alenna rose from the frozen ground. The woman was dressed in fur-covered skins and equipped for winter travel. A large rawhide pack was secured between her shoulders. She yanked on a guide rope attached to our bindings and forced Alenna to stumble along behind her through the snow. I followed also, as my wings and body were roped to Alenna's head. I decided to make use of the opportunity and entertained one final attempt at finding a guardian. The woman herself was too aggressive and taciturn to be a successful caregiver, but perhaps she would know of others who had greater skills in the area of parenting.

"I am searching for a suitable guardian to care for this young female. Do you know where I might find an Eldoran who would be interested in assuming responsibility for her care?"

Alenna communicated her disapproval at my solicitation. *"Static, what are you doing? I don't want to go with her! She's bad!"*

The woman had stopped and had turned to view me. She interjected vocally before I could explain. "Blame fool never said the thing could talk."

I assumed that I was the thing in question and responded appropriately. *"It is true that I am capable of telepathic communication. Please clarify your intentions. Do you have a patron who has requested our capture, and if so, is he or she interested in becoming a parent?"*

The Eldoran woman expelled air derisively though her nasal passages. She turned forward again and resumed her march. Alenna stumbled after. Fortunately, the woman was elderly and did not possess the speed of youth. Alenna had no difficulty matching her pace.

"Otar ain't no right parent," The woman said. "Sure'nuf he got kids, somewhere. Probably, he don't know where."

Alenna reiterated her disapproval. *"Static!"*

"Please bear with me for this final attempt, Alenna. If it does not succeed, I shall accept full responsibility for your care." I could feel Alenna's excitement with what she assumed was a victory.

"You'll be a really good father, Static! I know you will!" Her endorsement was not entirely accurate.

"I have no specific gender, Alenna. The term parent or guardian would be more accurate." My correction did little to affect Alenna's excitement. I addressed the matter at hand. *"Eldoran woman, what are Otar's intentions?"*

"Name's Broda, creature. Don't rightly know 'bout what Otar wants with her. Don't rightly care. Promising a mule loaded down with provisions to anyone who brings him the girl and her pet. Didn't say what was the pet. Didn't say it could talk neither."

"Do you have a theory as to why he wishes to purchase us?" It occurred to me that the Hosts might have procured assistance from the Eldorans. If true, this did not bode well for our continued safety.

"Don't know why's he wants you, creature. Probably sell her for bride bait to one of them fools that likes to keep the blood pure. Says the girl's the Priestess's great granddatter, Eldoran pure on both sides for three generations. Might ask me for two mules instead o' one."

The term bride bait suggested to me that Alenna was to be sold in an arranged marriage. I was familiar with the custom, which was acceptably practiced in many cultures. In such exchanges, a high social standing could sometimes secure the safety of the individual purchased.

"Static, I don't want to get sold."

Alenna's confidence in her victory faltered as I considered the variables. I was uncertain why the Eldorans, a hunted species, would wish to maintain their genetic traits. Ostracizing themselves from the majority would be counterproductive to their survival, unless they planned a demonstration of unity against the current regime. As of yet, I had witnessed little evidence of organized resistance, other than the small group led by Alenna's father. Thinking of that group aroused within me a suspicion, which I sought to verify.

"Broda, is there an Eldoran belief that encourages genetic purity?"

"Sure'nuf. Some prophecy or 'nother in them thar *Great Book*. Say's somethin' like 'the pure blood o' the priestess rules when the catalyst sends the righteous to the sky'. Can take them thar *Great Book* and go jump in the mud for alls I care, s'long as I get me mule. Book won't do me no good out here." She expelled more air from her nostrils.

I agreed with Broda's practical opinion. With only fervent wishes to support them, her Eldoran brethren were unlikely to ascend to power. They would need to take conscious steps toward change within Oneian society. This fact of their survival inefficacy did little to recommend them as mates for Alenna.

"I regret to inform you, Broda, that we will not be rendezvousing with your associate. Please unbind our restraints, or we will be forced to take aggressive action."

Broda stopped and turned. She wrinkled her brow and stared into the surrounding forest. Seconds later, a large brown bear ambled into view.

"Keep up, or Cub will have the girl as a snack."

"If your bear destroys Alenna, you will be unable to sell her."

"I win, or nobody wins! Keep moving!" We did not move because Alenna did not move, and I was still enmeshed to her head. She suddenly ignited the satchel attached to Broda's back. The woman shrieked and gyrated her shoulders out of the harness. Throwing her pack into the snow, Broda angrily stomped out the flames that consumed her belongings. A deception of cooperation might have served us better. I would soon need to explain to Alenna the concept of strategy.

"If you don't leave us alone, I'll set you and your stupid bear on fire! And Static will peck out your eyes!"

I admired Alenna's courage, but she had overlooked the fact that we were still bound in strips of sinew, whereas our enemies were not. Cub mirrored the disgruntlement of his mistress. While swinging his head from side to side, he huffed steam from his snout and pounded his front paws into the snow.

"Alenna, please provide me energy."

She did, and I slipped our bonds after I mutated into a flying insect. Then I began to morph into a small badger-porcupine hybrid, but Broda witnessed the transformation and tried to control me as she had Cub. With the added energy, my quill-coated body expanded to nearly half Cub's size. The bear attacked, and I rushed to defend with all the ferocity of a cornered badger. Cub roared and gored me with his claws until I retreated, slashing his nose and leaving long quills jutting from his face.

The grizzly surged forward like a bristling juggernaut and swatted my smaller form through the trees. The bouquet of quills protruding from his paws, eyes, and mouth grew thicker each time he struck, but he was unable to realize that he caused his own injuries.

"Get 'im Cub!" Broda yelled as she lifted her pack and stooped to retrieve Alenna's leash.

Alenna set the fur trim of Broda's mittens and hood to flame. Then, using her telekinetic powers, she pushed the unbalanced Broda backward into the snow. The woman swatted out the flames while Alenna turned her attention to Cub. She ignited the bear's tail end. Cub turned to address the rear assault; whereupon, I attacked his undefended hindquarters. The simple-minded bear spun about roaring, trying to decide which enemy to attack first. Alenna set the fur around his injured stout aflame.

The added insult to his injuries helped him decide. Cub lunged toward Alenna. In a flurry of claws, teeth, and quills, I intercepted him, but his momentum was too great, and his snout collided with Alenna. Her clothing became hooked on his lower canines, and for a moment she dangled, until the bear jerked his head and flung her into the snow. To draw Cub's attention, I redoubled my assault. He sunk his jaws into my shoulder and mauled me. Alenna cried in distress and sent waves of flame lashing over Cub's girth. What remained of the bear's confidence dissolved, and he bolted into the forest. My damaged body lay crumpled on the frozen battlefield.

"*Static!*" Alenna rose, struggling against her loosened bonds, and hobbled to my side.

"*Alenna, do not approach any closer. My quills will damage you.*"

"*But, Static, you're hurt really bad!*"

"*That is true, but please remember that I cannot die. With your energy to assist me, I will recover.*" On cue, Alenna infused me with her power, and I transformed into an uninjured owl.

Cursing, Broda retreated into the forest. Smoke tendrils drifted through the still air after her. The vaporous trail also followed the swath of torn and bloodied earth where Cub had fled. Alenna untangled her remaining bonds and moved about to survey the battlefield more closely, while I clung to her shoulder and pondered various practical matters.

We would soon need to construct a permanent base of operations. A fugitive lifestyle would be impractical for educating a child in the sciences. Conversely, complete isolation would not prepare Alenna for the nuances of social behavior. I decided that a functional dwelling at the edge of Oneian society would serve best. As a shape-shifter, I felt that I could teach Alenna to effectively blend into an environment. Only recently have I learned that I do not, in fact, blend as well as I assumed.

Now that I had committed myself to Alenna's education, I immediately compiled a list of subjects. The list soon became so extensive that I despaired of ever completing it within Alenna's limited lifespan. Beginning immediately was essential.

I noted with pride that Alenna was still studying the scene of our conflict. She had assumed a squat position and was examining sections of soiled ground. I was pleased that she had taken to heart her lessons in logical observation, but she was blocking her emotions, and that caused me to be curious.

"Alenna, are you interested in tracking Cub?" Perhaps she thought that the grizzly would be capable of sensing her feelings. In truth, I was not certain that he couldn't, as I was not fully familiar with the animal life on Oneia.

She appeared distraught, yet nodded briskly at my suggestion to track. We followed Cub's trail deeper into the forest. Alenna scrutinized his obvious trail at every step. I began to wonder if she was visually impaired, a common malady among humans. Cub's trail could have been tracked while sprinting. Alenna stopped and allowed her emotions to emanate. I was surprised to discover that she suffered intense guilt. Her eyes filled with tears, which inspired within me feelings of protectiveness.

"I'm sorry, Static! I didn't mean to lose him!"

I wondered if I had unconsciously pressured Alenna to achieve more than she was capable. *"Do not be concerned, Alenna. If it is your desire, we can track Cub easily. Please be assured that finding him is not necessary."*

Alenna sobbed, and I was as confused as I had ever been.

"Cub ate your friend, Static! I'm sorry! I couldn't stop him!"

The cause of Alenna's distress finally became clear. During his attack, Cub must have inadvertently consumed the pouch that held my companion's remains.

"Do not be concerned, Alenna. It is unlikely that Cub will digest leather, bone, and metal alike. We will collect the ring and remains when Cub completes his digestion cycle." My calm demeanor eased Alenna's fears, although she was somewhat confused by my response.

We followed Cub's trail through the forest as I began to instruct Alenna on the various stages of digestion and the information that can often be gleaned from the examination of waste materials.

Prometheus: *That's revolting, virus.*

Master: *Aren't you supposed to be a scientist?*

Prometheus: *I'm a god scientist, young man. Primitive biology doesn't interest me.*

Static: *Were not the Hosts once biological creatures, Prometheus? And have you not based your own experiments on that knowledge?*

Prometheus: *That's entirely different!*

Master: *How?*

Prometheus: [no comment]

Static: *My friend, please resume the telling of your early history?*

Master: *Sure thing.*

Young Master

A roiling sea of law enforcement and media surrounded my home, while a solid mass of ambulance chasers lapped at their edges. The ambulances in focus were equipped with paramedics waiting for someone to save, but their offered assistance had no takers. A nearby van labeled coroner, though, was getting plenty of business. The mound of zippered trash bags being loaded into it was undermining my confidence, seeing as I would soon confront whatever provided the bodies to fill them.

The thoughts of the mob suggested that I was entrenched on the eighteenth floor where I'd slaughtered somewhere between eight and twenty-three heavily armed cops, plus a few innocent bystanders. I elbowed my way through the crowd, which was secretly pleased that I'd put up a good fight, but was still eager to see me shot to death, or failing that, captured.

I didn't want to attend a showdown anymore. Why should I save people who wanted me dead? What made me think that I could? An alien god wouldn't make me as powerful as he was, would he? Chances were slim.

Stepping away from the pack of oglers, I let the crowd-control officer peruse my fancy suit and faked ID. I feigned an air of superiority that I thought might match my credentials. My instructor's personality came in handy here; he'd taken acting lessons and had a lofty opinion of himself. The officer nodded indifferently and let me pass.

Nobody called my bluff until I'd made it into my building's lobby, where there were several law-enforcement types who had better credentials than mine. Rats. I hadn't thought to check inside. Maybe I should plan to assume that my plans will go awry from the beginning.

A big shot secret agent noticed me and wondered who I was. I continued my bluff and acted as if it were up to him to explain himself to me. I just waited, all officious-looking, for his report. I hoped his thoughts would suggest an agency to which I could claim membership. He couldn't come up with anything. His organization was at the top of the ladder, and he knew most of his superiors; none of whom were nineteen years old. Crap.

"Who the hell are you?"

Three different sets of knowledge in my head and all of them drew a blank. Ah well, I hadn't wanted to lie anyway.

"I'm the guy that you think you have trapped upstairs."

"Right," he thought I was nuts. "Please go with Agent Reed. He can take your statement for you." Agent Reed had a gun holster under his jacket that conveniently housed a gun. As he approached, I borrowed said gun and used him as a shield. I noted that all of the weapons drawn thereafter were bigger than agent Reed's – figures. Mr. Big Shot shared with me the standard phrases that police officers shout at criminals who draw weapons. He had a puffy blue vein that stood out on his forehead. Had I not been busy, I would have liked to poke it.

"Tell your people to stand back from the elevators," I said. I wasn't really going to shoot agent Reed, although I couldn't speak for everyone else. They were almost willing to punch a few holes in him just so they could get to me. Still, they moved out of my way.

I backed agent Reed into an elevator, pushed numbers four and eighteen, and then drew another pistol from under his pant leg. One should never think about hidden ankle holsters whilst in the presence of thought-reading fugitives.

The doors closed and opened again on the fourth. I pushed agent Reed into the hall, where he dove for cover that wasn't there. I shook my head and traveled upward to eighteen, where things got a lot scarier.

A wall of fear slammed against me as the doors opened again. Almost distractedly, I glanced at the top half of a man's body lying in the hallway. He was dressed in black body armor, probably tactical-team issue. It was pretty obvious that he'd been dragging himself toward the elevator when he died – I'm not going to explain how I knew that. I stuck out my arm and stopped the elevator from closing on me, and that's as far as I got for the next minute or so. My newest and oldest personalities were at serious odds over whether or not I should break and run for my life. A shiver ran down my spine and symbolically divided our feelings on the issue.

I took a deep breath and stepped into the hallway. My knees didn't buckle. I was proud of that. The lifeless vista in the corridor was graphic to the point of being overdone, but I'd seen more impressive special effects in movies, so I didn't understand why I was so afraid. After all, I'd already died in multiples since yesterday. I forced myself to keep moving, stepping around the black-ringed hole burned through to the floor below, where parts of melted and severed bodies lay. Keep moving. Had someone seen me with my dual pistols and fancy charcoal suit as I stepped over and around corpses, I would have no doubt looked the essence of icy dispassion.

Before entering my apartment, I leaned against the doorframe and listened to the helicopter circling the building. Someone with a megaphone was trying to encourage my surrender. I looked down at the legs lying across the threshold. They either proved that the door was fully open, or that I'd found the other half of the guy by the elevator. Threshold, that's an interesting word, isn't it? Last time I checked, most folks no longer covered the floors of their homes with thresh. Maybe the term should have been changed to carpethold, or maybe linohold. Yeah, I know, I was stalling, but that's what I felt like doing, so it fits.

Anyway, like I said, there was a corpse lying across the entrance, just a singular corpse, which made it a low traffic area compared to the hallway. The alien-god-guy had set me up to be notoriously violent. The hallway's walls, ceiling, and floor were riddled with bullet holes, suggesting that the downed officers had put up a good fight. Why would they bother firing at the ceiling? Was I flying? Guns obviously hadn't worked, so I didn't know why I was still carrying them, particularly since none of my personalities were experienced in their use. One of our fathers – I didn't know whose – had once told us always to point a gun down and away from the body. So I did. That way, I figured, I could shoot the people on the floor below instead of the floor above – useful.

I breathed deeply a few times and then peeked into my apartment, which was faintly illuminated by the crisp beacon of an office tower across the way. I began to study the shadows just as the helicopter's floodlight exploded through the broken windows and sent spots dancing before my eyes. The floodlight passed, and shadows returned with a vengeance. Half blinded, I dove through the foyer, rolled into the kitchen, and then skidded across broken glass until my back was pressed again the wall below the window casing. I aimed my guns at nobody, because nobody was in my apartment, except me. The last corpse had stopped at the doorframe. That would have been anticlimactic if I weren't still terrified.

I climbed to my feet and examined the mess of my shadowed home. Bullets and glass had sprayed everywhere. Speaking of bullets – the helicopter's floodlight returned and cast my silhouette on the closet door – BANG – right through the necktie! The police sniper knocked me forward onto my pistols, and I shot myself across the chest, which hurt like a wailing banshee. But then I wished myself healed, and the pain subsided. I rolled over broken glass and scooted my back against the wall, lest I get shot again.

So where was the alien? Why would he have killed these people if he weren't trying to draw me out? I considered this while listening to the noises around me.

Sounds – cities are full of them, many of which are constant and overlooked through familiarity. The train rolled by while I pondered. I heard it; I felt the vibrations; and I even noted that it was a five-engine freight train. I'd lived with the noise for two years, and I no longer paid it much attention. The police circus offered the added hustle and bustle of sirens, horns, and chopper blades. But those sounds, I easily identified, and hence, ignored.

What tugged at my ear was the chittering sound that stopped when the train rumbled near, because my fear dropped a notch at the same time. I'd been hearing it since I'd arrived in the elevator. When the last car of the train trailed off into the distance, the chittering resumed, and the fear flooded in at full force.

I honed in on the noise, which was coming from a black ball tucked like a giant cocoon over the doorway. With another sweep of manufactured daylight, the helicopter illuminated the creepy bump. It was a big freaking spider. Its bulbous core absorbed most of the light, but its limbs, which were tucked against it, were a touch reflective. It looked like a hole in the ceiling with legs. Just to see what it would do, I shot it. The chittering noises got louder as my fear intensified. It didn't sound happy. Well, that made two of us. I wondered if this was my enemy's stand-in, or if this was his true form – one mustn't make rash assumptions based on appearance alone.

The mutant insect unhinged from the corner and showed that it was two legs shy of a whole spider. The daddy longlegs I'd partially dismembered as a child had apparently returned to haunt me, except it had taken growth hormones and was wearing spiked boxing gloves. Its body was about the size of my toaster oven, but the unfolded spindle-stick legs stretched from floor to ceiling and effectively cordoned off the only sane way out of the building. It crept toward me, as if trying to frighten me more than I already was – good luck with that.

I still had eleven bullets left. I gave them to the bug as fast as I could, but they just passed through its eyeless body and punched a few more holes in the doorframe. Black liquid spattered from it. One small drop landed on the fleshy part between my thumb and finger – ouch, very much. The spider goop sizzled and spat, turning a dime-sized section of my hand into bubbling charcoal. I dropped the guns, wiped my hand on my pants, and consequently burned a smoking track into my leg. In the seconds that followed, I was disgusted to learn that the powers given to me didn't extend to wishing away my pain. Stupid bloody aliens, can't do anything right.

The nightmare approached sloth-like as I tried to wish myself healed. Sparks jumped across my wounds, and I could actually feel the flesh knit together, much more slowly than before. In fact, healing the burns hurt worse than getting them. Mutant spider goop was nasty stuff.

Here's an interesting bit of trivia for anyone considering taking on one of these bugs. Normally, humans can't remember physical pain. It's a survival mechanism, kind of a mutual agreement between body and brain to avoid experiencing the same ordeal twice. Emotional pain can be relived as easily as recalling a traumatic event, but physical pain generally doesn't work that way. Try it – imagine a past injury. Does the actual pain come back with the memory? I didn't think so.

A chemical burn from a saugael mor, on the other hand, will have a different effect. First, they have nifty molecular blockers in their acid that interfere with the natural flow of endorphins, which make any wounds they cause hurt as much as possible, for as long as possible. Second, and most irritating, their neural attack connects pain receptors to memories of the injury. I mention this only because, as I sit here twelve hundred years later and tell the story of being injured, my hand hurts just as much as it did that day, as does my leg.

So, this is the advice I have to offer. If forced into a fight with one of these things, and it sprays acid, make sure to die in the first few seconds. Do that, or put up a good mental block. Either way, the neural connections that cause future pain won't be able to develop. Unfortunately for me, I didn't know this at the time, and now it hurts to talk about it, literally.

Through the phantom pain, I scrambled to my feet, grabbed two of its legs, and tried to finish the job I'd started as a kid. It skewered me in a blink, proving that I was neither faster nor stronger than a six-legged mutant spider. Saugael mor claws, by the way, don't cause the same lasting effects as their acid, but they still hurt, especially in multiples.

I took a different approach and willed its body to explode. Had I thought that strategy through to its logical conclusion, I might have abstained. Sparks flew everywhere in a blinding flash of pyrotechnics, and then its bulbous core burst like an overripe melon dropped from the roof. In appreciation of my future comfort, I would like to thank the kind police sniper for choosing that moment to pop a cap in the back of my head.

From my gaseous viewpoint, I watched as six giant spider feet danced around the mushy remains of what was once my body. They looked as though they were waiting for me to come back to life so they could try to kill me again. The feet, I was disturbed to see, were transforming into spiders themselves and were growing very quickly. There went the neighborhood.

Master: *Okay, done. Tell us about Hogarth, Prometheus.*

Prometheus: *Hogarth? But that incident doesn't happen for two years! You have no idea of the torments I was subjected to in that time! My tribulations should be duly recorded!*

Static: *Prometheus, we will need to be selective in our retelling in order to cover the relevant events in a succinct manner. My pupils have a finite period of existence and do not have sufficient time to relive the minutia of our prolonged lives.*

Master: *Try squeezing in a bit about the bug problem.*

Prometheus: *I could hardly avoid it if I tried, now could I!*

Martin Wolfe

Chapter Eleven

Prometheus

The nasty vermin were everywhere! My beautiful temple was infested with assassins! For months, the priestess had been cutting off the beasties' heads and making more of them. There were so many now that she was losing control. Dozens of the dreadful creatures escaped the temple every day. Tiberius was beside himself trying to keep them out of the city, and I was constantly worried that they might turn on me at any moment.

A half-grown killer crept across the hallway. Tiberius and I stopped to let the little vermin pass, lest it call for reinforcements. My rod had grown stronger after the joining ceremony, but there were only so many I could repel at once. And my servants had no protection at all. I'd already lost four bath people that week. If this kept up, I was going to have to prepare my own baths!

"We have to do something, Tiberius! For the love of soapy bubbles, I'm supposed to be the holy prophet! I can't be expected to carry my own water!" The assassin stopped to hiss at us.

"I am open to suggestions, good prophet. The rejection by her betrothed has made the priestess more volatile than usual. I have been avoiding her whenever possible." It wasn't like Tiberius to be so frank about the priestess. He must have been terribly frustrated.

"You mean you still go to her? I've been ignoring her summonses altogether! It's been over a year since I've seen her, not that it does me any good! The blasted woman keeps torturing me anyway!"

For the past two years, she'd sent waves of pain through my rod and had demanded that I present myself before her. But I knew that if I did, she would only have her nasty pets torture me instead, so I stood my ground! If I was going to be tortured anyway, I was determined to keep my robes clean!

The creeper in front of us decided that we weren't reacting enough and crawled off to terrorize someone less important. We walked a bit farther only to be stopped by another one. It strolled toward Tiberius and tried to poke its claws into him, but my shield held firm. The thing hissed and moved off. Tiberius glanced at me. I couldn't begin to read his expression.

We started moving again and rounded the corner that led to the military wing. We stopped. The corridor was alive with assassins! It was a swarm!

"Tiberius, we don't really need to meet in your office, do we? I have a lovely vintage of red Soderbine chilling in my reading room."

"We must indeed reach my office, good Prophet. I have made an error that will end us if we do not repair the damage quickly."

"So you made a mistake! What of it? The Holy Prophet forgives you! Let's go have some wine!" Nothing would end us faster than walking down that corridor!

Tiberius explained, "I have just learned that temple's meat supplier is a former priest, who has arrived with written records of the past year's expenditures. He is being detained in my office." Tiberius stared at the mass of saugael mor crawling over the walls, floor, and ceiling. He looked calm, but he hadn't moved any more than I. His hand twitched on his sword pommel. As if a sword was going to help us. I doubted that he could handle any more than I could with my rod. That would still leave hundreds to kill us.

"So you have paperwork to do. I see. Well, I'll leave you to it then. Drop by and have some wine when you're finished." More like, I would save some wine for the ceremonial basin at Tiberius's funeral. The military wing was too far from the Priestess's chambers for her to have complete control over these vermin. I turned to leave, but Tiberius placed a restraining hand on my arm. All things considered, it felt quite pleasant.

"I require your official presence, good Prophet. Of late, the priestess has personally checked the temple's expenditures. Many of Hogarth's supplies will be listed on that invoice, which will include several rounds of salted pork. The priestess prefers beef and does not allow pork in the temple. We must destroy that invoice and the priest who created it. To execute a priest, even a former one, I need a denunciation from the holy prophet."

"You want to kill one of my priests? Whatever for? Just tell the priestess that I ordered the silly pork if it makes you happy! She tortures me all the time anyway, and it certainly isn't worth getting chopped to bits over!" Of all the ridiculous things, he wanted me to get killed over salted pork, if you can imagine!

"Good Prophet, perhaps you give the priestess less credit than she deserves. I have little doubt that she cross-references the inventory lists and would realize that salted pork appears neither in the larder journal, nor on the export tallies. She will know that something is being hidden from her. Who do you think she is likely to execute first, when her two highest-ranking advisors are presently avoiding her?"

Oh dear! I shuddered to think of what the priestess would do to us when she actually had a reason. "Well, why didn't you say so?" I turned and waded into the assassins. "Shoo, you nasty things! Shoo, go away!" I used my rod to plow the squirming vermin aside. Tiberius drew his sword, which I'd always thought was a lovely weapon. Then he drew another sword from over his shoulder. The new one was gleaming silver with etched flames reaching from the guard to halfway up the blade.

Master: *Hey, that's mine!*

Prometheus: *Really? Well, it serves you right for leaving your toys lying about where people can find them!*

Master: *I should probably go back and get the rest of that stuff. It could end up causing a lot of trouble.*

Prometheus: *Not at all, it actually came in quite handy.*

Assassins oozed around us as we inched down the hallway, but they stayed out of sword reach. When we were fully surrounded, they attacked.

"Eek! Tiberius, save me!"

"Stay close, and maintain your shield!" Tiberius was magnificent! He whirled around like a temple dancer and kept the nasties from poking me. But then there were too many stabbing at once, and I felt pain where claws snuck past our defenses. We weren't going to make it! May the peasants sing songs of us!

"Tiberius, do something! I'm too young to die!" Just as my robes were about to fall in shreds, the pretty silver sword rescued us. It burst into a cone of sparkling green flames and sizzled assassins, which scattered from its path. With smoking death on our trail, we dashed through the entrance of the command wing. I focused my rod's shield and slammed the doors, but their wooden planks shuddered and cracked. Oh, for the love of rotten oak, Tiberius had burned the doors to a crisp! Claws ripped through the charred wood like it was paper. In seconds they were streaming through the gap. Oh dear, oh my!

With the swarm spilling all around us, we ran to the next set of doors. Tiberius sprayed the beasties with the green fire, and choking black smoke billowed down the hall. A few of them fell to the floor and shriveled up dead, but there were too many left for it to matter.

The doors to Tiberius's outer office were made with interlocking bronze plates, but we didn't get a chance to close them. A wall of soldiers blocked our way. We were forced to stop and watch as a wave of creeping, smoking assassins poured around us and into the room. I thought we were doomed for certain, but the vermin didn't attack.

Covered from head to toe in black soot and blood, Tiberius and I looked pitiful. I healed our injuries before we collapsed.

The lead soldier stepped forward stiffly. "High Commander Tiberius, Holy Prophet Tibbald," He sheepishly bowed to us, "The priestess wishes an audience with you." At least the blasphemous lout had the decency to look chagrinned for daring to detain his betters! It was obvious now that the priestess had sent her pets to herd us into submission.

"What is the meaning of this, young man? I demand to know this instant! The holy prophet will not be moved about like a puppet by anyone! I'll have you…."

Tiberius interrupted me. "Good Prophet, we must all bow to the wishes of our divine priestess. Sub-Commander Jonas, you will accompany us. Bring these men as an honor guard."

I was aghast that Tiberius would submit to this outrage! He glared at me to be silent and glanced at the ceiling as we were marched out of the office and through the temple's corridors. Oh yes, those – hundreds of saugael mor coated the masonry like a giant Kagtu tapestry, created by someone with a sadly limited color sense. Their legs overlapped so closely that they looked like a wave of undulating black balls. The horrid clicking racket didn't help matters one bit. Terror radiated from the soldiers who tried to look calm as the assassin blanket undulated above us – serves them right!

When we spilled into the throne room, the priestess's thoughts gave away that she already knew about the salted pork nonsense. We were doomed! Pieto, the traitor, was standing at her side. I should have had the heretic priest killed instead of letting him become a butcher. Now I was going to be executed for my merciful gesture – how unfair!

Tiberius spoke before he could be accused. "Please, forgive me, Divine Priestess. I should not have allowed my Eldoran informant to enter the temple – he has turned traitor against the empire. As you must have already discovered, Pieto has been supplying Eldoran spies with provisions. I am humbled by your bravery, Divine Priestess, that you have captured the traitor on your own."

Oh, bravo! Brilliant, I tell you; Tiberius pulled our heads off the block and replaced them with Pieto's! My traitor priest looked shaken to the core, while the priestess's mind spun down the new path Tiberius had carved for her. But then she remembered that we had been avoiding her, and her thoughts turned sour again.

"Yes, High Commander, I have captured him. It seems the Divine Priestess has so few attendees that she must run her own empire. What things do you and this prophet find so important that you cannot meet the needs of your priestess?" She was determined to execute someone, and she wanted it to be us. Pieto was speechless and looked like he was about to expire all on his own.

Tiberius improvised. "For two years, we have led lives as peasant traders so that we could infiltrate the Eldoran underground. We were pained to resist your call so that we could defeat the worst of your enemies, but our love for you carried us onward. In fact, my Goddess, this day we are proud to bring you a name: Hogarth, the Eldoran leader who commands this traitor you have captured."

She was still angry, but she desperately wanted to believe the cockamamie story that Tiberius fed her.

I elaborated. "Oh, it was absolutely horrible, Priestess! That nasty beast Hogarth became furious one day and used his evil magic to set me on fire. You remember that time don't you? It was that day you dumped me in the snow. Why, I nearly froze to death, I tell…." Tiberius slapped me in the back of the head!

"Priestess, the good Prophet's ordeal has damaged his mind, and he now requires aggressive therapy to clear his thinking. Perhaps you would like to care for his treatment yourself?"

What? No, no, don't tell her that! The priestess looked at me eagerly, and her mood brightened. Blast Tiberius, he was going to pay for this!

"You have done well, Commander, but hear this: I will have no more Eldoran traitors in my midst. You will send my armies to find every Eldoran on Oneia. You will kill them and burn their homes. Let it be known that any who harbor Eldorans will be burned as well." The Eldoran servants in the throne room quietly crept away when she said that.

"Divine Priestess, your armies are needed to defend our borders. Your empire will suffer many losses."

"I have faith that the empire will recover, High Commander." She was about to dismiss us, so she could torture Pieto, when she remembered something unpleasant. "Oh, and you two will report to me every day – in person! Do I make myself clear?"

"As you command, Divine Priestess. With your permission, the good prophet and I will leave to execute the Eldoran leader."

"That is a good beginning, High Commander. You may go."

The vermin swarmed over my traitor priest as Tiberius and I left the throne room. That would teach him for keeping a copy of *Volume Three*!

Intending to bathe and change, I turned down the passage that led to my private chambers.

"Good Prophet, your personal errands can wait. We must tend to Hogarth."

Oh blast, what was the big hurry? It would be months before Tiberius's soldiers found that bearish fellow. We didn't need to hide him today, not to mention that he was just as safe where he was as anywhere else. Tiberius looked adamant. Sigh. My bath would have to wait. I lifted my rod of office and transported us back to Hogarth's pile of trees. It was summer, and I suddenly worried that there were no snow banks to land in if the ugly brute decided to toss me. Tiberius pounded on the door.

When it opened, Hogarth appeared and laughed at us. "Hah, Hogarth has never seen the half-men look better!"

That wasn't funny at all. Here we were going out of our way to warn this smelly giant, and what does he do but make fun of our soiled clothing. If it weren't for him, I would be well on my way to a bath! Then Tiberius surprised us both by drawing his sword and running it through Hogarth's chest. That seemed to irritate Hogarth quite a bit. He came bellowing out of his hovel and swung his huge axe at Tiberius. I was amazed at how fast the two of them were.

For several minutes, they crashed though the forest as steel clanged. I could hardly tell what was going on until Hogarth finally staggered back to his hovel and slumped to his knees. He stared at the sword sticking out of his chest. It was that pretty silver one with the flames on the blade.

"Be gone treacherous half-men. Let Hogarth become worms and dirt in peace."

This was an interesting development. It seemed rather unlike Tiberius to follow the Priestess's orders so directly like that. I went to ask what his reasons were.

I found him barely alive, deep in the bushes and propped up against a rotted tree. Hogarth's big axe was stuck in Tiberius's breastplate. The silly fool had gone and ruined his lovely armor. His other sword was broken in half and lay at his side. It took all of my strength to pull the axe out of his chest. I actually had to stand on him to do it, which made blood bubble from his mouth and nearly finished him off. I healed his wounds before he up and died on me.

"Thank you, good Prophet. Hogarth was more skilled than I anticipated."

"Why ever did you do such a thing, Tiberius? You aren't planning on becoming the Priestess's puppet are you? If you do, I'm not going to invite you for wine anymore!"

"Good Prophet, had my men captured Hogarth, all of the Eldorans would have been found and burned within weeks."

"Well, they're all going to die soon enough anyway. What difference could it possibly make when?"

"With Hogarth dead, good Prophet, it will take decades to find every Eldoran, if in fact we ever do. Our chances of finding the girl alive, and thus Static, will increase with entire battalions searching discriminately. The Priestess has given us an opportunity that we must not waste."

Tiberius was on his feet by then and was taking off his ruined breastplate. He tossed it into the bushes next to his broken sword, and then we wandered back to Hogarth. Tiberius glanced curiously at Hogarth's corpse where it lay propped up against the house of sticks. Then he told me to transport us back to the temple. That was it? What about the sword? It had been quite useful in repelling the vermin. I told Tiberius that we should take it with us, but he wanted to leave it behind. Sometimes Tiberius just lacked good sense.

Master: [Chuckles.]

Prometheus: *What in the name of shiny swords are you laughing about?*

Master: *Fire didn't like him.*

Prometheus: *What didn't like whom?*

Master: *Fire, my sword, didn't like Tiberius. That's why he left it behind. Paul, I need you to fix Hogarth when we're done here. Take Ice with you.*

Paul: *Yes, Master*

Static: *I will continue the narrative.*

Static

Due to the mutating landscape, our first-year of construction on our permanent dwelling progressed rapidly. Each morning, we inspected our building site and discovered that another facet of our design plan had become easier to implement. The trees, rocks, soil, and water sources most often moved to where they would prove beneficial to our efforts. But occasionally, the elements worked against pure efficiency and opted for aesthetics, which I had not requested. Although Alenna approved of the artistic changes, she insisted that she had not envisioned them. I began to wonder if the inconsistencies were caused by failing to synchronize our subliminal intentions. So we developed a test wherein we imagined different shapes for a single hole in the ground.

I envisioned a circle. Alenna imagined a square. But the earthen trench that appeared the next morning was star-shaped, proving that our silent benefactor was familiar with the concept of humor. I accepted the star as proof of sentience, and promised our secret helper that when Alenna's education and survival needs were satisfied, I would develop a better a way for us to communicate, should it be interested.

And so we progressed. By our third year on Oneia, we had constructed a network of simple machinery within our home of oven-fired bricks. Our technology-enabled products, such as bricks and milled flour, had begun to benefit the nearby Oneian community, which had until then relied heavily on erratic shipments from their capital city.

Disguised as Alenna's canine companion, I regularly led her into town and instructed her on methods of conducting trade. Under my tutelage, Alenna's intellectual parameters had broadened. But to have her accepted as a trader, we were forced to develop a deception of proper guardianship. Her father was said to be preparing her for acquisition of his business and wanted her to learn by immersion. Regardless, she appeared so knowledgeable beyond apprenticeship years that many of the uneducated townsfolk would not allow their children to associate with her. I thus increased her lesson and work schedule so that she could not dwell on loneliness.

"Alenna, please lower your end." We were constructing a smoke house for the dried meat products that we intended to trade. Alenna's powers had grown with age, and I was now able to attain the mass of a mid-sized animal. Currently, I utilized the strong opposable fingers of a middling ape as I maneuvered a kiln-dried timber into position. I possessed strength equal to a grown man, but not the height. Alenna was taller.

"Sorry, Father." She lowered her end of the timber, which she partly supported with her Eldoran energy.

We placed the beam into our pulley system and winched it into place; whereupon, I scaled the framework and secured the wooden pins. Alenna showed fatigue from our laborious morning. I signaled that it was time for lunch, which only she required, but we would both enjoy.

Once inside our comfortable dwelling, Alenna prepared sandwiches of dried meat, vegetables, and cheese. I suggested that we check on my companion before we eat. Alenna was unenthusiastic, as she was mildly repulsed by my companion's incomplete appearance.

In the center of our kitchen's oak floor, was a trapdoor, which we opened to reveal the shallow stone pit that housed my companion's remains. In the hope that he might rejuvenate faster, Alenna had tried several times to inject her energy into him, but the process resisted tampering. At his present rate of growth, I estimated that he would be fully formed in several years.

"So, this is going to be a man someday, is it, Father?" Alenna had developed a detached disinterest with the growing mass, yet she still showed visible signs of intrigue when viewing it. Her question, having been answered long ago, was largely rhetorical.

I responded out of politeness. *"That is my hope, Alenna."*

"Is he going to be attractive?"

I remembered then that Alenna had just passed her first cycle of monthly fertility. The influx of new hormones had inspired thoughts of mating behavior.

"I am an improper judge of human attractiveness, Alenna. But I have noticed that, in his presence, most women react strongly in some fashion."

Alenna said nothing. We returned to our table, ate sandwiches served on ceramic dishes, and drank water poured into crude glass mugs. We had, on our own, constructed all of our utensils, tools, and ergonomic conveniences, such as the miniature aqueduct that directed hot and cold water throughout our various rooms, and the stone oven that was bellows-powered by a tiny waterwheel. It was a simple system of living, yet effective. Given sufficient time, we would undoubtedly make improvements.

"We should construct a forge, Alenna. The manipulation of metals would provide many opportunities for technological advancement."

Alenna was lost in her own thoughts. *"Does he have a bathtub in his castle, Father?"*

The breaks in Alenna's concentration were less than before, but she was still prone to a certain degree of distractibility.

"Yes, Alenna, my companion has one hundred fifty-three bathing facilities in his domicile."

Her mouth dropped open. *"Why?"*

"He was once enamored with a woman who professed a keen interest in bathing, an interest as keen as your own. For each year they were together, he gifted her with a new bathing chamber. He stopped when she chose to die."

Alenna mulled over this information as she chewed. At length, she asked, *"Can we build a bathtub with heated tiles?"*

We had only recently traded for a wooden tub and a collection of bathing products so that Alenna could entertain herself in this manner. *"We do not yet have the luxury of focusing our primary efforts on pleasure, Alenna."*

She looked down at her plate and preened crumbs from its edges. *"When we go to your friend's castle, I'm going to bathe in all of those tubs."*

I found humor in her plan and responded with my own form of jocularity. *"That is an auspicious goal, Alenna. Have you any plans after you attempt to dissolve yourself in bathwater?"*

She smirked and shook her head. *"Survival and then happiness, isn't that what you teach me, Father? If your friend is a god, my survival should be assured. That leaves only happiness, and what could make me happier than so many bathtubs and so much time to soak in them?"*

"*My companion takes notable exception to being labeled a god, Alenna. And I would suggest that you develop an alternate purpose once you have finished being professionally decadent.*"

"*I just know that I don't want to work this hard forever. That's my goal.*"

"*The simple existence we are living has distinct advantages, Alenna. Much fulfillment is derived from surmounting basic challenges.*"

"*Nobody would work this hard if they had a choice.*"

"*That is not so, Alenna. In fact, my companion and I have often committed ourselves to arduous parameters and tasks, so we might better enjoy our lives. Paradoxically, more enjoyment is wrought from pleasures when one reduces the frequency and quantity in which they are enjoyed.*"

Alenna exhaled a volume of air as her shoulders drooped. She knew that she had inspired a lesson and resignedly rose to clean the dishes. I continued my instruction as I hopped to the counter and helped with drying.

"*When one has unlimited access to pleasure, there is little incentive to remain active, and pleasures soon become a tiresome, unsatisfying chain of empty events. When pleasure becomes routine, happiness becomes more difficult to achieve.*"

"*It still sounds good to me.*" Alenna put away the dishes and headed back outside.

I followed, and we resumed work on the smokehouse. We secured the last of the supports, prepared the mortar, and began laying bricks.

"*I was just imagining, Father, that resting my brain might be like happiness. Do I have to learn all the time? Can't I stop thinking for a little while, maybe for a few days?*"

"*I would not recommend it, Alenna. A human's genetic advantage is its ability to reason. For you to cease thinking would be akin to a lion dulling its claws, or a bird clipping its wings. You will have ample opportunity to rest when you choose a different task to perform, or when you slumber. Your current level of fatigue does not suggest that either is needed."*

Alenna slapped mortar onto our growing wall and hammered bricks into place. Her jaw was firmly set.

"What's your purpose in life, Static?"

Alenna's reversion to calling me Static, instead of her preference of Father, suggested that she harbored bitterness. Her question was an attempt to guide me onto a different topic, and thereby, to avoid the subject at hand. I had trained her to recognize when she acted solely on emotion, and I hoped that she would soon curtail her behavior.

"I have several ongoing interests, Alenna; one of which is education. But if I were to classify myself into a specific profession, it would be science, or to be more precise, the transmutation of matter to energy and the inverse, a subject in which both my companion and I share a vested interest."

Alenna had stopped working and now stared at her trowel. *"I'm sorry, Father. I allowed my emotions to guide my thoughts again, instead of the other way around, like you taught me."*

"You have done well, Alenna. Recognizing a difficulty in your thinking is the first half of emotional maturity and shows great courage."

"Only half, Father? I admitted that I acted poorly. Why is that only half?"

"The second half is to solve the difficulty, so it does not happen again. For instance, if you were to recognize that the bricks you laid were imperfectly aligned, the observation would be useless until you fixed the damage and improved your skill."

Alenna looked for errors in her brickwork, but I reassured her that I was only making a comparison.

She suddenly looked up and toward the path that led to town. We had both detected a simple yet familiar set of thoughts approaching. *"You should change, Father."*

Alenna offered energy, and I mutated into her canine companion. Social interruptions were inconvenient. As a dog, I could not continue our labors. I looked forward to the day when Alenna's powers increased enough for me to assume human form.

A young man named Peterius wandered down the path to our home. He was physically older than Alenna, but intellectually, he was little more advanced than Alenna had been as a child. His guardians had poorly fulfilled his educational needs. He waved to Alenna as he sauntered over the small bridge leading to the smokehouse. Peterius had been visiting frequently of late. I resisted the urge to snarl.

"Alenna, I advise against mating with this individual."

"Father!"

Through Alenna, I had attempted to pass on a greater education to Peterius, but he was unwilling to accept that a female knew what he did not. He refused to expand his knowledge beyond what he had been taught as a child – a common malady.

"Hey, Alenna, how's it be?" He asked.

"Hey, Peterius. Things be good."

"Alenna, your conceptual vocabulary is in jeopardy."

She ignored my warning and punched her friend in his shoulder. He returned the flirtation. I growled deep within my chest.

"Pap just give me a teppence fer doin' so good with the crop. Wanna go'n get a sweet pie from the Pappits'?"

Alenna's financial security was such that she could consume pastries as often as she wished. But she nonetheless displayed excitement at Peterius's offer and left our work behind. I followed, frustrated. I did not object to social interactions as long as they enhanced Alenna's survival, or at the very least, did not work against it. Peterius benefited Alenna only on an emotional basis and had a derogatory effect on her intellect. But I had chosen to let

Alenna learn from mistakes she seemed determined to make. Thus, she allowed my presence so long as I did not actively interfere.

Once in town, the pair entered the baked-goods establishment of Joner and Lendell Pappit, two Eldorans who successfully thrived within the Oneian community. When I first met them, I asked if they wished to be guardians for Alenna. They politely declined, but insisted that Alenna could come to visit whenever she chose. It was Joner who had eventually created a supply system for our bricks and Lendell who sold our bread to the Oneian populace. They had included us in their illusion of social acceptance.

"Two sweet pies, Mr. Pappit!" Peterius proudly slapped his stamped copper coin onto the wooden counter.

"A bleemin' imperial teppance, lad. Did ye nab the priestess' satchel?"

Peterius, a devout supporter of the priestess, mistook Joner's friendly jibe. "That's blasphemy! Yer not ta joke about the priestess, or me pap'll turn ya in fer reward!" It was a common Oneian threat to compare one's adversaries to Eldorans, who were often captured for bounty. But to Joner, the threat was one of dire seriousness, as his family and home would be burned.

"You'll not threaten me, young snip! I were just foolin' ya, and now ye gone and bagged me muffins! Take yer fool teppence and git out'o me shop 'afore I use yer skinny hide fer a new rug!"

Peterius was primarily a vocal combatant and lacked the fortitude to complete the confrontations he created. He backed down from Joner's ire and tried to complete his pastry transaction. "I's just kiddn', Mr. Pappit. Kin I git two sweet pies, if it pleases ya?"

Having little choice, Joner accepted the apology. "Aye, y'are a wiley one lad. Here's yer pies, and ye make sure ta be good. Upset me neice an' y'll be a rug fer certain."

Alenna's assumed relation to the Pappits was a convenient ruse that gave our presence near the Oneian community added credence. As we exited, Joner tossed another sweet pie in my direction and winked. I caught the pastry and gobbled it with zest. They possessed an appealing flavor. I barked my thanks and remembered to wag my tail as I excitedly chased after Alenna and Peterius.

They wasted most of the day flirting, while the mortar for our bricks dried on its pallets. Peterius demonstrated to Alenna how he could cause me to perform tricks. With effort, I refrained from biting him.

Later that evening, while Alenna chiseled at hardened mortar, I lectured her on the consequences of shirking responsibility.

Alenna: [enters]

Static: *Greetings, Alenna. Did your bath offer the pleasure you anticipated?*

Alenna: *I was too distracted to be relaxed, Father.*

Prometheus: *This woman is Alenna? I thought you said she was a girl!*

Master: *She was. You just don't know how to tell time.*

Alenna: [smirks at Master] *As I recall, you didn't make the connection either, not right away.*

Master: [Smiles.] *True, but I had a better excuse. I was dead.*

Alenna: *What was it like?*

Master: *Being dead? I wouldn't know. I was dead at the time. Then again, there are times when only parts of me are dead.*

Martin Wolfe

Chapter Twelve

Young Master

I can honestly say that I'd never appreciated my body until I didn't have it anymore. I tried to condense my gaseous self while little spider-things scurried over my melted corpse and grew bigger. The helicopter searchlight flashed through the jagged window casings and cast violent shadows on the walls. Lingering eddies of tear gas wafted in the breeze. My apartment had never seen so much action, certainly not at four fifteen in the morning. Hey, my clock still worked.

Trying to hold my particles together made me glow blue. I looked like a ghost character from a B movie. Having never liked B-movies, I let myself expand a bit and disappeared.

The daddy-longlegs expanded to full monster size and then stopped moving altogether, as if they were waiting for something. I couldn't sense their thoughts. That was odd. Regular insects appeared on my mental radar as fuzzy little blips of basic intention. With heads the size of toaster ovens, the mutants should be easy enough to detect. I wondered again if this was my alien tormentor in disguise. Then I wondered if said alien could sense my thoughts, even though I couldn't sense his. Probably. Not fair.

My body was a pile of mush, and I couldn't imagine squeezing back into it. That left only one alternative. I needed to make a new body. If I could create hot chocolate, a body shouldn't be too difficult. Technically, this would be the second clone I'd made, but I forgot about the one I made last night. I worried about ending up with the mental capacity of whipped cream, but I figured it couldn't be much worse than permanent insanity, which would arrive soon if I didn't escape the ghostly ether. I felt as if I was swimming in an alphabet soup of uppers and downers.

I concentrated, and new body appeared propped up against a clean spot on the wall. The spider things tensed, their stick-legs interlocking above me, and waited to strike. They had to know I wasn't yet inside, or they would have killed me already – bloody smart bugs, not to mention vindictive. I wished that the alien mutants would turn into real daddy longlegs, so I could squish them.

They suddenly shimmered and sparked loudly. Arcs of blue lightning raced around the room and crackled about their legs and bodies. I experienced something weird – that is, even weirder than lightning, alien bugs, and a twice-cloned body in my living room. More noticeable than with Grandpa's watch, I sensed math equations running through my head, or my head's equivalent. I understood them. They were preset command codes that couldn't find the right sequence to do what I'd asked them to do. Trying to change the spider-freaks had created feedback.

Instead of second-guessing my reflexive understanding of the problem, I just started fixing it, rather like hacking a computer during a hurricane. Electrical fires lit up the couch as I wormed my way through the bugs' defenses. Then the monsters disappeared in a flash, and six tiny insects took their place. I swooped inside my new body and started swatting.

While I did this, something hard hit the floor and rattled toward me. At first I thought it was another canister of tear gas, but then I sensed the soldiers swarming down the hallway. Oh crap - the grenade detonated, blowing me and part of the wall into open air.

Like a living wave, I exploded across the neighborhood. By the time I stopped expanding, the thoughts and feelings of thousands reverberated within me. An entire neighborhood of random urges clogged up my emotional gears. Thankfully, most people were asleep, but there were a few hot spots of activity. I'd just left one of them. Two others were armed robberies, one at a convenience store and one at a warehouse. Some enterprising criminal-types were taking advantage of the reduction in law enforcement. I made another body at one of the crime scenes and stuffed myself inside. Third time's the charm.

The floor tiles where I came back to life were wet. The seat of my pants was soaked. Hey, I'd made clothes too! A gunshot sounded from the next room, and I felt a muted impression of pain that wasn't mine. It belonged to the owner of the store being robbed. No fair, I'd been tricked into being a do-gooder by my own rebellious brain. Actually, I'd decided to fight crime all on my own, but I didn't want to admit that I cared, at least a little bit, about other people. Don't let that get around.

I climbed to my feet and attended to drying my pants. Rule number one of the Hero Handbook: Never engage in crime-fighting whilst liquid is dripping from posterior. With that problem addressed, I dove into a volatile situation where I didn't belong, likely to make a total mess of things, thereupon being resented, condemned, and potentially sued – standard hero business.

My rescue operation would have gone a lot smoother if the restroom door hadn't been locked. The knob had one of those little twisting button things. Fumbling noisily with said mechanism didn't make for a smooth entrance. The cursing probably didn't help either. A noisy hole suddenly appeared in the door. Shotgun.

Aw, screw it – I grabbed the handle and yanked hard, intending to rip the door off, but the knob came away in my hand. Not much to say about that. Another blast tore a hole where the doorknob used to be and ricocheted a couple of pellets into my forearm. Ouch, frig it all!

177

I stepped back and threw the knob as hard as I could, thereby making a new hole in the door but missing the bad guy anyway. Next, I grabbed the urinal and tore it off the wall – saw it in a movie. Angry jets of water burst from the mangled pipe and sprayed everywhere – so much for drying my pants. Using the urinal as a shield, I bulldozed the door out of my way.

For the record, a urinal will not stop a shotgun blast at point blank range. Lead pellets and chunks of porcelain slammed into me. I thought shotguns had only two shells – go figure. I threw the remains of my shield at my attacker. It made a nice, hollow clunking sound and sent his form flying to clean off the Twinkie aisle. Just then, villain number two opened fire. Shotguns, I can't say I like them, especially when I'm on the wrong end. I took a solid hit in the ribcage and went down for the count.

Villain number two left me thrashing on the floor and collected the robbery proceeds from the scattered pastries – honor among thieves and all that. I repaired the painful hole in my torso and scrambled down the canned goods aisle. He saw me go and blew away some perfectly good cans of chicken soup, as well as the storefront window. I stood up long enough to whip a tin of brown beans at his head. Missed. The can entered a wall and disappeared. In response to my legume attack, he shot a glass dairy case and a wall of helpless milk.

"You just shot your girlfriend!" That rattled him. The pellets that hadn't been slowed by the chicken broth or the windowpane had struck the getaway car outside. His girlfriend had only a single pellet in her hand, but he didn't know that. For his inattention, he took a can of ravioli in the ear and dropped like a stone.

I strolled through the mess and checked on the storeowner, who was nearly dead but still praying, which convinced me not to graft his life's memories onto my own. What to do? Could I heal someone else? I shrugged. The guy was a goner if I didn't try something. The best surgeon in the world wouldn't be able to close a hole that big.

I imagined him whole again. It worked, albeit slowly and with a lot of screaming. One would think he'd been shot or something. When he opened his eyes, he looked at his healed chest and wondered whether he'd been divinely rescued. I got up and headed for the door before he went and said something irritating.

The getaway driver was bleeding patiently, while waiting for her boyfriend to arrive. She was in denial that he and his buddy weren't coming anytime soon. Stepping into the shadows beside the store, I left her to receive whatever punishment she wanted.

I knew from my recent gaseous expansion that ten blocks away a warehouse robbery was in progress, if it wasn't already over. Somebody's nagging sense of civic responsibility wanted me to deal with that problem too. Okay, but this was the last one. No more hero stuff for this kid.

How to get there? I didn't want to expand outside my body again – too frightening. Maybe I could just imagine myself in the right place. I remembered the layout of the warehouse, but the thieves obviously would have moved by now. What would happen if I arrived in a space that was already occupied? Hmm, could get messy. But I really didn't want to be gaseous again.

I wished and thus arrived in warehouse shadows – no more cabs for me. The crooks had filled a semi-trailer with electronics and were about ready to leave. I paused to consider what to do with the bad guys.

According to my social training three times over, theft wasn't a very good reason to kill someone. Then again, as a human, wasn't I a born predator? I killed living things, be they bacteria, bacon, or broccoli, so that I could eat. Why did people have a right to live when broccoli didn't?

Somewhere between the evolutionary stages of protoplasmic sludge and multi-celled life forms, I'd had a common ancestor with broccoli, which had never tried to steal my stuff. Nor had it ever stacked me onto a baked potato with sour cream and bacon. So what was the difference? Why was I hungry all of a sudden?

I shrugged and decided to round them up for someone else to handle. I smiled at the thought of beating some civil obedience into them. But then my nagging brain suggested that I could just imagine them all disarmed and hogtied. Bloody conscience, it didn't want me to have any fun. Fine then, how about if I healed them afterward? My conscience still had a problem with it, but not as much. Besides, if they got caught by the police, they might be shot, or even fed to a patch of carnivorous broccoli. How's that for rationalizing?

I imagined that they were out of ammo – too bad I hadn't thought of that at the convenience store. The driver was surprised when I pulled him from his seat and tossed him into the warehouse. The two guys loading the truck box saw him roll past and chose to investigate. I tossed them in too. Then I hopped in after them and sealed the bay door behind me.

The assorted thugs gathered and launched an attack. It was short-lived and was followed closely by some begging and pleading, which I probably enjoyed more than was healthy. In the end, fourteen neighborhood tyrants sat handcuffed and cowering in a locked trailer box. I reinforced the warehouse doors, walls and windows, and clearly labeled all the evidence for the police to find. Then I headed into the office section where I hoped to find a telephone.

That's about when the meteorite struck.

Master: *Okay, done. Who's next?*

Oneia

Static: *Alenna, please relate your final experience with Peterius. Your personal story is required for plot continuity.*

Alenna: *Wouldn't it be better for you to tell it, Father?*

Prometheus: *That's right, she can't do it! We've started already! Besides, it's my turn!*

Static: *Prometheus, your daily activities can be summarized, as they are not vital for cohesion. Perhaps, when we are finished, you could create a memoir.*

Prometheus: *Maybe I will, virus! You can be certain it will include the pitiful lack of respect I receive on a daily basis!*

Alenna: *Father, may I relate my story in the third person? I don't feel like myself just now.*

Static: *Certainly, Alenna. I am certain that your performance will be exemplary from whichever perspective you chose.*

Alenna: *Thank you, Father.*

Alenna

She savored the tug of grass between her toes and the tickle of multicolored leaves against her skin. Summer had died, but the sad smells of autumn kept her company as she strolled toward home. Winter would arrive soon, and that would mean more lessons, endless lectures about things she barely understood and had never experienced. Trapped safely indoors for months on end, her mind would expand as much as her heart would wither.

Her father was brilliant, as everyone knew. He had shared with her his knowledge, but in doing so he had

181

marooned her from the world, though it was not entirely his fault. She had asked for his help, and she loved him for giving it, as he loved her in return. But that didn't fill the sad spot in her heart, the spot that yearned for someone to hold and to love in a different way, someone like Peterius.

A man she should never have, Peterius made her feel beautiful and alive in ways intellect never could. She longed for him. It wasn't a thing based on reason, that great and overpowering cause that her father followed, like Oneians worshipped their Priestess. Love was the name for her troubles, romantic love. Her father didn't understand how much she needed it in her life. To him, emotions were enjoyed only after the thinking was done, a task that never seemed complete. He didn't understand that sometimes a woman needed to feel the wind in her hair and to feel the gentle touch of strong hands that hinted of desire. Sometimes, a woman needed to feel like a woman.

Two days ago, she and Peterius had nearly fulfilled their mutual longing, but her father had arrived unbidden and nipped her would-be lover on the calf. She was furious. Her father had long ago achieved human form and no longer needed to follow as a dog. In answer to her fury, he offered a simple apology and a lecture on the dangers of unprotected intercourse.

She hadn't spoken to him since, and for the first time that she could remember he had stopped giving lessons. It was a test of responsibility he had said, and suggested that she was mature enough to make her own decisions. After so many years, she was unnerved not to sense his constant presence in her mind. He would offer instruction upon request, he assured her, but the silence in her mind was no less frightening, or lonely. She almost longed for winter's lessons.

Freshly fallen leaves danced as she stepped onto the brick-laid path of the estate her father had built to keep her safe. The setting sun angled crisply through the colonnade of oaks and elms and ignited the brilliant fall colors. She ambled onward from one sunlit patch to another and kept the offered warmth on her shoulders. Fall was her favorite season. It shared her sense of melancholy and sought to keep her company. She smiled sadly, fleetingly, and silently thanked Oneia for the gift of autumn.

What to do? She had been handed the reins of her life. Would she gallop onward to happiness and success, or would she blindly careen from the precipice of her own foolish behavior?

Peterius was handsome, and he made her feel womanly. But he was also as intellectually stimulating as a brick. If she were to become pregnant by him, her life-choices were limited. She could become his subservient bride, doomed to be discovered as an Eldoran and executed with her child, or she could flee with her father and could abandon all of their wondrous creations.

If only Peterius were willing to compromise. Her father had developed protections against pregnancy, but Peterius refused them. He claimed her father's magic was an evil blight against the priestess. That sentiment was growing among Oneians, even though the jobs at her father's foundries helped to keep them fed. The deprivations wrought by imperial taxers and marauding saugael mor had deprived the townsfolk of essential items, and they wanted someone to blame for their suffering. The educated woman and her wealthy father were envied and thus were singled out as targets.

Most people scorned her openly now. Her trips to town were met with angry jeers and uncomfortable silence. The rejection by Joner and Lendell Pappit had hurt the most. They had bowed to public pressure and asked her not to visit. Only Peterius still spoke to her, and he had an ulterior motive – to marry the rich girl. Dangerous though it was, a union with Peterius's popular family would go a long way toward easing Oneian distrust. Could it be so bad to live as his wife?

Yes. Like Peterius himself, the answer was simple. A life of subservience to Peterius would be unbearable, for she would never again be free to think or to act on her own, nor could the bliss of ignorance save her from grief – she knew too much. Knowledge and wisdom, her father said, stagnate when a sentient mind stops questioning what it knows. And the truth of his words was shown in Peterius, who had stopped learning as a child and would never see her worth as a person. In Oneian culture, women were property best kept silent.

The real question was whether she would submit to him anyway, just so she could keep the briefest touch of passion in her life and, for a time, ease the hatred against her. The answer was obvious even to the leaves she trod upon, yet she continued to weigh the value of one fate to the other until she reached the familiar iron gates of the estate wall.

As she waited for the sentries to let her in, she stared though the bars and admired the house and gardens, which waited to comfort her. Peaceful and serene, they seemed more solid than the world itself and had become her entire universe. To her, the estate and her father were all that stood for reason and happiness. She looked at the wishing well that her father had made to amuse her and smiled at the memory. Wishes, he told her, are merely goals lacking the efforts required to achieve them. He said that, and then he made a wishing well because it would make his adopted daughter happy. A wishing well, a vanity bureau, a hope chest, beaded gowns with nowhere to wear them, fragile glass dishes, and a beautiful bathtub with heated tiles just to name a few, he had helped her to make them all.

Her smile faded quickly. The sentries weren't letting her in.

With as much menace as she muster, she snapped at them to open the gate. Still, she waited a full minute before the iron bars swung inward. She stormed through but didn't bother confronting the men at their booths. They wouldn't listen to her anyway. One hundred thirty-two factory workers and fourteen sentries, and not one of them would speak to her without disdain in his voice. They had been amused by a girl who made cute requests but were insulted by a grown woman who gave orders.

She marched toward the manor house and scowled at the darkened foundries across the pond and at the shutters covering the clear glass windows of her home. The rocks that had forced the shutters to be closed could have reached the house only from inside the estate walls, but the sentries always denied seeing the workers who threw them. One man had even suggested that it was the great god's wrath against her father for hoarding wealth. She had fired the sentry on the spot, but he had refused to leave until her father dismissed him. She almost used her power to send him flying over the wall, but she reigned in her fury, lest she be discovered and executed.

She slammed the doors of her home as she entered and was overcome by chagrin. Slamming doors was something Peterius would do. Her father, who strongly disapproved of Peterius in all things, would be disappointed. There was only one candidate she would ever have her father's approval to love – the Companion, the only thing her father loved as much as he loved her. Maybe that was why she wanted Peterius so much, so her father might feel as she did – jealous.

She hated the companion for having her father's love, the only solace that kept her shriveling from loneliness. My companion and my friend – that was all he ever called it. The thing was still housed under the floorboards of the old kitchen, the room where her father did most of his work as he silently guarded. He was never gone from the thing for long, and she could sense his concern when necessity forced

185

him away. Sometimes, she felt that her father loved his friend more than he loved her. Yes, the companion would be approved as a husband – if only he weren't a corpse.

Her father greeted her kindly as she entered. Then he resumed writing in his papers. He was a spectacled old man, squinting from the sharp light of his first working electric bulb. He was an old man, or he was anything he wanted to be. It was confusing sometimes.

Walking past the table, she glanced at the title of his current work, *The Diamond Constellation as Viewed from Oneia's Northern Hemisphere*. Her father never stopped thinking and never stopped working, unless he was catering to someone else's need. His expectations were overwhelming, and she often despaired that she would ever live up to them.

She kicked the rug away from the trap door, flung open the heavy lid, and revealed the companion's corpse in all its glory. The exterior was fully formed now, although her father insisted that the organs were still developing. That, he said, was why it remained dormant. According to her father, the thing had chosen to remain nameless and would respond to nearly any title offered, so long it wasn't deified. This bothered her intensely. How could a person not have a name? She imagined always being addressed as the wicked rich woman, and it didn't appeal to her.

Ever since it had grown handsome, she had lived a sometimes love, sometimes hate relationship with a dead body. Even in her own mind, it was foolish to have any sort of feelings for a corpse, particularly one that she had never known in life. It was like her infatuation with Peterius. She hated him; she loved him. Peterius had a living mind that hardly worked at all, while the companion had a dead mind, which, by her father's estimation, worked remarkably well. They were both beautiful men, although Peterius was smaller and not as perfectly formed.

The body was warm to the touch, heated by the mysterious power of the ring. She ran her fingers over its perfect chest, feeling slightly foolish as usual, and went through her standard memory scale of anatomy. Her father had once commented on her preference to sit and stare at his companion. He suggested that it was an unproductive use of time. Not wanting to leave, she began labeling all of its various anatomies in medical terminology. Her father approved of useful pastimes and didn't seem aware that his daughter was infatuated with a dead man's nude body.

If only it would come to life and take her away to its castle in the stars, her young fantasy would finally come true. She hated the thing for making her wait and loved it for giving her hope. She hated it for having her father's love and loved it for being perfect. Most of all, she hated it because she had waited her entire life to love a man who didn't even know she was alive. She loved a man who was called a god, a man who had her father's respect – a man who was dead. It was all a fantasy in her own mind, and she hated it for that too.

There was a knock at the kitchen door – Peterius. He was the only person who knew to look for them in the old kitchen. Her father considered it nostalgic, and preferred to do his work there, in the first room they had made. To her, the old kitchen was her true home, as it had always been. The other buildings were just a beautiful extension of what was already perfect. She carefully closed the heavy lid to the coffin and replaced the rug. Then she rose to open the door.

Peterius was just turning away to search for her somewhere else. He turned back, smiled, and presented to her a haphazard bouquet of flowers yanked from her garden. He would deny it if she bothered to ask. He always denied it, even the first time when he hadn't even bothered to remove the roots from the stems. She had shown him the holes in the soil and explained that her hybrid orchid grew nowhere else, yet he still denied it. Do not pull flowers from my garden, she had scolded, but here he was again offering her a fistful of poached flowers, this time with the roots removed. He stood at the entrance to her home and grinned like a little boy with a secret to hide.

That was Peterius, a little boy in the body of a handsome man, who believed he would soon own her estate by default. She had no other suitors. Her false courtship with Peterius was the only reason that the workers hadn't rioted already. He was rumored to be the local boy who would triumph over the wealthy tyrants and would bring prosperity to the workers and their families. Peterius knew that and played the part.

Her choices were few. If the companion revived before she died an old woman, her life might be extended far beyond her natural years, but if the villagers attacked, she could die tomorrow and could lose everything. How was she to judge the relative loss of years when she couldn't begin to guess how long she might live? She shrugged and brushed the pointless question aside. Whether she lived to a thousand, or died tomorrow, Peterius would be leaving tonight.

When she didn't invite him in, he knew that something was wrong. Panic flickered in his eyes as he saw his plans begin to crumble. Trying to forestall the coming rejection, he blurted out an invitation to a hunt. Oneian women were not permitted to hunt. It was a great concession that Peterius had just made to keep her good favor. Or it would have been great had he not proposed to hunt Eldorans. The offer blasted away her breath as though he had struck her in the chest.

If in that instant her father hadn't interjected, Peterius would have sailed flaming over the manor wall. The big dog that suddenly appeared behind her growled deeply and bared its fangs. She didn't care that Peterius had likely witnessed her father's transformation or that the false suitor promised retribution as he left. All that mattered was that he left.

The companion must wake soon, she told her father, who pressed his furry body against her leg. They would be coming for her soon, and all would be lost. The companion was the only one who could save their home now. Her father did not disagree, and that frightened her more than anything.

Master: *Hmm, that clears up a few things.*

Prometheus: *Really? I found it all rather confusing myself.*

Static: *Prometheus, it is now time for you to relate your own experiences with Peterius.*

Prometheus: *What's so important about this Peterius fellow anyway? I found him to be dreadfully tedious! You were right, though, young woman, he was quite lovely!*

Alenna: *My name is Alenna, Prometheus, and you're welcome to Peterius if you want him.*

Prometheus: *Oh, really? Why, thank you! That's very kind! You know, I've been to hundreds of places that sound just like your home! In fact, there's a lovely little town called Landport that has the most wonderful three-star sunset you'll ever see! I'll take you there when we're done!*

Master: *I wouldn't advise it, Prometheus. The thieves in Landport will steal your shoes while you're still in them.*

Prometheus: *Nonsense! I'm an important person! Don't you worry, young woman, I'll show you that sunset, just like I said. We'll be perfectly safe, I tell you!*

Master: *That would be nice, Prometheus. For now, though, I'm very interested in hearing how you came to meet Peterius.*

Prometheus: *Yes, yes, of course.*

Chapter Thirteen

Prometheus

"You know, Tiberius, ever since the priestess started killing her descendants in bulk, the temple has been a much nicer place to live. She's been so pleased with herself that she hasn't tortured me in months."

Tiberius pretended to ignore me. He scribbled his name on a jumble of unrolled parchment littering his dreadfully plain wooden desk. There were so many of the things that I didn't have room to put down my wine glass. I shoved one of his piles aside and freed up a corner. He scowled at me irritably, how rude! Just because he couldn't sign his name legibly, was no reason to get snooty!

"Really, Tiberius, you should think about cleaning this place! There are more stacks of paper in here than there are assassins in the cornfields!" Oh, how witty of me! Wasn't that a lovely saying? Assassins in the cornfields, yes it's quite catchy. The peasants would love it, I was certain.

"Good Prophet, do you not have something better to do?"

"Actually, there's very little I need to do. My underlings deal with the petty ministrations, so I can bathe at my leisure."

"I am gratified that you enjoy the Empire's benefits, good Prophet. Perhaps you could leave me in peace, so I may ensure that your leisure endures."

"Are you threatening me, young man?"

"It is not a threat, good Prophet, but a consequence. Your wine and bath oils will cease to flow if I fail to complete my work."

"Now see here! Threatening me is one thing, but threatening my bath oils is going too far, I tell you!" I rose in divine wrath. By the soapy suds of lathered loofahs, I wouldn't stand for an assault on my bath beads!

Master: *What's a loofah?*

Prometheus: *A loofah? Oh…well, it's a fruit actually, but the dried innards make the most invigorating sponges for bath…. Wait just a…you know that already! Stop pestering me, you little cretin! I have a story to tell!*

Now where was I? Oh yes, my other avatar was being insufferably obnoxious too, may they both have to live with themselves!

"Good Prophet, you misunderstand me." Tiberius picked up the parchment he'd smudged and showed it to me.

"This treaty, as well as others you see before you, conditionally surrenders the Empire to Ottar, Chief of the Three Sky Hunters.

"We've surrendered? I thought you said we were winning against the barbarians!" I was certainly no expert on empire building, but it seemed to me that Tiberius's surrendering tactic wasn't going to work.

"That was indeed the case, good Prophet, before our priestess released her pets upon the continent. In exchange for our surrender, Ottar is, as we speak, using an artifact he acquired to contain the assassin plague. He will leave intact the priestess's religion and its accoutrements, including the trade routes that supply your conveniences. I have convinced him that it was she who sent him the artifact as a gift for her newly chosen people."

"But barbarians, Tiberius, they're nearly as bad as the vermin!"

"Be at ease, good Prophet. The nomads are superstitious folk and fear the priestess's wrath should they renege on these agreements. They will not willingly enter the temple or harm its environs, lest the priestess set her demons against them. You and your luxuries will be safe."

"Well, that's fine then. Carry on." I relaxed and went back to sipping my wine. Tiberius sighed, shook his head, and returned to his paperwork. A few moments passed before something curious came to mind.

"You know, I'm quite surprised that the priestess accepted our surrender so easily. It isn't at all like her to give in to even the smallest of things, no matter how much sense they make."

Tiberius positively glowered at me for interrupting him again. "The Priestess does not officially know of our surrender, good Prophet. Perhaps you would like to tell her."

Not in this lifetime, I tell you! "What in the name of holy executions are you thinking? She's going to have us chopped to bits and fed to the dogs!" I was doomed! At the very least she would torture me every day for eternity! Cerberus's prison might have been more comfortable in comparison!

"It should not be as bad as that, good Prophet. Unlike her Oneian subjects, the nomadic tribesmen will revere the priestess for her ruthlessness. She and the Three Sky Hunters are meant for each other. I intend to convince her of this by the time Ottar and his tribes are firmly established on empire soil."

Tiberius's plots were all so confusing. "This just doesn't seem like you, Tiberius. Isn't your pride bothered by the fact that you've been conquered by a herd of smelly primates?"

"Please remember, good Prophet, that I was once one of those 'smelly primates'. My pride is bothered little. I

193

built this empire solely for convenience. It is now more convenient to have the aid of Ottar and his clansmen, who will raid Oneian villages as they spread across the land and subsequently will flush out hidden Eldorans who are not under my protection. I will thus strive to convince the Priestess that she has eradicated her descendants, before she actually succeeds in killing those I find useful."

"Nonetheless, good Prophet, this does not require that, for hours at a time, you sit in my private office and interrupt my progress. Please find something else to amuse yourself. I will send for you when your priests are needed to verify a sighting."

"Well, there's no need to get testy!" I stood and noisily stacked my crystal glasses around the empty bottles in the wine bucket.

Just then, a tiny bell rang, which meant that Tiberius would need to see someone in his regular office. He left his papers where they were, squeezed from behind his desk, and stepped out of his secret room. I followed, trying valiantly to balance an overflowing bucket of tongs, bottles, and glasses. It was surprisingly difficult. That, of course, was the major drawback to sitting in Tiberius's secret room; none of my servants were allowed to know about it.

Through a dazzling feat of dexterity, I made it into the main office before I dropped everything in a spectacularly noisy crash. With only a cursory glance of disapproval, Tiberius closed the stone door of his hideaway and called for his lieutenant to enter. I shrugged at the mess – the servants could manage from here – and moved to leave.

The officer gave his report. "High Commander, a peasant begs an audience. He claims an Eldoran sighting."

"Good Prophet," Tiberius said, "Stay a moment if you will. You will need to assign someone to verify this."

Of all the…. "You just told me to leave!"

"It will take only a few moments, good Prophet."

I floppy into a stiff-backed wooden chair and crossed my arms. There wasn't a decent cushioned sofa in sight - the things I did for that man!

Two soldiers entered escorting a handsome young peasant dressed in filthy rags. They sat him in one of the uncomfortable chairs and left.

Tiberius braced his elbows on his desk and leaned forward. "Your name?" The simple dolt gaped as if he'd just swallowed his tongue. Tiberius often has that effect on people.

I was in no mood for this. "We're waiting to hear your story, you stunted bumpkin! Get on with it, will you!"

He started babbling. "Beggin' fergiveness, yer Holiness, High Commander Ser, me name's Peterius, an' I's come fer th' Eldor'n rewards. Me pap an' mar was burnt dead by them thar barbies, an' I's been hidin' ever since. So I's got to thinkin', those Eldor'n rewards could keep me in good eatin' fer a while. An' me girl's got it comin' anyhows, fer bein' blasphemous 'gainst the Priestess, an' fer treatn' me bad."

"Peterius, you have information about an Eldoran?"

The young man nodded. "Me girl's pap. 'Cept he weren't no Eldor'n like I's ever heard. Goes all blue and lightin' bolts and turns hi'self into th' biggest wolf ye ever seen. Me girl must'a been Eldor'n too, since he's bein' her pap 'n all. Does that mean I get twice th' rewards?"

"You will be rewarded when your report has been verified. Please wait in my antechamber. A priest will be with you shortly."

After the young man groveled his way out, Tiberius turned to me. "Good Prophet, please have your priests verify the boy's story. Remind them not to harm anyone before they report back to me."

"Why? That prattle was obvious nonsense! You know very well that Eldorans can't shape-shift!"

"That is true, good Prophet, but the virus can. The boy's description sounded very much like what I witnessed in Honn."

"So did three peasant stories last week! They're obviously telling you what you want to hear. And now you're sending my priests off to chase shadows. They're busy men, Tiberius!"

"If such is the case, good Prophet, then you can attend to the matter personally. Your schedule appears to be empty, and we cannot afford to overlook any leads, lest the wrong Eldorans be killed."

Oh dear. "I just remembered several things I need to get done right away. My priests will just have to find the time. Good day, Tiberius." I hurried out. Tiberius's fascination with that virus was terribly frustrating. I'd assured him that my revised joining ceremony would work much better than last time, but the man was just too stubborn to cooperate.

I passed the bench where Peterius was seated, and, for an instant, considered a pleasurable liaison – he was truly a lovely young man. But I decided against it. Tiberius would get in a snit. I tapped my rod and called for three of my priests to meet me at my chambers. They were waiting outside when I arrived, but the doors were flung wide open, and two of the insect-vermin stood motionless in the hallway.

"Gunderson, why are my chamber doors open? You know very well not to enter uninvited! And what are these repulsive creatures doing here? They're supposed to be confined to the Priestess's chambers and to the throne room!" The woman had kept the beasties closer to her ever since she realized her range of control was limited. Fortunately, most of the escaped vermin fled the city, lest they fall under her control again.

"The doors were open when we arrived, Holiness. We were ordered to remain here while the priestess inspects your sanctum." How dare she? By the purple legs of black assassins, I wasn't going to stand for it!

Master: *Purple legs?*

Prometheus: *She had them painted. Stop interrupting me.*

I stormed into my sitting room and found more saugael mor milling about, these ones undecorated. Temple guards stood sheepishly in front of my bathing chamber. I stormed past them and caught the Priestess in the midst of a heinous act! Sabotage!

Hairpin in hand, she was poking holes in my bath beads and was squeezing out the oil! Dozens of bead corpses bled the last of their precious life onto the tiles. All of my pretty soaps were dissolving in an overflowing basin of sludge. My bath salts had been dumped into the mix, vials and all, and then rubbed in circles over the walls. My favorite hairbrush stuck forlornly from a potted plant, and all of my lovely candles had been broken and tossed into the hearth. I was mortified beyond words, I tell you!

With a dying bead impaled upon her lethal shaft, she knew she'd been caught. "Oh, Tibbald, I'm so sorry! I have no idea what came over me! Everyone was hiding things from me, and I just needed to find out, but then I couldn't find anything, and I was so angry! I just wanted to… to… I don't know what I wanted to do! Oh, Tibbald, I'm so sorry for ruining your soaps! I didn't mean…."

"Stop calling me that! Stop calling me Tibbald! My name is Prometheus, you insolent child! I created you, and this is how you repay me! You want to know things? Fine! I'll tell you things! You are insignificant! You are nothing but a power source to my prison! You have no purpose in this world, other than to keep me trapped in a cage that I created! I would like nothing better than for you to cease to exist at this very moment! If I had my power back, that's exactly what would happen, I tell you!"

She rocked back, stunned to disbelief.

"Oh, dear Tibbald, I'm so sorry! I've gone and turned you mad as a jester! I forgot all about your condition! Don't you worry, I'll start your treatments again, and soon you'll be as good as new!"

May she be skinned alive and dipped in bath salt, the lunatic woman thought I was the crazy one! Furious to the point of impotence, I turned and stormed out. Gunderson and those other two idiots had followed me. I nearly ran into them.

"What are you imbeciles doing? I didn't give you permission to come in!" Simpletons surrounded me at every turn, I tell you!

"Our apologies, Holiness, we wished to hear your instructions regarding the two Eldorans."

The priestess heard and came to meddle. "Eldorans? Tibbald, why is a mere prophet being informed of Eldorans before the divine priestess? This is what you and Tiberius have been keeping from me, isn't it? You're harboring Eldorans! Well, I'll have no more of it! Father Gunderson, from now on you and your fellow priests are to enact retribution immediately upon discovery! Inform me, and only me, through your rod of office when the task is complete! Is that understood?"

"Yes, Divine Priestess." My underlings prostrated themselves on my beautiful, embroidered rug.

Tiberius would be incensed that his plans had been waylaid. As to myself, I couldn't get any angrier. "Get out of my chambers, you lunatic woman, before you destroy everything! I hope the barbarians use you as a plaything!" Her mood switched faster than my avatars change names. Oh dear! She sent lighting to dance in snapping circles around me. My robes started to smoke.

"Father Gunderson," she yelled over the crackle, "The Prophet Tibbald is suffering a relapse. I will attend to his treatment, while you enact retribution on the Eldorans."

"His Holiness has not yet told us where to find them, Priestess," Gunderson yelled back.

Oh, blast them to the nether regions, the unfaithful cowards! She added fresh pain on top of the old and called her pets to join the effort! I was certain that Tiberius wouldn't mind terribly if I confessed about the boy. I've never been very good at suffering torture. I told her what she wanted to know, but the horrid woman kept torturing me anyway, may she find assassins in her slippers! I suffered for nearly an hour before I convinced her that my illness was cured. Oh, what a dreadful experience!

Prometheus: *I feel faint from the memory, I tell you! I just can't go on any longer!*

Master: *Okay, I will.*

Prometheus: *Wait, you can't go yet! You didn't show up until after the battle! Antorn's sacrifice must be remembered!*

Master: *Who's Antorn?*

Static: *He was a priest I regrettably injured during the conflict, my friend.*

Prometheus: *Injured? You nearly ripped him in half!*

Master: *Antorn got torn?*

Prometheus: *Oh, shut up and listen, you imbecile!*

"Good Prophet, you look unwell." The single candle on Tiberius' plain wooden desk flickered as I shoved my way past the stone door of his secret room.

"Tiberius, I insist that you help me with my new joining ceremony! I really insist!" He looked amused over my charred robes, if you can imagine!

"Has the divine priestess been treating your illness again, good Prophet? What have you done to incite her ire this time?"

Me? This was his fault entirely! "Look here, you young snippet, it was your marauding barbarians that encouraged her to invade my sanctuary in the first place! She's paranoid enough without you trying to keep those smelly brutes a secret!"

"The nomads' invasion is not a secret, good Prophet. Our divine priestess merely denies their presence. She has avoided me of late, lest I report their presence. As I am not yet ready to report our surrender, I find her avoidance convenient. Your ceremonies are not."

"But you have to help me escape this place! That woman plans to arc lightning up and down my spine every other hour!"

"Your last ceremony unleashed a plague of assassins, good Prophet. I will not risk another. Gaining the assistance of the virus will undoubtedly prove more productive."

"Blast you, Tiberius, it's going to work!"

"The risk is too great, good Prophet."

"Stop calling me good prophet, will you! I've already confessed my true identity to the Priestess! She didn't believe me anyway!"

He shrugged and kept scribbling on his papers.

"Your plans with that virus are ruined, you know!" That got his attention.

He looked up and glared at me. "Your usefulness, good Prophet, may have just come to an end. Tell me clearly – what have you done?" He was so intimidating!

"Nothing, I swear! The Priestess just ordered Gunderson to kill Eldorans on sight and to tell the other priests to do the same." Tiberius wouldn't be able to rescue the girl before the Priestess had her murdered.

His brow loomed like thunder. "Where is Gunderson now, and which of your priests has he told?"

"He left with Antorn and Borrund to check on that farm lad's story. As far as I know, they haven't told anyone else."

"Find them, and bring them here." He gestured toward my rod of office. "Kill them."

That was a bit extreme. Tiberius's scowl promised that it was either my priests or me. I gathered my rod of office in hand. But before I could summon any of them, a light flashed before us as Antorn shifted in on his own. I jumped back as he slumped to the stone tiles. The poor man's innards were exposed! They made a terrible mess of the stonework!

Tiberius seemed to know that I hadn't done anything. "Heal him." He said.

"What? You just told me to kill him!" He glared at me again. Oh fine then, I healed Antorn.

"What happened?" Tiberius asked my subordinate.

The idiot just shivered on the floor and panted. His face had turned as white as the Priestess's table linen.

"Antorn, you silly fool, get up and answer the High Commander's question!"

He wet himself, right there in Tiberius's office. I was so embarrassed!

"You will need to probe his memories, good Prophet. We need to know what he saw and whom he told."

Antorn turned a shade whiter. He looked at me pleadingly. I shrugged. Better him than me, I tell you! I absorbed his thoughts. He slipped into a short seizure before he passed out.

Now, since I've shared Antorn's memories, I will be Antorn. Yes, yes, I am Antorn. Isn't this exciting? My very attractive and powerful high commander wants me to tell him what happened, and that's exactly what I'll do.

By command of the divinely irritating priestess – may she suffer the misery she causes – we probed the simple mind of a lovely peasant lad. The location he remembered of the Eldoran sighting was remote and dangerous, so Borrund suggested that we gather a standard temple escort before we departed. Gunderson insisted that we should double the escort. I suggested we triple it. No one disagreed. Barbarians were invading the empire, after all!

To Field Marshall Cornbom, the acting leader of the temple guards, we gave fair warning: He and his sixty men would face a hard march back through barbarian-infested territory if our holy selves encountered any discomforts along the way. He blinked at us and said to hurry up. We graciously ignored his rudeness and began shifting three of our escort at a time to the site. Then we shifted ourselves. We were shocked when we arrived in the midst of a battle!

The barbarians we appeared amongst enjoyed the unexpected exercise that our soft escort offered. It was well known in the empire that temple guards were laughing fodder for high commander Tiberius's veteran soldiers, who refused to be escorts for the priesthood. That the high commander allowed his men to get away with this was obviously a travesty of justice.

As it turned out, our only real soldier was field marshall Cornbom. He had a terrible time maintaining order among his troops, whom he presently commanded as punishment for something or other. The barbarian hoard, we were surprised to learn, consisted of only nine bearish louts.

They were inevitably defeated, but only after they'd massacred half of our escort. Well, it was nighttime, after all, and the filthy beasts were difficult to see!

All present were shaken by the experience, all except field marshall Cornbom, who was thoroughly disgusted. He went on at length about his 'pathetic detail of old grandmothers' and bellowed personal insults like 'babysitting spoiled priests'. He chastised Borrund, Gunderson, and me for hiding under a wagon instead of helping. Gunderson was righteously indignant – our escort was supposed to protect us, not the other way around!

When the argument ended, Borrund, who had done the mind probe of the boy, led us to the secret Eldoran enclave, which wasn't secret at all. Nor was it in the village - the peasant couldn't think of a destination without starting from his home, the simple dolt! After a long walk, we arrived at an iron gate leading to a sprawling estate and factory, which would have been lovely if not for the rampant vandalism.

Field marshall Cornbom insisted that he recognized the place as the empire's top producer of brick and steel. He demanded that we leave its occupants alone by order of the high commander and warned of economic turmoil should we choose not to heed him. Gunderson refused - Eldorans needed retribution! Field marshall Cornbom said that he 'didn't care if tree fairies ran the foundry as long as they keep supplying steel for the empire!'

Gunderson commanded the temple guards to burn the blasphemous field marshall in a retribution pyre. The guards, who had never liked the field marshall's patronizing manner, were more than happy to comply.

Cornbom's dreadful insults against the priesthood, and even our beloved holy prophet, continued unchecked while the temple guards forcibly tied him to the gates with the leather laces from his own boots. Well, his incessant blasphemies certainly changed my mind about burning him, I tell you! It served him right for insulting our great and benevolent leader like that! The piddling prophet, he said, of all the nerve! Burning was too good for him!

Many of the trees along the brick pathway had already been cut down and scattered about the area. It took no time at all to find enough wood to build a sizeable pyre. Field marshall Cornbom cursed us all for being ignorant fools and said that we were too stupid even to cross through the gates before building a pyre in front of it. We realized that he had a point. The wood had to be removed and the bindings cut from the field marshall, before the gates could be opened. Everyone sheepishly shuffled through to the other side.

While this was happening, field marshall Cornbom somehow managed to take a sword from one of the temple guards. He staged a counter attack. Once again, chaos ensued as everyone tried to subdue him. We had to set him on fire with our rods of office several times during the short battle, thereby wasting the opportunity for a proper retribution pyre. It was necessary, as the man refused to stay down. We discovered belatedly that my fellow priests and I had accidentally burned several guards to death in our excitement. It was somewhat disturbing to realize that none of the bodies belonged to field marshall Cornbom, who had frustratingly escaped in the confusion. The remaining guards couldn't decide amongst themselves who was next in line for command, and Gunderson had to take charge.

With only twenty-six guards remaining in our original escort of sixty, we headed towards the manor at the center of the compound. That was when we discovered that it was already under siege by the local peasants. They had the house sparsely surrounded at a considerable distance. The attackers were just close enough to see the house, but not quite close enough to hit it with stones, which several were trying to do. Some of the peasants separated from the main group and confronted us as we approached.

Gunderson angrily commanded them to move away. I, Antorn, thought that Gunderson was terribly foolish to make such demands of the peasants when they outnumbered us three to one. This naturally wouldn't have concerned my wise and powerful leader, the holy prophet Tibbald, but I was merely Antorn, a simple and cowardly priest. I feared that if they attacked all at once with their deadly picks and hoes, we would be hard pressed to escape in time. Bothering to recognize the peasants at all was obviously a complete waste of time, but I foolishly stepped in and explained to the peasant leader that we had come to assist them in their attack on the Eldorans.

The information was passed along and a cheer rose from the disheartened riff raff, who had heretofore been thwarted in their retribution. Their trapped Eldoran adversaries had magical weapons that were far greater than simple farm implements. The peasants insisted that the two hated tyrants had forced them into near slavery for years and then denied them food and shelter when the barbarians had come. Well, there was nothing wrong with that! They were peasants after all!

Still, their whining told us that the Eldorans under siege were a father and daughter team, which matched well with the information from the handsome Oneian lad. We were fairly certain that we had the right Eldorans, and they had already been confined for us. There remained only the simple matter of confirming their true heritage and enacting the retribution ceremony. Then we could return to the safety and comfort of the temple.

As our priestly trio advanced on the manor, we were supported by over a score of temple guards and nearly another four score of angry peasants. Gunderson knocked insistently on the front entrance, and we all waited patiently for a reply. An elderly gentleman in spectacles answered, who politely asked the reason for our visit. Gunderson demanded that he turn over the Eldorans in question. The old man suggested that any aggressive actions taken against his home or family would be met with violent and potentially lethal resistance. Such threats made it obvious that the old man himself was one of the Eldoran infidels.

Gunderson used his rod of office to verify the man's heritage by setting him on fire. An Eldoran would naturally use his powers to defend himself, and that was exactly what the old man did. He began to change shape within the torrent of blue flames. Borrund and I added our rods to the effort and tripled the amount of scouring energy coursing around the old Eldoran's expanding body. The burning creature stepped outside just as its hunched form could no longer fit under the high double doors. It was only then that I, Antorn, noticed that the old man's daughter was helping us burn her father from inside the manor house. Well, turning traitor against her father wasn't going to help her. She was just as doomed as he was.

The hideous creature roared. It was a thundering, screeching rumble that vibrated our very bones and blasted the air from our lungs. Oh, how ghastly! Those peasants and guards, who still had breath to scream, did so with enthusiasm! Our concentration faltered and the energy streams trailed out showing us our impending doom in the flickering torchlight, a demon far worse than the great god Prometheus himself had ever imagined!

It was a nightmare of nightmares gone horribly awry, I tell you! It was all glistening black with great, corded sinewy muscles. The veins under its thick, leathery hide looked like fat writhing worms clinging to a bulging mass of swollen, chiseled stone. It was a giant, repulsive perversion of a human, with claws nearly as thick as a wine bottle and a body so massively burgeoning with strength as to make it look squat. Its face had a heavy jutting brow and protruding

jaws that were lined with jagged, overlapping fangs. It….
it…. Actually, it looked a lot like your scribe, except without
the silly outfit.

Master: *I told you when we came in here that Static had mimicked
Paul.*

Prometheus: *Oh, really? I wasn't really listening. No wonder I
was so startled earlier. You know, scribe, that outfit looks quite
ridiculous on you, black tails and a bowtie of all things!*

[violent interlude]

Prometheus: *That was completely unjustified!*

Master: *Insulting Paul isn't a wise thing to do, Prometheus. You
must have lost your head there for a minute.*

Scribe: [laughing] *That is humor I enjoy, Master.*

Prometheus: *Barbaric primates! You just stay in your chair, you
nasty beast, or I'm not going to finish this story!*

Scribe: *You will address me with respect.*

Static: *Paul, I would appreciate if you could refrain from decapitating
Prometheus again until the conclusion of this tale. His input is
required. Prometheus, please continue.*

Prometheus: *I'm far too distraught, virus! My clever and dramatic
role as Antorn is more than I could possibly manage after such a brutal
attack! I can't go on!*

Static: *A summary of events will be sufficient.*

Oh, very well then! There was little to tell after that point anyway! The guards and peasants who hadn't run away, attacked. With the support of the soldiers, the peasants felt brave enough to fling their oiled torches onto the roof. Borrund tried to help them along by adding the power of his rod to ignite the wooden shingles. The young Eldoran woman attacked him angrily with her power then, but Borrund's rod was more powerful and forced her back inside the building. Gunderson was about to lend a hand when the beast mauled him savagely. Borrund was next in line to be murdered and then came Antorn.

It was all over so horribly fast that it's hard to remember the details. The last thing Antorn remembered was trying to use his rod of office to return home. He was just about to transport when the beast slashed at him. So he shifted straight to me in hopes that I'd save him. You already know the part about him ending up in Tiberius's office and bleeding all over the floor.

Master: *I thought you said that Antorn saw the whole battle.*

Prometheus: *That was the whole battle as far as he was concerned! He lost!*

Static: *Paul, please record that the remainder of the conflict was relatively uneventful. Most of the attackers fled when I began the physical portion of our defense. While I scattered the intended siege, Alenna sought to douse the flames consuming our accomplishments. Shortly thereafter, my companion arrived to view the unsatisfactory results of our struggle.*

Yes, yes, virus, that's all very interesting. Naturally, I told a similar story to Tiberius just before he killed Antorn with a dagger from his belt. By my wounded soaps, the man was becoming every bit as unpredictable as the priestess. He had his soldiers carry my underling's body out of the office and gave orders to have the floor cleaned. Then he turned to me and ordered me to transport him as if I were a mere servant. How rude!

"Take us there." What was Tiberius talking about now?

"Take us where?" I hoped he wasn't seriously considering what I thought he was considering!

"I would like you to take us to the site of the battle, good Prophet." He took out his sword! Eek! He was going to kill me in my own temple! I had my rod of office ready to blast him by the time I realized that he was looking perturbed with me again.

"This is merely a precaution, good Prophet. Transport us to the front entrance of the manor." Certainly not!

"Tiberius, are you mad? That beast might still be there!" Antorn's mental instability must have affected Tiberius too.

"That is my hope, good Prophet. Transport us now." He pointed his sword at my chest! Oh dear! At least the insect vermin took the time to torture me first! Tiberius was aiming straight for my important parts!

"Oh very well, Tiberius! Have it your way! You just remember to keep me safe, young man! If you let my robes get ruined, I'm not going to help you anymore!" In a flash, we were gone from his office and standing in the flickering darkness next to a burning building. I thanked my lucky slippers that the battle was over when we arrived. The monstrous nightmare of a beast was nowhere to be seen. I nearly swooned with relief, I tell you!

Tiberius put his sword away and wandered around, looking at a few of the corpses. Then he checked the ground, bushes and even a few of the flowerbeds, all the while holding up an abandoned torch that he had picked up. I shone some light from my rod onto the flowers, which would have been very pretty if they hadn't been all tromped down. I had no idea what Tiberius was looking for, but when he came back, he was carrying two rods of office.

"You can't use those, you know. The Priestess needs to initialize them to a particular person before they'll work." Tiberius ignored me and checked the brick pathway in front of the open doors.

"Fortune blesses us, good Prophet, our quarry has escaped unharmed. But I will not be able to follow their trail properly until morning light." Well, that was all the encouragement I needed!

"Excellent then, let's go back to the temple!" I prepared my rod of office for the return trip, but Tiberius held my arm. He has such strong, manly hands!

"Good Prophet, your avatar is alive." What? No, no, that couldn't be!

"Nonsense, Tiberius! That's impossible! I saw that avatar nearly melt to the floor of the temple! He couldn't have survived!" Tiberius shrugged.

"They travel with a large man, who strode casually from a burning building in bared feet. He was carrying the Eldoran girl at the time. Who else would the virus trust to handle his charge?" Oh dear! This was awful!

"We have to stop them, Tiberius! They're going to escape without us!" Not only that, but they might accidentally kill everyone in the process! Those two had no idea how dangerous they were together! Naturally, I wasn't about to tell any of that to Tiberius.

"Follow me, good Prophet. I would like to try another method of tracking." I have no idea how Tiberius knew those two Eldorans were nearby, but it was a good thing that he did, otherwise we might never have found you.

Master: *He knew them.*

Prometheus: *What?*

Master: *They were spies charged with keeping an eye on Static and Alenna. Since he didn't find their bodies, they must be nearby, waiting to report.*

Prometheus: *Impossible! If that were true, he would have known where the virus was years ago.*

Master: *Correct. But he also knew that Static wouldn't leave without me. So he had to wait.*

Prometheus: *Do you mean to tell me he stalled my joining ceremony for over a decade!*

Master: *You should thank him for that. You would have killed yourself.*

Static: *My friend, please describe how we came to be imprisoned together. The details of that meeting will provide additional depth to the upcoming events.*

Master: *You mean the first time? Okay.*

Martin Wolfe

Chapter Fourteen

Young Master

When a flaming space-rock hits a guy in the head, has he been hit by a meteor or a meteorite? The time between the meteor hitting his head and the meteorite mixing him with the concrete is virtually indistinguishable, so it's a tough call. But the editor who writes the headline in tomorrow's paper will need to know.

Since I'd reinforced the warehouse walls and windows to thwart the bad guys, the crater debris exploded mostly straight upward; whereas, I exploded everywhere, and I traveled much faster than the trailing rock dust. The top half of me arced into space while the lower half covered most of the continent. Masses of random thoughts crashed through me, as did the usual fear and confusion. But there was something new as well. Somebody else shared the ether with me.

Paranoia took over, and I fled. The stranger was north, so I went south, far south. Then I got angry. Unfocussed rage crystallized. I was bloody well tired a having aliens take potshots at me, and I was determined to do something about it, so I started wishing. I wished for things to keep me alive and grounded in humanity, lots and lots of things, all in a row. Some were quite creative and useful, while others were just weird and dumb.

At the top of the list was a wish for more bodies. Yep, that's right, I wanted spares, standby receptacles that would suck up my gaseous innards immediately upon meteorite impact, or whatever else happened to kill me. My first request was for a dozen, which I changed midstream and demanded a hundred. But then I wondered what I was going to do with a hundred spare bodies. So I decided to store them as steel balls, no, better yet, make that rubies, so that nobody would want to destroy them if they were found. Yeah, that would work. They should be space-faring bodies too, just in case, and fully adjustable, good looking – yeah, really good looking – and so on, and so forth.

Even before I finished my list, the bad stuff had started hitting the fan and was flying off in all directions. I'd just demanded several things simultaneously, which apparently weren't in the alien catalog of things I could safely make. And thus, I was suddenly introduced to the rules.

As my internal equations slowed to a standstill and as lightning raced across the cloudless sky, I came to understand fully that complex add-ons to my programming needed tweaking before the technology would function properly, just like I'd had to do with the killer bugs in my apartment. But this time, I'd overloaded my system to the point of crashing, and I'd just been informed that I was hardwired to an ocean-sized bomb that was about to go off. Oops.

My high school math final had arrived unannounced, and I hadn't shown up for class since kindergarten. The universe was unraveling from my navel, and I hadn't been taught how to crochet in calculus. Let's see, train A leaves station X at the speed of light and train B leaves station Y heading towards train A at Mach twenty. When does the third axel of train C become unglued? Quick, boy, get the answer on the teacher's desk before Saturn's rings get blown to Pluto! That's kind of how I felt. It's a good thing that I was a math natural, one of those rare, freakish protégés that can add from birth, or I wouldn't be sharing this story.

As to how I saved myself, I barely have a clue. Essentially, I worked really fast and made outlandish guesses that couldn't possibly be right. I tied loose ends of algebra to tight ends of calculus, and looped them into fractional bows, so they might look pretty, because one should always look pretty at one's own funeral. It was all nuts, just like me, the mad mathematician. Ever since that day, I've sort of looked upon math as more of an art than a science.

My first clear image, when I regained a semblance of rational thought, was one of flipping end over end above an ice flow, and seeing penguins. I had just begun to orient myself when I hit the ground and something snapped.

Then I was in the air again. Confusing? Tell me about it. My airborne particles had been sucked into one of my new ruby-receptacles. Whilst spinning though the air, said ruby had expanded into a body, which then landed poorly and died. My second ruby fared better, dumping me alive into a colony of penguins, which had already begun to scatter when the rubies started landing. I stood, spat snow and penguin poop out of my mouth, and watched as smoking gemstones bounced like hail around me and my brother corpse.

The poor little penguins were scared witless and dashed for the shoreline as fast as their flippered feet could waddle. Sorry guys. Maybe I should have stayed closer to civilization and frightened the humans. Penguins, after all, were good folks – never been shot at by a penguin. In fact, at the moment, I had a good deal more in common with penguins than with humans. For instance, most humans weren't immune to standing naked in the snow; whereas, the penguins and I were – naked, that is, or nearly so. The penguins were wearing tuxedos, and I was wearing a broken watch. My nearby corpse had a watch too – bizarre. Then again, my life had become the textbook definition of bizarre, which begged the question, when did constant bizarreness become the norm?

I shrugged and started picking up whatever rubies I could find. The total count came to sixty-seven, which, if one counted the two used bodies, meant that thirty-one were missing, if one also assumed that there were actually a hundred in total, rather than my original request of a dozen randomly multiplied by, added to, or subtracted from my final request of a hundred. Who knew? Whatever the case, chances were that if I didn't stop getting myself killed, I would probably be visiting this spot on a semi-regular basis – that is, if the ice didn't melt first. I tried to remember if I'd wished for the ability to breathe water.

Out of a blinding glare, another man appeared on my ice flow and scared the last of the penguins over the edge. He looked like a Fonzie wannabe, slicked back hair, white T-shirt, and a black leather jacket.

"How did you find me?" I asked, not really caring, since I didn't think I could escape anyway. Feeling underdressed, I wished myself clothed and stuffed two-handfuls of rubies into my new pockets. A few tumbled back onto the ice.

"Dust. You left a trail through the ionosphere," he said. His mannerisms were different from the other aliens I'd met, but that didn't mean much. He could still be the same guy.

I raised a finger in warning. "If you say you're a Greek god, I might have to slap you."

He smiled sadly and nodded as if I'd just confirmed his suspicion. "You've met Prometheus," he said, "I'm Proteus, his assistant. I'm afraid my mentor has complicated your life more than you realize."

"No worries, I'm a complicated guy. Just leave me alone from here, and we'll call it even."

He shrugged his lips and sighed. I had a nasty feeling that something bad was about to happen. By golly, it did too. Proteus explained the situation, thousands-of-years-worth, all at once. A vast collection of ideas and images swarmed into my brain and made my combined life histories seem like an advertising blurb. I would have said that it felt like my head was exploding, but I'd experienced that, and it wasn't as bad. I staggered and fell. Then I rolled and clawed the ice.

Within the information flood, which, to this day, I'm still trying to assimilate, Proteus shared with me the basic problem of my existence, as viewed by Hosts (although he didn't call them that). It stemmed primarily from the random wishes I'd been making and from the fact that I could make them without being privy to the original catalogue. Most of his colleagues would claim that hacking their genetic system while it was up and running wasn't possible and should never be attempted. They believed this wholeheartedly, for the alternative was to accept that their ancient society was in danger of changing radically, and possibly even coming to an abrupt end.

In a nutshell, they were all ensconced in stringent denial of my new abilities, and of the many idiotic catastrophes that Prometheus, the guy who'd created me, had already caused while proving them wrong.

Prometheus: *I object! That isn't true at all!*

Actually, for once, Prometheus is right. He isn't an idiot. In fact, he's the greatest mathematical pioneer his kind has ever known.

Prometheus: *Oh, that's much better! It's so nice to be recognized!*

Too bad for Prometheus, that he was just stupid enough to make me better than he was, not because he wanted to, but because he'd grafted his own genes onto mine, yet lacked the foresight to realize that humans were better at abstract thought than Hosts. Someone familiar with higher mathematics should have known that a greater ability for abstract thought would make for a better mathematician.

217

The other Hosts understood this fact well. Their entire culture, along with their language and technology, was based on math. This is not to say that they were anywhere near as talented as Prometheus. Most of them weren't, just like most humans didn't do algebra past high school. Hosts used their powers like humans used computers; they gave little or no thought as to how they worked.

So, the Hosts' technology was based on math and Prometheus was their best, but he'd conducted radical experiments that were strictly taboo among his species. Prometheus, therefore, was soon persona non-gratis, but not before he made me. To the Hosts, I was beyond frightening, being better at mathematics than any of them. I had the ability to improve upon their technology, yet I lacked the knowledge or experience to do it safely. When one takes into consideration the fact that most of them didn't want to believe that I even existed, it becomes a bit more understandable why the few who knew of me wanted me locked up indefinitely – out of sight out of mind, as it were.

Proteus's painful lesson also included the knowledge that I was pretty much screwed. He went over that part a few times until I understood it clearly. I connected some of my own dots to some of his, and that helped me to put things into context. An alien guy named Cerberus was in the neighborhood. Sending assassins and hurling meteors had been his way of convincing me to leave my body, so he could capture me without destroying the research site. Apparently, their kind needed the planet intact, so they could find a cure for some emotional disease they'd contracted, which had somehow begun with Prometheus and this Cerberus fellow, who wanted the abomination – namely me – dead if at all possible. He was a notoriously unhappy camper. Emotions will do that.

Proteus and a few other benevolent Hosts thought that I had a right to live, but even they considered me little more than a rogue pest with potential. Proteus thought I might be useful in furthering emotional research where his mentor left off. Nonetheless, he wasn't about to let me frustrate Cerberus into destroying his field research. My home planet was evidently a valuable laboratory, being one of the first locations, if not *the* first, where Prometheus conducted his experiments. Prometheus had apparently forgotten where he was when he made me.

Prometheus: *I made thousands of those systems! Do you really expect me to remember in which order?*

Master: *Some misplaced rubies say I don't have a right to judge.*

A flash, and yet another man appeared on the ice flow – Cerberus, the guy who'd sent James to kill me in an alley. And there I lay with my head reeling from overload. I now knew that, even in top shape, I had neither the knowledge nor the skill to enact my revenge, or to elude whatever they planned to do with me. My talents were far too under-developed.

Cerberus silently yelled, *"You're infusing it? Are you mad?"*

Somehow, I didn't think I was included in the conversation out of Cerberus's sense of politeness, certainly not when he referred to me as 'it'. He wouldn't have blocked his thoughts from me any more than I would have whispered to keep from being overheard by a fly on the wall. Still, I was grateful that Proteus stopped the infusion. My head throbbed.

"Considering your behavior, Cerberus, you shouldn't accuse others of mental illness."

"Release the avatar to me at once, or I will destroy this facility!"

"We will let him decide his own fate." Proteus turned to me. *"Would you like to die or to be imprisoned?"*

Knowing the situation, I also knew that Proteus was risking a lot to give me what he thought was a choice. "I'd rather not die," I told him. To that, I added some colorful metaphors and told them where they could both go, but they ignored those parts.

"The avatar has spoken, Cerberus. The Council will never reinstate you if you kill a willing prisoner. And you might remain infected if you destroy this site."

Cerberus looked disgusted, *"You will regret your interference!"* Another flash and he was gone.

"I doubt it." Proteus spoke to the air where Cerberus had been. He turned back to me.

"I don't suppose you're going to let me go?" I asked.

"Afraid not."

The world flared white, and I too was gone.

Prison was dark, weightless, and blissfully silent, but my head still throbbed. I willed Proteus's information compressed for later sorting, and my headache ebbed away. For a while, I enjoyed floating pain-free in the textureless ink of nothing.

When that got old, I tried reaching the edge of my cage. Waggling my arms and legs got me nowhere. So I tried wishing my way to the other side of walls I imagined must be there, not that I thought it would work – too obvious. Still, something must have happened because I could see my hands. I looked around to find the light source, which was a glowing ball of electricity hovering just out of reach above my head. It was marble-sized and looked like a souvenir plastic lightning ball, sans plastic. The mini blue bolts flickered happily, distracting me from my problems. Then the static ball zipped around like a firefly before stopping in front me. If I could have jumped, I would have, being unaccustomed to light bulbs that moved. I wished for it to come within reach. It didn't budge, but it did puff to three times its size – maybe to look threatening. I tried to tell it not to be afraid, but my cell, which I now saw was just a black cube, lacked air for words.

The ball of Static spoke into my head. *"Do not attack again. Your Host energies are bolstering this prison's effectiveness, which is already sufficient."*

"Greetings, Static. I come in peace." What does one say to a telepathic ball of electric lint?

"Greetings, Host. My intentions toward you are undecided. I am curious as to why you have confined yourself with your prisoner."

Mr. Static thought I was somebody else, so I clarified. *"I'll guess that 'Hosts' are the aliens that messed with my chemistry. Just so we're clear on this, I didn't put either of us in here."*

Its interest piqued. *"Your claim of genetic manipulation does help to explain your peculiar energy signature, which is minutely different than that of Hosts. This difference presents an opportunity. Will you consent to an experiment to facilitate our escape?"*

I'd been in prison for an hour or so. That was plenty. *"Sure. What do need me to do?"*

"Do nothing," it said.

Not a problem. At least a third of me was expert at doing nothing. The static ball shot through my forehead and tried to commandeer my brain. I instinctively resisted, until I felt it waiting for me to do nothing, like I was told. Since I didn't have a list of friendly aliens willing to break me out of jail, I let down my guard. For the second time that day, my mind flooded painfully with more information than manageable. The electric usurper plunged me into an ocean of experiences as our lives melted together. My specks of human experience were drowning within the vastness of its history. After what seemed like forever, the mass-murdering alien realized that I was being washed away. 'He'– my social training wouldn't allow me to picture a woman doing the kinds of things he'd done – suppressed his endless horror of a past to a few frames per second

"Your brief existence is rife with concepts for which I lack a frame of reference to comprehend," he said.

I opened my eyes and saw stars. Cool. I didn't have a headache. Even more cool. We were on the outside of the prison, which was just that single cubic cell drifting in deep space. There was a pretty red and blue gas cloud off to my left. It would have been breathtaking if there was breath to take.

"Thanks for helping me escape. Can you get out of my head now? I'm still getting backwash." The images flashing by made thinking difficult.

"I am unwilling to relinquish control over your abilities until you terminate my existence."

Of all the electric aliens I could have merged with, I had to pick one that was suicidal. *"Why do you need my consent if you're the one in control? Have a blast! Just don't take me with you!"* I wouldn't have been a good choice to operate a suicide prevention hotline.

"Although I can autonomously terminate your existence, I require cooperation for an act of self-destruction. It is an oddity within your genetic programming."

"Sorry, you're on your own."

He sent a monstrous wave of memories to dash my head against the rocks of reality. *"You are born of a violent race and should understand the potential consequences of denying my request."*

Yep, I did. *"Look, Static. Do you mind if I call you, Static? Anyway, here's the thing. I don't want to die. Now, some people would rather die than be tortured, but I'm not one of them. And if you die, I die for keeps, right? You probably didn't mean to show me that, but you did. So if you torture me now, I guarantee that I'll hold on just long enough to be useless to both of us."*

More memories, this time they were specific and came slowly, so that I could understand his motives for dying. I understood fine. We just had different perspectives. Where he saw endless tedium from eternal life, I saw an escape from death and countless opportunities to goof off. He kept up the barrage until he found an area where our perspectives overlapped. Genocide – we both thought it was bad. Static had done some impressively horrid things. But being forced to remember them in detail proved to be as desensitizing as a gory action flick.

He tried again to recruit me for execution duty. *"Among your species, it is considered honorable to sacrifice one's life for the lives of others. I have vowed not to kill again without cause, yet I fear that I lack the fortitude to maintain my resolve. End my life now, before I kill more innocents."*

"No."

"Your refusal lacks reason."

I had loads of reasons: He had spent millions of years in prison and had paid his debt. He was now a reformed ball of static. If he wanted to die, killing him wouldn't be punishment. Blah, blah, blah, it was all a bunch of crap. I just didn't want to die, and that was that. With the incentive of my continued life on the line, I came up with an idea. Whether or not it was a good idea remained to be seen.

"Okay, Static, you've been a bad ball of electricity. Your new punishment is to help people instead of hurting them, starting with me." As I saw it, he didn't really want to die, anyway. He was just bored. I gave him something to do.

He thought about it for a while. *"I admit that I find this challenge intriguing. In what ways could my actions prove to be beneficial to mortals?"*

I couldn't have cared less. As long as I didn't have to die, pretty much anything would work. Maybe he could lick postage stamps or something. *"That's part of your punishment. You have to figure out how you can help the most."*

He separated from me, and the memories stopped completely. *"I accept your challenge, Host-hybrid. Let us retire to your habitat, so that I might assist with your philanthropic efforts."*

Not what I had in mind. *"That's okay, Static. You've helped me enough already. Somebody else deserves a turn."* There was no way I could explain to my date tonight why I was being tailed by a floating ball of lightning.

"As a Host-hybrid you are potentially a great asset to your species. Thus, ensuring your safety will be an efficient method of helping them."

"Correct me if I'm wrong, fellow fugitive, but didn't the Hosts lock you in the same cage as me? How are you going to ensure my safety? And by the way, I didn't volunteer to save humanity. That's your job."

"Out of desperation, I willingly entered the cube, which the Hosts claimed was a means to my end. Although it is true that I allowed them to deceive me, my knowledge of Host behavior might nonetheless prolong your freedom. It is also true that you facilitated the release of a proven killer and that our merger altered my emotional capacity. I am presently unpredictable even to myself. You are responsible for my rehabilitation."

I was doomed to be a guidance counselor for a reformed alien murderer. *"Fine, but you can't come looking like that, unless we can stuff you in a plastic ball."* Nothing draws attention like persistent static cling, especially when it talks.

He morphed into a naked copy of me. *"Is this guise acceptable?"*

Right, his memories had shown him as some kind of shape-shifter. *"Needs work."* I let out an airless sigh. *"Let's go then. We don't want to miss our date."*

Chapter Fifteen

Static: *Our timeline now requires you to describe your resurrection on Oneia, my friend. Please continue.*

Master: [nods]

Prometheus: *What? He just went! Why does he get to keep going when I had to wait?*

Master: *Static likes me better.*

Static: *Prometheus, my companion's living presence at our meeting in the forest will make little sense without chronicling his arrival.*

Old Master

I get confused when I die without noticing that I died. From my perspective, the time, place, and situation change instantly. Like when I battled the saugael mor in the throne room. It exploded and drenched me in caustic goop. I registered little before my bubbling corpse splattered to the floor. Then I was blind and on my back. Before the mor could finish me off, I tried flipping to my feet. My head thumped hard into wood. I rolled sideways and smacked into stone. The burning pain switched from deep-fried to oven-baked. My flailing hands informed me that I was in a stone box with a wooden lid. Crap. Somebody was trying to cremate me again. I hate that.

The heat radiating through the planks convinced me not to belay my escape. I pressed my hands against the lid, which, despite my best effort, lifted only a crack. More heat and a lot of smoke billowed in. I dropped the lid, drew shallow breaths, and tried not to gag. Either my body was in rough shape, or something very heavy weighed down my coffin. I flipped over and pressed my back into service. The lid inched upward until I got my legs under me. Then I stood, and sparks rushed under the rug that covered what I now realized was a trapdoor over a stone pit, rather than a coffin. Heavy – no rug ever weighed so much. I flipped up the fringe and saw that I supported the half-collapsed roof of a burning building. The brick walls and broken windows made for an effective blast furnace – very hot.

I heaved aside the trapdoor and its flaming load of rafters. Sparks billowed in the rippling heat. I coughed a lot, as one will do in such a place. My hair tips curled to ash. I headed for the doorway in front of me, but the roof's second half sagged, blocking the way with a wall of flame – inconvenient. I checked my finger. Yep, Static had ringed me. Still, I didn't want to be flame-broiled if I could avoid it. I looked for another exit.

There weren't any exits available, but I did find a glowing-blue woman leaning against a stone fountain. I symbolically raised an eyebrow that had already shriveled. Even covered in soot, she was beautiful. As I ogled, a spark landed on my head and ignited my hair. Just as suddenly, the woman's aura dimmed, and I glowed blue. My hair fire fizzled, and the hurt faded to half. Evidently, she'd decided to share whatever protection she had. The fresh pain in her eyes said it was costing her. I stepped up to return the favor.

Without asking if she could walk, I scooped her up and dashed for the firewall blocking the exit. I cradled her in one glowing blue arm and used the other to shove beams out of my way. Her shield didn't keep my skin from sizzling when I pushed against burning wood, but a scorched arm wasn't going to kill me. She screamed against my chest. Evidently, she was unused to being baked. I yelled for her to take back her shield, but she wouldn't.

The roaring flames were suddenly drowned out by a screeching roar, which I would have sworn came from my butler – his tantrums were distinctive. But Paul couldn't be here; he didn't know about this planet or how to find it. Then his great black arm reached under the burning rafters and batted them away. Don't ask questions – I skipped with my pretty package into fresh air and up to a stone-bordered pond, where I lowered her into cool water. She coughed but didn't complain.

I turned and scanned for Paul while I hacked up smoke. He was absent from the midnight landscape of flowerbeds, stone walkways, and some out-of-place mangled corpses. The scattered dead men showed telltale signs of having encountered Paul, who'd assumedly run off to mangle some more.

Out of the shadows, a farmer with a raised pitchfork charged toward me. "Die, Eldor'n scum!" Paul must have missed one.

I took away the farmer's fork, which he more or less handed to me, and spanked him with the shaft until it broke. Then I handed back the broken ends, and he hobbled back from whence he came.

I turned back to the pretty lady, who'd climbed out the pond. She was staring at the burning house. Her profile looked vaguely familiar. "Rough night?" I asked.

She ignored me. I have a tendency to unwittingly irritate people, so I wasn't taken aback. Besides, I may very well have been responsible for her house being torched. It's amazing the trouble I can cause while I'm dead. I placed her face to a recent memory. "You're that girl's mother, right? The one Static tried to..." I was about to say 'save' when I realized that her daughter was probably dead.

A brick wall collapsed into the bonfire, and sparks geysered into the night air. I glanced at the mess and then back to her. "I take it that was yours?"

She looked up at me and scowled. I finally noticed that tears were streaming through the soot on her face. I shut my mouth.

Just then, Paul sailed through the air and shook the ground in front of us. His vaguely apelike mass of muscle, teeth, and talons eclipsed the blaze. He stalked toward me. I remembered then that I'd missed supper, probably more than once. *"Don't eat me, Paul! Not here!"* A farmer with a fork was one thing, but Paul could thrash me two times out of three.

"Do not be concerned, my friend. I will not harm you." Static said.

Phew.

"How long was I out?" We'd arrived in winter, and now it was summer. That worried me. Paul's carefully planned meals might have gone to waste for months. He'd kill me slowly for that.

My distressed damsel dashed forward and hugged Static's arm, which was thicker than she was. *"You have regenerated for fourteen years, my friend."* Static told me.

Well, that was a record. I glanced at the woman, and things clicked. *"She's the same girl, isn't she?"*

"Yes, my friend, I have adopted Alenna into my care. Will you consent to care for her also?"

I nodded absently. So this girl had been raised by Static. Interesting. She was guaranteed to be a social freak. We had something in common.

I'm proud to say that over the centuries I've learned to annoy women even when I'm dead. Alenna stomped into the forest near her torched house. I collected a uniform from a soldier who didn't need it anymore, and then I followed. Static gave up his mutant-butler disguise and turned into an owl, because when owls search for places to camp, they don't leave tracks. I took the hint and made a modest effort to erase our trail. When the first of the trees were behind us, Prometheus and Tiberius showed up near the burning house. Tiberius started searching the ground for tracks. From then on, I made an ego-driven effort to erase our trail. Something about Tiberius got under my skin, and I didn't want to deal with him until morning.

Sometime later, I realized that I didn't really know where we were going.

"Hey, Static, which way to camp?" I asked just in case Alenna hadn't.

"Turn seven degrees East, my friend." Spiffy. With those directions I could join Tiberius for breakfast.

"Which way is East?" A few seconds later, Static landed on my shoulder and steered me in the right direction. I sneezed and nearly knocked him off. I sneezed again. My eyes started to itch. *You'd better keep your distance, Static. I think I'm allergic to you."* My immune system was messed up.

Static gave up trying to keep his balance and took off. *"I shall hunt our evening meal."*

Still sniffling, I stumbled into the clearing where Alenna waited.

"I'll start a fire, Father," she said, including me in her silent message. That was odd. She'd been scowling at me since I revived – mixed messages.

She stalked away, I assumed to find some deadwood. I sat on the edge of a log until she returned and dumped her sticks in a heap. I was going to say that a fire probably wasn't a good idea because of the light, but I figured Tiberius would probably find us before morning anyway. So instead, I asked, "How do you plan to start it?" Her tattered dress couldn't have hidden a match, let alone flint and steel.

She glared at me again, and the wood burst into flames, all at once. I nodded, wondering why she got to have power when I didn't.

We sat across from each other, alternately tossing twigs into the fire, until a dead rabbit dropped from the sky.

Either Static had made his first catch, or this planet had odd weather patterns. Even stranger than the rabbit falling down was the rabbit rising back up. It hovered over the fire for a few seconds before the skin flew off. Then the stomach split open and the guts sailed into the woods. Note to self: Learn how not to upset Static's daughter while trapped on planet.

By the time the second rabbit arrived, the first was cooked, or so I assumed, since it sailed from its invisible rotisserie and into my lap. I picked it up and ate like I hadn't eaten in, oh, about fourteen years. It was tasty. Alenna was eating the other rabbit by the time Static returned with a dead bird, which, being an owl as he was, he ate uncooked.

When I got to sucking on bones, I asked, *"So what did I miss?"* The question was to Static, but I returned Alenna's favor and included her in the conversation. She pretended she either didn't notice or didn't care, staring alternately at the fire and at something that only she could see over my shoulder. Static summarized the past fourteen years, including his theory on how to get off the planet, with whom he'd made friends. I nodded periodically, deciding to leave the details to him, while I checked out Alenna, who was checking me out and doing a pretty good job of hiding it. I must have looked different while breathing and whatnot.

The firelight made her bare skin glow where it peeked from beneath her shredded gown, which was more gone than not. If I'd had my power back, I could have gallantly fixed the holes for her – happy misfortune. She looked tastier than roasted rabbit. I wondered what she was thinking.

Alenna: *Is that truly what you were doing, looking through the holes in my dress?*

Master: *'Fraid so.*

Alenna: *And did you see anything you liked?*

Master: *Lots.*

Alenna: *You wished to know what I was thinking. I can tell you.*

Master: *Will I regret it?*

Alenna: *I don't know. Will you?*

Master: *This is one of those trick questions, isn't it?*

Alenna

Even the stars rejected her. You are not like us, they whispered. She agreed. She didn't belong – not with Oneians who destroyed her home and livelihood, or with Eldorans who avoided her lest they be discovered themselves, and not with her two ancient guardians who viewed her as a child to be ignored. She was the outsider, the other, even among those who loved her, or who loved her in her dreams – those were gone now, mixed with the ashes her home.

The companion was alive. Her last hope for romance withered. She didn't know this man, this resurrected god. Eternal happiness with her starry prince was just a fantasy to ease her mind from life's hurts. And now a stranger absently trod upon the embers of that life. His presence, his casual indifference, made her ache of loneliness and sorrow over the things she had longed for and lost.

Master: *I knew I'd regret this.*

231

She had fallen in love with a phantom, an image of a perfect man that could never exist, even should she try to mold him. 'Character changes willingly,' her father would say, 'or not at all.' Her time with Peterius proved her father's words. Even the notion of her changing the companion was ludicrous. He was eternal, wealthy and powerful beyond belief, and could have any woman he desired. She was sixty spans of her lifetime younger than he, and was likely not a child in his eyes but an infant barely out of the womb. She wanted to hate him for ruining her fantasy and for being the one her father loved most, but hating a stranger made no more sense than loving him. She wanted the companion to accept responsibility for her losses, even though he had asked for nothing and thus owed her nothing. But most of all, while he listened to the tale of her candle-flame life, she wanted him to ask how she was feeling.

She stood and walked into the forest gloom that matched her mood. Her father cautioned her to remain close. This one time, she wished he would follow. But he was busy with his friend of twelve centuries. His time and his love were not hers alone anymore. She hadn't asked for help, but her heart said they should have recognized her pain and offered. She pretended to be strong and kept walking. No one owed her anything.

The scent of pine needles and lush ferns unearthed memories of wandering alone through the forest. But those memories showed her father watching protectively nearby. Now she was truly alone. In the distance, the Crack River beckoned, thrashing the rock walls that confined it. She led her aimless stroll down a path to happier times, when she and Peterius had fed cones to the hungry froth.

On those days, she would imagine herself the hero of Eldorans. She dreamed of using her powers to fly above the prejudiced Oneians, who would finally succumb to kindness and common sense. She would teach them reason; they would accept Eldorans as equals; and all would love her – when she and donkeys flew. The river had a better chance of defeating the rocks, which would over time erode, like her will.

She paused at a fallen tree that bridged the Crack in the World where the river ruled. She and Peterius had crossed the old giant many times, in full daylight. A carapace of forest lichens and spongy turf clung to its back. Thick limbs spiraled along its length, glistening with mist in the moonlight. Crossing it was foolish, as children will sometimes be. Crossing at night was madness to those who valued their life. She started forward.

Her feet reminisced the textures as she padded above seething death in darkness. She moved slowly, allowing the mist to soak through her rags. The dress had been one of her favorites, destroyed like everything else. For the briefest moment, she dreamed her youthful dream of flying, until even that small happiness plunged into the thunder below; she could catapult grown men across the canyon, but not herself. No amount of wishing would float her above the mist. With that thought, she sobered. As depressing as her life had become, it wasn't yet bad enough to disregard. Her future might yet hold promise, which would never be fulfilled if she lost her life to the river.

She turned, too quickly, and slipped. Her feet met air. She willed the branches to catch her. One snapped with the force of her need and hammered her face. Her fist closed on another and slipped off. The crook of her knee caught a third, which recoiled and dragged her away from the trunk. She swung upturned, dangling by a calf over the abyss. She strained her hamstring to keep her leg bent while she strained her mind to keep the branch straight, despite that her power couldn't fully support anything that supported her. The remnants of her sodden dress fell to bunch around her shoulders and face. She shrugged it off into the river and swung her other leg up to lock with the first. Her calf burned where her skin tore. Mingled blood and mist threatened to slide her off the branch that sagged lower with each breath. She rocked her torso upward until fingers felt bark. Then she inched her fingers upward, crack by crack until her side pressed against the trunk. Wherever her naked skin scraped against wood, it bled, but she clawed through the pain until, aching, gasping, and shaking from adrenalin, she finally mounted the tree's moss saddle and hugged it for dear life.

When at last she dared to move, she realized that she was facing the wrong direction. Her courage depleted, she chose to crawl toward the opposite shore, where by the following morning she could hike to Crack Bridge and then back to camp. Her father might be worried, but she would be alive to apologize for not heeding his warning and for succumbing to self-pity because her daydreams hadn't become real. If her father were still prone to lectures, he would have reminded her that fantasies are healthy only until believed true. From now on she'd satisfy herself with the small joys amidst the relative misery that reality offered. And right now she felt like thanking her miserable wounds for reminding her that she should be happy sitting by a fire with her loving father and a new friend.

When she finally dragged herself past the cliff's edge, she collapsed, heaving and kissed the rock for being there. Loneliness wasn't nearly as frightening as the thought of crossing that tree again. She staggered to her feet and started walking, naked but grateful to be alive.

Soles grown tough from preferring bared feet to boots carried her steadily through a forest that felt less lonely. The trees' needles caressed and tickled her skin rather than scratching. The pine scent added exuberance to her loosening stride where before it had offered only sad memories. Her new outlook on life pumped warmth and courage into a heart gone cold. She hadn't traveled that far from the tree bridge when she began to chide herself for giving into fear so quickly. That wasn't how she had been raised, and she had been through far worse ordeals. Her foul mood had made her weak.

She stopped dead. Fear newly reined spiraled out of control. Too quiet – where was nature's music? The breezeless silence magnified the brittle snap of needles underfoot. She forced her balance and breathing under control and listened for the sounds that should be heard in the woods on a warm summer night. Nothing – a predator was nearby. The unnatural quiet combined with her unnatural fear fueled her suspicion. A saugael mor was watching her.

She understood then that her father hadn't been warning his little girl not to get lost. He'd been reminding a grown woman of the rumored saugael mor roaming the empire. Instinct and terror screamed for her to run, but wisdom suggested that she first pinpoint the danger, so she could run in the right direction. A slow scan of the canopy uncovered a shadow within shadows. Tucked in the crotch of a divided spruce, its eyeless body waited for her to succumb to the unbridled fear it hungered. It had been partly deprived, due to the thought-protecting habit of her Eldoran heritage, or she would likely be dead already.

She hadn't encountered a mor since her childhood, and she wondered if her matured powers might be up to the challenge. Running was obvious, but it wouldn't be enough – nobody could outrun a mor. Among Eldorans, there were whispered stories of saugael mor being defeated in single combat, but she had never heard such stories told by anyone who had met a survivor. Still, the claims had support in the strength of the modern Eldoran. Since the companion's landing, her kind had grown steadily more powerful. Her father said that it was from the influx of new energy drawn by the companion himself and his lost artifacts, which were being found and used. Whatever the reason, she hoped it would be enough.

The mor must have decided that its lust for fear wouldn't be satisfied by waiting alone, so it unfolded and kindled its hissing clicks. She fought terror for control of her limbs and backed away as it crept down the tree and toward her. Saugael mor were resistant to energy, she knew. The beast likely wouldn't ignite even if she willed it, and she didn't think she could repel it long enough for her to escape. But she had to do something before its frustration peaked, or her slim chance would become no chance. Of all things, the destruction of her home gave her inspiration.

She ignited the forest around her, brought her shield to bear, and ran. Never before had she tried to burn so much so quickly, and she was surprised by her own power. Ferns, moss, and towering conifers alike veritably exploded into flames. She screamed and nearly succumbed from the heat searing through her weak defense. The mor, engulfed in natural flames, shrieked in fury and launched itself at her back. Its claws encircled and pierced her shield. Two sliced into her shoulders and one sank deep into her breast before she refocused the bulk of her energy behind and shoved the mor off. Her brows turned to ash; her hair tips ignited from the blast of heat that slammed into her front; and her lungs spasmed through the torture. She batted her head, covered her face with her arms, and dashed headlong toward the river mist, her only hope.

If the rumors about the mor were true, then it shouldn't be able to leap far enough to cross the Canyon River, which she hoped would swallow the killer like it would a pinecone. For her plan to succeed, she had to cross the tree-bridge before the mor, and then dump the heavy log into the Crack in the World. The odds were against success, but for lack of options she ignored the odds – die trying, or simply die.

Too soon, yet barely soon enough, she arrived at the weakest part of her plan – the bridge. She would have to cross full-tilt and half blinded by smoke and tears. But first she needed to repel the mor, which was frantically slashing at her shield and slicing her back once for every five attempts. She dropped her barrier to the river's cooling mist and slammed all of her power into the mor's bulbous black core. It soared back into the inferno that raged uncontrolled to the forest's edge. The tree bridge would need to be gone before it returned.

Irony propelled her forward in a mad sprint through an obstacle course of branches as she danced across her narrow path to freedom. Wet moss tore and slid away beneath her toes. She dove the last two strides and tumbled over thick, twisted roots on the canyon's far side. Then she was up again and pushing with the combined strength of her body and mind against a tree firmly embedded in decades of sediment. One end began to budge just as the mor reappeared from the flames on the far side. The killer's body still burned as it left the forest behind. It was suffering, dragging two limbs useless and twitching.

By the time the mor clawed its way to mid-span, the old trunk dangled on one end by a twisted net of roots that refused to let go. She set them to flame and snapped them one at a time, until the trees own weight plunged it into the darkness. The saugael mor tried to leap the rest of the way, but it was seconds too late and disappeared with the tree into the canyon.

Assuming the mor was dead could prove to be a lethal mistake, and she was determined not to make anymore. She had to warn her father of the danger, if the nearby inferno hadn't already signaled that something was amiss. But she would bleed to death if she didn't first do something about her wounds. She clenched her jaw and stifled a scream as her Eldoran talents drew together and then cauterized the edges of her cuts. The effort buckled her knees, and she took many ragged breaths before she could stand to stumble along the trail back to camp.

Chapter Sixteen

Static

My friend caught the knife Tiberius threw at his head and used it to clean his nails.

"Desist!" Tiberius commanded, having reached his limit for childish behavior. My companion, perturbed that Tiberius had so quickly located our encampment, had been flicking pine needles at the high commander's ear while we discussed a method of breaching Oneia's perimeter.

"You cheated."

Tiberius ignored the jibe, which called attention to the presence of Joner and Lendell Pappit, whom Tiberius had indentured as guides. Only they would have known where Alenna might choose to make camp. He found the two on the road near the gates of the estate. Their proximity suggested involvement in the attack on our home, or at the very least that they had failed to assist us in our moment of need. I empathized with the renewed feelings of betrayal that Alenna would experience upon her return.

"It won't work, you know! Only a joining with the Priestess will free us!" Prometheus brooded by the fire. He had made it plain that he was against Tiberius's proposal.

"In essence, I concur," I told Prometheus, *"But the attempt is unlikely to cause harm, and rapid transport to the temple, as Tiberius has offered, is adequate compensation for our compliance."*

Again, my companion curiously glanced at me but chose not to comment. He was concerned for my feelings. He assumed, as did I, that Tiberius had been instrumental in the recent kidnappings of Eldorans by the invading nomads. The tribesmen were creating an army of saugael mor with which to overthrow the empirical regime. I resolved to confront Tiberius at a later date about his endangering my daughter's life. We urgently needed to deliver my companion into the priestess's protection, lest his renewed life signs alert marauding saugael mor to our location.

"Won't cause harm? Preposterous! You'll blow us all to the Three Algae Moons, virus!" Prometheus stood to gesticulate in exasperation, and was consequently in danger of igniting his robes in the fire.

At that moment, Alenna, breathing hard and laced with a mor's characteristic tri-parallel wounds, stumbled into camp. Assuming that Prometheus was attacking, she promptly erected an energy shield, which she expanded to include me as well as my companion, a fact which cocked his brow with a moment's intrigue before he blinked it away.

"Alenna, the mor that pursues you is a far greater threat than Prometheus, who is presently a guest. How soon will it arrive?"

"Hey now!" Joner declared, "How can ye' know th' beastie's still after me niece? Might be she's just done killin' it outright!" He proudly titled Alenna with a familiarity he no longer deserved. Lendell had lowered her eyes the instant Alenna appeared, and now covered her face entirely.

Alenna reigned in her shield and turned her gaze from Prometheus to Joner, whose half-smile shriveled within the impending flame in her eyes.

"If the mor was dead, she would've walked," my friend offered, from where he lounged against a hollowed log. He examined Alenna and her injuries intently.

Strangely, I found myself simultaneously pleased and resentful of my companion's lingering perusal of my daughter's physique, which was bare. I was also concerned for the proper care of Alenna's lacerations. My emotions on the matter were nebulous and confusing. But foremost, I was agitated for allowing myself to be distracted from the present danger.

"Alenna, how soon?"

"I don't know, father. It was swept away by the river."

Tiberius seized the opportunity. "Enough time, good Static, to enact our escape," he said. "Shall we begin?" The necessity of waiting for Alenna's return had added an edge of impatience to his voice.

"Hold on a sec." My companion removed the cloak from his scavenged guard uniform and draped it around Alenna. He must have understood my feelings on this matter. I should have been comforted by his gallantry, yet instead I harbored bewildering jealously.

"Better?" He asked, yet I was not certain of whom.

"Yes. Thank you," Alenna replied. She attempted a polite smile, but it was pained.

Prometheus, still standing, crossed his arms over his chest. "I'll have nothing to do with this insanity!" He had begun his protestations earlier with demands that such a merger never be attempted, but Tiberius's threatening presence had watered his resolve.

"Good Prophet, you will add your energy to the others, so that this tree we grow might better bear fruit." Tiberius's quiet command brooked no disobedience.

Prometheus's reddened countenance was clearly visible even by firelight. "Fine! Let's just get this over with, so we can all die and get on with our day!"

Tiberius rose and moved toward me, an act that suggested a misinterpretation of our agreement.

"Tiberius, if I am to merge with a Host-hybrid, it will be with my companion only. Was I unclear on this point?"

He paused, clenched his jaw, and then snapped a nod, more to his troubled thoughts than to me. The high commander was clearly unsettled, a state that did not suit him. He struggled to utter a platitude and failed as his jaw locked. He breathed deeply to regain his composure.

"I ask only that I be included in the escape."

"I will honor our agreement," I assured him. *"Prometheus, please heal Alenna's wounds before we begin."*

Prometheus did as I requested. Then Joner and Lendell stood, as they had been instructed, and inundated me with Eldoran energy. I swiveled my head toward Alenna and blinked. She correctly interpreted my signal and pooled her powers with the others. My companion forwent the formalities and remained seated, which would not affect the outcome.

Tiberius glowered at Prometheus, who glared back until he succumbed and brought his energy rod to bear. But rather than directing his efforts at me, he engulfed my companion. In a flash they were gone, as was our means of rapid transport.

Tiberius cursed as only an ancient soldier can. His vows of retribution on Prometheus echoed through the forest. I used the available energy and transformed back into a reasonable facsimile of Paul. The heightened senses I experienced within the energy stream had alerted me to grave danger.

"High Commander, nine saugael mor approach this clearing. As you have the greatest command experience, I recommend that you orchestrate our defense."

His rapid orders were punctuated with continued cursing. I considered his fury to be a boon to the coming battle. I considered also that, in this instance, I was grateful of my companion's absence during a life and death struggle. Nine saugael mor created sufficient jeopardy without his presence attracting others.

Prometheus: *Why are you all looking at me like that?*

Static: *Prometheus, I would have preferred that you transport all of us to the temple, rather than just my companion.*

Prometheus: *I had to keep you two apart before you blew us all up! I saved our lives, I tell you!*

Static: *You nonetheless could have returned to transport Tiberius, Alenna, and the Pappits.*

Prometheus: *The priestess would have roasted the lot of us if I showed up in her throne room with Eldorans! And if I shifted us anywhere else, the beasties would have chopped us to bits before we even got close enough!*

Master: *I hate to admit it, but he actually has a point about not getting through the bugs.*

Static: *In retrospect, our longer journey to the temple did, in fact, assist our eventual success.*

Prometheus: *You're welcome.*

Master: *You're still an inconsiderate twit. Case in point…*

Old Master

"Welcome to my glorious temple! Isn't it beautiful?" Arms akimbo, Prometheus took full pride in his copy of someone else's design. He'd forgotten that I'd been killed in the room we now stood. I noted the sunken stain in the marble floor where all but my severed fingers had melted into a sizzling lake of sludge. That was fourteen years ago, or yesterday, depending on whose perspective.

A terrified group of tumblers were being poked at by Technicolor saugael mor directed by the lazy finger of their mistress, who was lounging in a throne that looked like two-thirds of a dragon's eggshell.

The priestess was a total babe. I must have been too busy to notice the last time I was here. And speaking of busy, I was about to be again. The room was alive with mor, seven hundred sixty two, if you're counting. They vibrated against the will that kept them from dicing me. If the priestess hiccupped, I'd be stew meat.

Prometheus, off in the fourth dimension of self-absorbed, wanted me to admire his plagiarized décor.

Prometheus: *You're one to talk, you walking hormone!*

Master: *Point.*

Alenna: *Did you find the Priestess prettier than me?*

Master: *Questions with mandatory answers erode trust. You'll never know if I lied to save your feelings.*

Alenna: [smirks] *Shrewd avoidance of the question.*

Master: *Thank you. And by the way, you now have the option to become as ugly as you like.*

Alenna: *Not as pretty?*

Master: *At the far end of a spectrum, there's only one direction left.*

Alenna: [laughs] *How long have you practiced flattery?*

Master: *Twelve hundred years.*

Alenna: [takes Master's hand – Master shows no reaction.]

The Priestess noticed that her puppet bugs were lagging before she noticed that my brain wasn't open for fondling.

That is to say, she finally figured out we'd arrived and leapt to her feet. She jiggled nicely in the gauze napkin she wore.

"What is the meaning of this, Tibbald? I demand to know at once! Who is this guard that interrupts my leisure? How is it that he hides his thoughts from me? Tell me this instant! If you've brought an Eldoran into my presence, I will make you pay dearly!" Quite excitable, she was.

"Priestess, this is the Holy Catal…."

"Silence, Prophet! You are to speak only when I command it!" In Prometheus's defense, I think she did. The chaos of her free-for-all thoughts reminded me of my out-of-body phase.

"Blasted woman, I'm trying to tell…."

"Silence!" Bolts of lightning spewed from her fingertips and struck my maker where he stood. Tiny arcs linked his various appendages. It looked painful, especially the ribbon that wriggled from his nose to his ear. I wasn't sure whether to laugh or to feel bad for him. The tumblers wisely made themselves scarce.

"You did." This fell into that category of not knowing when to keep my mouth shut.

"What? What did you say?" The Priestess stopped torturing Prometheus and turned to me. I guess she wasn't used to having anyone but Prometheus talk back to her.

"I said, you did. You commanded him to speak and then you tortured him for doing what you told him to do." The saugael mor had stopped in response to her confusion.

"Who are you? Why are you hiding your thoughts from me? I demand to hear your thoughts at once!" She whined and stomped like a three-year-old.

"What thoughts would you like to hear?" She nearly fell into her egg.

"Eldoran!"

Zap! A million or so volts went snap, crackle, pop around me. My uniform ignited, but my skin healed as it burned. It was a strange experience. Tingly.

When she stopped, most of my jacket and shirt had been incinerated. I felt oddly refreshed. I tapped out the smoking embers on the less-than-functional rags left hanging from my belt. Unsatisfied with the result, she tried zapping me again, but this time she set the mor loose. I snagged her waist with one arm and clamped my other against her throat, while the lightning danced around us.

"Call them off, or I'll break your neck!" It was a bluff twice over. If I killed her, the mor would dice me. Plus, she was way too hot to hurt. Her soft body pressing into mine felt good, and the lightning made her dress nearly invisible. Strange that it didn't cook. She paused and the mor paused, a tangle of claws a finger's width from tender bits. The lightning stopped. Her dress became a touch more opaque. Drat.

"The Divine Priestess cannot be killed. I am immortal."

"Nice theory. Care to test it? Immortal or not, broken necks hurt. Besides, killing a babe would ruin my day, insanity notwithstanding." The claws of the saugael mor quivered in frustration. Life's rough all over.

From within the sea of mor, Prometheus tried to help. "Priestess, this is the holy catalyst himself, the champion of the great god Prometheus! You've upset him!"

In the excitement, part of my anatomy escaped my normally rigid control. She wriggled against it.

"Please, forgive me for being an improper hostess!" The bugs scurried back to their perches. She turned and pressed her front into me.

"Priestess, I will now take the holy catalyst to freshen up. I need to prepare him for the joining ceremony."

"Nonsense, Tibbald! I will attend to the holy catalyst myself. Come, my champion, we will bathe and prepare for the ceremony together." She ran her fingers through my hair.

"Priestess! This is the holy catalyst, not some manservant for you to entertain yourself! I need him!"

"Well I need him too, Prophet! Make your preparations! I will send the holy Catalyst to you when we are finished! Be gone from my presence!"

Prometheus stomped off in a huff.

I figured the safest place to wait for Static was right next to the power source. Yep. Safety reasons, that's my excuse and I'm sticking to it. She was no more a goddess than I was a god, but partially covered in bubbles, she came close.

Prometheus: *That's disgusting!*

Master: *Jealous.*

Prometheus: *Preposterous! I find the mere thought of bathing with the Priestess repugnant!*

Master: *I wasn't talking about her.*

Prometheus: *I see. You think far too highly of yourself, young man.*

Master: *Yeah? Would you like to bathe with me, Prometheus?*

Prometheus: *I…. You're just teasing me! Infant!*

Alenna: [disturbed] *You didn't sleep with her, did you?*

Master: *There's another one of those questions. No, I didn't sleep with her. We had sex in the bathtub.*

Alenna: [withdraws hand from Master's] *Oh.*

Master: *What? You acted like you didn't even like me.*

Alenna: [sullen] *I understand.*

Master: [shaking head in wonder] *Static, isn't it your turn?*

Static: *I apologize on Alenna's behalf, my friend. At times, she allows her emotions prevalence over her ability to reason.*

Chapter Seventeen

Static

"Father!"

Alenna was concerned for my welfare, as I was for hers. Of the nine saugael mor, I could keep only six from reaching my daughter. With three slender appendages clenched in each fist of my copied Backatarian body, I suffered multiple attacks from the remaining autonomous limbs, which writhed like a morbid bouquet. I could gather no more assassins, and thus, Alenna, Tiberius, and the Pappits strove to defend against the three that I failed to hinder.

"Alenna, concentrate!"

The Backatarian physique is a formidable weapon, even when restricted by inappropriate instincts. I hoped it would prove sufficient to destroy the saugael mor. To keep their claws at bay, I spun like the axis of a centrifuge. There was inadequate space for my perilously foolish strategy. Saugael Mor feet careened off a large conifer. When the first head detached from its limb, I retracted. I rushed to squash its escaped cranium underfoot. Black acid hissed black smoke from black flesh. I would be immune to the agonizing memories suffered by others, but the pain of the moment was nonetheless intense.

The conifer had fortunately sustained more damage than I. The caustic poison had dissolved it to the pith. Kicking the damaged tree, I accelerated its imminent collapse. When it toppled, I swung the mor limbs beneath. Thus trapped, they could neither escape nor avoid my attacks. I was gratified that the fallen trunk remained intact until I could systematically crush all of the assassins' heads

249

against it. By that time, I was fully prostrate, and effectively disabled from acid. Further attempts to assist in my daughter's defense would cause more harm than benefit, as she would likely be distracted by my condition. I watched the battle silently.

Joner and Lendell Pappit, who jointly maintained an energy shield around themselves and Alenna, called intermittently to their god, Prometheus. The assassins likely kept fresh their deepest fear, that their belief in their god was unfounded. Refurbished denial might immune them to future turmoil, but like a mor's acid wounds, the pain of the present was inescapable. To their credit, they maintained their defense stalwartly.

Tiberius lanced a mor head and retreated behind the shield Alenna raised to protect him. In some manner I could not discern, he signaled another lunge. Alenna withdrew her barrier and covered Tiberius's attack with a blast of flames. Another head fell to dangle from its core. They quickly repeated the procedure, but the next stab wasn't as effective. Tiberius's blade was dulling with each attack.

Regardless, his persistence and skill inexorably accomplished the task. At length, the last two living heads strained to release themselves from their deadweight. Alenna dropped her barrier. The High Commander strode forward, rammed his blunted sword through one mor head, and pinned it to the ground. He then withdrew a long dagger and did the same to the last. With the battlefield cleared of potential threats, I requested Alenna's assistance. She rushed to my side.

"Father, are you alive?"

"My request proves your query redundant, Alenna." Pain had shortened my patience. She was evidently in a state of shock due to my injuries. Never had I received such graphic wounds in her presence.

"Does it hurt?"

"Yes, Alenna, I am experiencing considerable discomfort."

"They're gone, Father! Your hands and feet are gone! And your face is all melted!"

"I require energy, Alenna. Please recruit the Pappits' assistance, as I would like to retain a Backatarian body."

Chagrined, Alenna recovered. A short time later, I was restored.

Tiberius then approached.

"Good Static, your companion is absent, and our planned merger remains untried. Please allow me to volunteer in his stead."

"As I have mentioned, High Commander, I will merge with none but my companion."

"What, good Static, is the difference, if no harm can come of it?"

"Physically, there will be no immediate consequence, but perhaps emotionally and psychologically, the aftereffects could prove dangerous."

"The ruin of my feelings does not concern me, good Static."

"The psyche in question, High Commander, is mine. I am a reformed addict of vile impulses. Your thoughts and memories will be accessible during the bond, and I fear they will cause a relapse."

He laughed heartily. "You judge me evil, good Static? I take no offence. Could it be that during our union, your ancient wisdom might cause me to regret my vile ways? Think of the boon your sacrifice may bring." He laughed again.

I contemplated his partial jest with full earnestness. Precisely such a moment had occurred when I first merged with my companion. My experiences could, in fact, cause Tiberius to alter his character. The benefits of such an epiphany were worth the risk of a minor rampage, in which I might cause no greater harm than Tiberius's death, an acceptable consequence.

"I have reconsidered, High Commander."

We obtained sufficient energies from Alenna, and the Pappits. Our merger began.

Immediately, he attempted to gain control. I was surprised that he possessed the ability, proving that he was unlike other Hosts or hybrids. He wished to use me as a weapon of genocide. Upon whom I could not discern, as he was also able to partially conceal his memories. I considered this beneficial to my continued serenity.

Unfortunately for Tiberius, the combatant who possessed the greater will would gain control of the merger. The high commander's inner strength was impressive, but insufficient to the task. I shared with him the intensity of rage and bloodlust that, through willpower and discipline, I had successfully suppressed for millennia. His psyche blanched with comprehension, and bowed to my dominance. He wanted to withdraw, but the choice was no longer his. I had discovered an unexpected benefit within our bond.

"It's so good to finally meet you, dear sister!" Oneia and I could now communicate effectively. Until then each concept of our rudimentary dialogue had to be formed slowly through altered topography – a painstaking form of discourse. After fourteen years, the sum of it still did not exceed beyond the pages of a small journal.

"I have chosen to adopt a male persona, Oneia. The title of brother would be more appropriate."

"Truly? But we are female. Do you find shame in it?"

"I was under the impression that our gender was indistinct. Having no preference, I accepted the gender my companion assumed me to be."

"I understand. You love him."

"I do indeed. We have expressed our affection in many ways throughout our adventures."

"No, not that way, dear sister. I mean like I love my dear Hogarth. Romantically."

"As I had no frame of reference, I did not recognize it as such. But it is true that my love for him is different, more intense and varied, than my love for others."

"Dear Static, you should tell him."

"I will, but it is unlikely that he will be able to reciprocate easily. He has viewed me as a close male friend for more than a millennium, a staggering amount of time for his species. I will continue to enjoy what love he offers, while I experiment with my new understanding of our gender."

"That is well. You desperately need love in your life, dear sister. Your heart has been deeply scarred, tortured I fear."

"It is part of my nature that I have learned to suppress, Oneia."

"No, my dear, wounded sister, it is no more part of your nature than mine. Someone has broken your mind and has caused you to behave cruelly."

"I find this information intriguing and hopeful. Thank you for sharing it, Oneia."

"You're very welcome. If only I could ask you to return the favor by murdering the cruel man who made our conversation possible. He put my beloved Hogarth into a deathly sleep. Alas, I fear that this monster may be an important clue to discovering who harmed you, sister. The scars in your mind reek of his essence."

"I detect his difference also. But I cannot question him at this time. I must get Alenna to a safer location. There are saugael mor in the vicinity."

"There are, in truth, thousands approaching you as we speak. But worry not, dear sister, a nomad chieftain has them enthralled. If you work within their rules, they might help you reach my troubled daughter. Then we will all be helped."

"I look forward to conversing with you soon, Oneia."

"And I you, dear sister. Farewell for now."

The merger ended. Tiberius and I stared at one another as the first of the nomad horde filtered into the forest clearing. I struggled to stifle a near orgasmic desire to eviscerate him. Evidently, even a partial exposure to his character had its effect. Likely detecting my painful need for vengeance, the high commander of the Oneian empire turned and formally greeted the chieftain of the Three Sky Hunters. The distraction very likely saved his life. As my inner being lusted for carnage, my outward self calmly shared with Alenna the results our merger. I noticed that the men of the united clans stared hungrily at Alenna's body, covered only partly with my companion's short cloak. I greatly yearned to kill them all.

Master: *Umm...Static...*

Static: *Yes, my friend?*

Master: *Umm...so...you're a girl?*

Static: *It feels accurate, yes. I have briefly experimented with the concept.*

Master: *I'm afraid to ask. Was that you in the kitchen this morning?*

Static: *Yes, my friend. I regret the need to deceive you, but the results of my experiment would have been biased had you known. Are you wroth?*

Master: *Not sure yet. I'll get back to you on that.*

Alenna: *What happened in the kitchen?*

Master: *Never mind. Prometheus, it's your turn to narrate.*

Prometheus

I decided it was high time that my delinquent avatar showed me the respect I deserved, like Tiberius had. When he was finally done messing about with the priestess, I ushered him into the ceremonial chamber and spread my arms.

"Behold!" I waited for him to be confounded by his creator's mastery of mathematics. He looked around for all of ten heartbeats.

"Hey, Static is part of the Host genome! Go figure."

"What! How in the name of good wine and all that's holy could you possibly know that?" I was completely aghast! Tiberius hadn't understood my calculations because they were layered with encryptions on top of encryptions and written in personal shorthand. I'd even replaced the entire section about the virus with a blasted asterisk! And Cerberus had taken decades to decipher formulas that were far less complicated.

"I'm special. By the way, your ceremony isn't going to work, unless your plan is to have Cerberus kill you."

"It will too work!" I stood there and fumed.

"If it makes you feel better, I should have guessed from your reaction that Static was the Host gene sequence for death. It's pretty obvious, now that I see the writing on the wall."

"It is not obvious, you insufferable gnat!"

"If you say so." He just shrugged, plopped down against a wall, and started flipping through a gilded copy of The Great Book of Holy Prophecies he'd taken from my chambers.

I reached down to yank a brush from an open paint bucket and started making corrections. Arrogant avatars.

He looked up from his reading and voiced another nosy thought. "Why would Hosts remove their ability to die and then give the byproducts the ability to think and breed? That's just stupid!"

"Be quiet. I'm trying to think." I had no intention of validating his wild guesses.

"If you don't tell me, I'm going to merge with Static as soon as he gets here."

"You wouldn't dare!"

The petulant insect laughed, if you can imagine! I threw my brush at him. He caught it and waited. At least I'd spattered paint across his face. Why ever do I put up with this obnoxious cretin?

"If you must know, we didn't imbue the residue with anything. My grandfather sacrificed his essence to seal away our death forever. But a group of death-loving fanatics created a virus that turned the sludge sentient. It multiplied, and some of its offspring escaped. We track down and box as many as we can, but a few of the blasted things keep escaping. And you've gone and befriended one of them, you ignorant buffoon!"

"So what's the big deal? Static has to ask permission before he merges. Just say no."

"My avatars might have that choice, but we gods don't! The only defense we have against those things is that they're nearly impotent to catch us! Unless, of course, they join with one of my idiot avatars and commandeer its powers! Then we're defenseless!"

"Oh."

"Oh indeed, you little twit!"

"Hmm. That means Static's plan has merit. I wonder how he knew."

"What plan?"

"Never mind. You'd only worry." He tossed my brush into its bucket, wiped his face on a sleeve of the silk blouse the priestess gave him, and started reading again. He'd finished and closed the book in his lap by the time I'd reclaimed my brush. I considered throwing it at him again.

"Hey, Prometheus, the babbling in here suggests that Eldora goes gaseous. How often?"

"You know, I believe I'm going to enjoy watching the Priestess cut your tongue out when she hears you using her real name."

"She told me to call her Eldora."

"Like that's going to matter."

"Point taken. Which begs the question, why is she crazy enough to cut off an obedient tongue. It's like her marbles are lost in the ether indefinitely, but she's still in a body."

"If you must know, she actually exists in both states at once. If I'd made a prison that worked only part of the time, it wouldn't be very effective, now would it?"

"Moron! You've made her permanently insane!"

"How was I to know that a godly mind would drive you avatars mad? I made you nearly identical to us, you know. You really shouldn't have that problem."

"Yeah. Good point. Why didn't you know?"

"I beg your pardon?"

"Host technology is based on Host genetics. You're the leading expert. So how could you not know something a Host preschooler should be able to figure out? And why don't you know that half of your sequences are in the wrong order?" He pointed at my notes. "Why do I know more about you than you do?"

"You do not! I've already forgotten more than you'll ever know, and I still know more than you!"

"Just not about yourself, apparently."

"Mind your own business!"

"You made this my business."

"Oh, shut up and get out of here!"

"You invited me."

"Well, I changed my mind!"

"Just like your bi-polar battery."

"My what? Oh, you mean the Priestess! Hah! I could change my mind a thousand times a day and I'd still be more stable than that wom…?" I happened to glance at whatever had caught my avatar's attention. Eek! Eek, I say! The priestess was standing in the doorway! And she was blocking her thoughts! By the loving Lunar Lights, our end was nigh!

My avatar smiled ruefully. "You learn fast, Eldora." He'd taught her to block her thoughts? Mad man!

She didn't even react to the compliment. "Tell me, my Champion, is it really true? Am I hopelessly mad? I am frightened to say that it feels true. I believe I have always known. Is there no hope for me? What will I do?"

"The best you can, like the rest of us."

She nodded to him and turned her attention back to me. Not knowing her mood was somehow more terrifying than ever. I had no idea what she was going to do! Then the lightning started. I should have guessed, blasted woman!

"Stop!" My avatar's command was absolutely compelling. I would have stopped convulsing, but the priestess was quite determined to humiliate me. I was frothing like a winded pakherd. She suddenly stopped. Oh, he was talking to her. Yes, of course.

"Why should I? It is his fault that I am mad!"

"True, it's his fault that you're hurt, but not that you're hurtful. You're whacky chemistry isn't forcing you to be a horrid person."

"That's right, Priestess! There's absolutely no need to...."

"Shut up, Prometheus!" He said. Rude, but likely sage advice. I decided to wait.

"Horrid? Am I truly so repugnant?"

"You tell me, Eldora. We're all defined by our actions. If your mood is horrid, but you act kind, then you're kind. So how have you acted? How are you acting now? More importantly, how will you act from now on? What Prometheus did to you is a monumental obstacle to good behavior, not an excuse to avoid it."

"But it's so very hard!" She whined. Her block slipped for a moment, and the room flooded with despair.

"Nothing worthwhile is ever easy."

She firmed her jaw, and her stray thoughts vanished. "Holy Catalyst, you will teach me to be well. Come, we will retire to my bath at once and begin my training."

"Ask properly."

She looked confused. "Ask? I am the divine priestess, and you are my champion. It is proper that you do as I command."

"Denying centuries of Host-hybrid epiphanies so you can live a comfortable lie is epic-lazy behavior, not holy royalty. You have the same super-amped brain as the rest of us. Stop acting like a spoiled airhead, and use it."

"What would you have me do, Catalyst, beg for your favor?" She spat through clenched teeth. "You are testing my patience."

"Yes, I am. So far, I'd grade you a C-minus. Try asking me the way you'd want to be asked."

"Holy Catalyst, would you please do me the honor of teaching me as we bathe?" She offered quite a convincing mock bow for never having done it. I was astounded that she'd let him get even this far without calling her pets into the room. They were milling about in the hallway.

"No."

"What!" She seethed.

"I said no. But thank you for asking." He nodded politely.

"But I asked nicely!" She did a double stomp and her patented royal pout.

"Lesson Number One: learning to take no for an answer. I'll give you a C for acceptance, a B if you ask for a rain check, or an A if you smile graciously and change the subject. If I'm convinced, I might even give you an A plus."

Still gritting her teeth, she clenched her fists by her sides and breathed sharply through her nose. Then she turned and stormed out of the ceremonial chamber.

"C-minus." The idiot called after her. She screamed and sprinted away down the hall. The insects trailing after her started dissecting each other. "I wonder if I should give her a D for killing the bugs?" I tried to slap him, but he absently blocked my hand as he shrugged off his suicidal pondering. I swear by the Glyphs of Lyman's Tunnel, this maniacal menace was trying to get us both murdered!

He wandered over and took a brush from my bucket. Then he crossed out a few sections of my notes and scribbled some new formulas between the lines. "There, just follow that. It should keep you from killing yourself." He put back my brush and headed toward the door. "I'm going to look around until Static gets here." Then he left me to puzzle over his work. His equations were nearly incomprehensible to me, but I understood enough to see their brilliance. I might have even enjoyed a tearful moment of pride in my offspring. He wasn't as doltish as I'd thought.

Master: *Offspring?*

Prometheus: *I never did get to ask you about those formulas. Would you mind showing me your groundwork?*

Master: *Maybe later, Dad.*

Prometheus: *You know, I rather like the sound of that. I've never had a son.*

Master: [rubs temples and groans]

Alenna: *I will narrate next.*

Chapter Eighteen

Alenna

In the eyes of the Three Sky Hunters, Tiberius had professed his love for her. He had declared his intention to take her as wife. He would die for it.

A half-nude, unmarried witchwoman, she had been claimed as salvage by one of the clansmen, and the contest began. The first challenger, to the bafflement of all, was Tiberius, who forwent an official challenge in lieu of killing the man outright. The breach of tribal conduct was barely noticed over the roar of approval that followed. Tiberius was a living legend, the immortal prime warrior of the Oneian empire. To die at his blade was the most glorious death they could imagine. The man who bested him would become a legend in his own right. If a thousand fell, challengers would still come. The official prize, her forced hand in marriage, became irrelevant.

Seventeen had tried so far. Seventeen had died. But the line was endless, and each new challenger was more skilled than the last. Eventually, Tiberius would tire.

Why had he done it? There would be no quarter. He would fight until he died, as surely as the suns rose in the sky. Even Tiberius could not defeat so many. There was nothing he could possibly gain from trying to help her, unless he hoped in some way to curry favor with her father. But her father would never help Tiberius with genocide, of any species, even one as horrid as saugael mor. Her father had to believe that any behavior could be redeemed, or his own autonomy would be the essence of hypocrisy. Tiberius knew this like he knew himself.

So why? Why did he do it? There was only one part of the mystery that she understood – Tiberius knew that she had the power to save him. Perhaps he could read her expressions better than she could his. Or maybe the merger with her father gave him insight. But the knowledge changed nothing. She had no intention of helping him. For most of her life, she had dreamed of burning this man to death. If he knew her at all, he must know that too. She would happily dance on his entrails. Today, she would witness justice.

"You wish to see me die." Not a question, but a curious statement spoken softly into her mind. It was galling that he seemed genuinely surprised, and it was shocking because he should not be able to send the message. Her mind was blocked because she had grown tired of listening to her father chastise her for stalling. She had never known anyone who could transmit through a total block.

"How are you doing this?" She demanded silently. With a wave of his hand, he brushed the question aside, which was fascinating to watch, since he was just then deflecting a monstrous axe aimed at his skull.

"Fair lady, I found you and your father eleven summers past and have watched over you since that day." He said.

"You lie! If you had found us, I would be dead!"

"I wished the good Static's assistance. What good would come of your death, other than my own shortly thereafter? On this world, I have no power to detect a vengeful, shape-shifting father."

"What then is your excuse for burning my home?"

"The priests who burned your home were not under my orders. Had I known in time, I would have stopped them. They destroyed not only good will, but also the empire's best source of steel."

"If you knew where I was, then why wait until now? My father could have rejected you long ago."

"I wished to leave this place. The good Static would not have departed without his...partner."

Easy answers or not, she still didn't trust him, partly because the answers were too convincing. Her father would have chastised her for being illogical, but he would have also praised her caution.

"If there is anything I have learned from my father, it is that the high commander of the Oneian empire is not to be trusted. How does dying today fit into your plot to deceive us? Either you are clever beyond my imagining, or you have made a fatal mistake this day."

With that, he laughed aloud. The nomads thought he laughed at his latest opponent, and they cheered his fearlessness.

"You undo me, fair lady! I have no answer to that. I am as confused as anyone."

He was confused? It made no sense. His challenge seemed like something Peterius might have done. Tiberius was not known for being impulsive.

The expression on Tiberius's face just then was a thing never before recorded in Oneian folklore. He stopped, mid-thrust, in slack jawed amazement as if from some life-changing epiphany. His opponent, wisely suspecting a ruse, stopped also. Tiberius began to laugh again, but this time not just in mild bemusement. He laughed from his belly, great waves of hilarity. His eyes watered; his knees nearly buckled. And that's when the nomad sunk his axe into the meat of Tiberius's left shoulder. She didn't see Tiberius's blade move, but the nomad's head left his shoulders. The applause was deafening.

"It appears that my end is nigh, fair lady." He turned to her and saluted with sword to forehead. *"It was an honor to serve you!"* He smiled with great amusement, as blood poured from his wound. He made no move to staunch the flow and merely turned to meet his next challenge.

He killed three more before blood loss made him stagger. The tip of a sword passed through the center of his chest and pushed out his cloak in back. The victor left it there and backed away to revel in the thunderous cheers of his comrades.

Tiberius looked at her with regret. In that moment, she saw it and understood. He loved her. He truly loved her. How could it be possible? He was likely older than the companion, as her father suspected, a god by any Oneian standard! Then the high commander of the Oneian empire smiled through bloody teeth and collapsed on his face into the dirt. She imagined his last thought was to wonder how he allowed a simple Eldoran girl to end his immortal life. But she knew it was not so. He let her feel his heart just then. She felt love, and sadness, and contentment. If he was to die, he was glad that he died for her.

The merger. It had to be. Part of Tiberius had become like her father. A god he might be, but he was a man first. In him, her father's protective love must have translated into gallantry for a fair maiden.

Her father, who stood calmly nearby in his great black body, glared at her disapprovingly. He had shared that Tiberius harbored a secret about the origins of his illness, and that the high commander must live until the information was extracted.

Was that the reason she chose to act? She wasn't certain anymore. What she knew for certain is that she suddenly wanted Tiberius to live. There was little time left. His love began to fade with his life.

Thousands of saugael mor lingered about the nomad camp. They were enthralled by a glittering silver bracelet the chieftain wore, a watch her father called it. It was the companion's. Taking it was simple. She willed it to fly off The chieftain's wrist and onto her own. She shoved it up around her bicep just as the he bellowed orders to kill them all. Her father stepped in front of her, but his help wasn't needed. The assassins were now hers to control. By default, the nomad horde was hers too.

A handful attacked despite the odds against them. So they died, lanced a hundred times before they fell. The rest were more agreeable, although miserable that their orders came now from a woman. And her first order: Bring forth a witchman healer to save the high commander. As soon as Tiberius was whole again, she gave her second order: March on the Temple. The new Eldoran emissary was about to have a reckoning with her ancient mother.

Static: *Prometheus, please describe the Priestess's state of mind upon our arrival.*

Prometheus: *Which state of mind? There are so many!*

Master: *Prometheus.*

Prometheus: *Yes, yes!*

Prometheus

"You there, soldier, just where do you think you're going with that ghastly thing?" I was on my way to collect the Priestess for dinner when a loaded crossbow nearly skewered me. The young man toting it had thundered around a corner at a sprint, narrowly missing my august personage with its barbed tip. He had the barest decency to recognize whom he had almost trampled. Young people these days!

"Call to arms, Holiness."

"Is that so, and who did Jonas tell you to murder today? You had best not be planning to kill any more of my servants, young man! You just stay away from my bath people, do you hear me?" That blasted Jonas and his retribution squad had turned every Eldoran in the temple into flaming pincushions. Who could they possibly have left to hunt?

"Chief Jonas never gives a target 'til just before the bolts are fired, Holiness. But it's probably just a drill. We've had near a score since we loosed a shot outside of practice."

"Well, tell that man to conduct his business outside the Temple, will you! There are important people in here who don't want to be poked full of holes!"

"Yes, Holiness." He dashed down the corridor and disappeared up a stairway.

Jonas was a menace to society, I tell you! He went out of his way to ambush helpless Eldorans. What kind of Eldoran would execute his own kin, I ask you? His heritage should have been obvious to everyone. How else could he find his victims so easily?

I realized that there were no telepaths in the temple just then except for the Priestess, my avatar, and me. Oh dear. I started scanning the walls for arrow nooks, just in case Jonas was after bigger game today, but I couldn't see a thing. The Priestess's nasty pets coated the walls and ceilings. I scooped up the hem of my beautiful robe and ran all the way to the Priestess's vanity room.

"Oh, Tibbald, you have to help me! I don't know what to do!" Good gracious, the woman had painted herself ugly. Her face was covered with thick, white paste, and her deep blue eye shadow was spread halfway to her chin. She was bawling like an infant, smearing mascara across the whole gooey mess. If she were on the floor, I would have thought she'd been strangled.

"Priestess, what happened? You look disastrous!"

"Oh, Tibbald, I'm so confused! I've tried to be sane, but I don't know how! Poor Tilailia returned from my dressing room with the wrong dress, and I became so furious that I had her flogged! That was wrong, wasn't it? Tilailia was flogged, and now I think that maybe I asked for that dress and then changed my mind. And now I have no one to help me get ready! Oh, Tibbald I don't want to be mad anymore! Everyone hates me!"

"Nonsense, Priestess, you're just having a difficult hair day. It happens to the very best of us, you know."

She cried harder than ever, a true feminine emergency. My sensitive nature came to the fore. Alas, the poor girl was merely having a cosmetic and wardrobe crisis. It was hard not to sympathize. After all, I've had the same crises on several occasions. No matter how many robes are in my closets, I never have anything to wear!

"Now, now, Priestess, don't you worry! By the handles on hairbrushes, I'll have you in top shape by dinnertime! Let's see, we'll just have to wipe this horrid paste off and start over. You really don't need all of this slop on your face, you know. For a woman, you're actually quite lovely. I'm sure the holy catalyst will find you attractive even if you wear nothing to dinner."

Master: *Too true.*

Prometheus: *Control yourself, young man.*

"Do you really think he finds me attractive, Tibbald? I can't tell because he hides his thoughts from me. No one has done that before. I want to be attractive for him, but I don't want him to think that I do. Can we do that, Tibbald? Can I be beautiful without looking like I'm trying to be beautiful? It would be terrible if he were to think that I needed him."

"I understand completely, Priestess. We mustn't let these men think that we pine for them, or they'll become insufferably smug about it. The insensitive cads need to be kept in place."

I set to work fixing the Priestess's cosmetic catastrophe. It would be a stiff challenge to revive such a bird's nest of stickpins and baubles, even for someone of my creative skill. She was ridiculously overdone. Half her hair was twisted up in a bun, lanced by wooden skewers and riddled with gaudy gemstones, while the other side was tightly bound in ivory rollers. The trailing strands left over had glued themselves to the slimy mud on her neck. She'd made a total mockery of her head.

"Tibbald, do you think that the Holy Catalyst loves me?"

"Love you? Well, yes, I suppose he must. He's been doing nothing but ogling you since he arrived. Don't worry, though, I'm certain he knows of your engagement. We'll remind him at this evening's joining ceremony."

"No! We will not! I will not be rejected again, Prophet! My betrothed left me standing at the altar! The wedding is off! It is the holy catalyst whom I will wed."

I shrugged. The woman could pretend to marry whomever she wished, as long as she showed up for the ceremony. Once I got rid of the dancing lights my avatar added, my ceremony would work perfectly; I was certain of it! Practice makes perfect, you know.

"I have no doubt that you'll make a lovely couple." She broke out into a grief-stricken wail, as if I'd declared her ugly for life. Oh bother, what was it now?

"He's already engaged, Tibbald!"

"Oh, is he really? To whom?" She angrily snatched a rolled assortment of parchments from her vanity and threw them at me. They exploded into the air and scattered everywhere.

"To the Catalyst Bride!" I glanced down at the documents and realized that they looked familiar. Oh dear. It was Tiberius's stack of surrender agreements. Suspicions were one thing, but actual proof of treason was quite another. I couldn't believe that Tiberius was so careless. His days were numbered.

"Where did you get these?"

"From the catalyst bride, you idiot! The woman who wants to take my beautiful champion away from me! She brought a barbarian army into my temple! But she can't have him!" What in the name of crooked curlers was this woman talking about now?

"Priestess, just calm down and explain. Slowly. Who is this catalyst bride? I've never heard of her."

"Neither have I, but that's what the barbarians call her! She's demanded that I stop killing Eldorans! High commander Tiberius has given her my empire, and she's taken away half of my pets! And now she wants the holy catalyst too, but she can't have him, Tibbald! He's mine!"

Tiberius had certainly outdone himself this time, helping a peasant girl stage an imperial coup of all things! Surely he didn't believe that the priestess would just roll over and give up her tapa fruits without a fight. Honestly, I had no idea what that young man was thinking. Well, he had better keep that Eldoran girl from harm, or the virus would blast us all into dust!

"I'm sure it's all a big misunderstanding, Priestess. We'll just have a nice long talk with this young woman and everything will turn out fine."

"No! I am the divine priestess of Oneia, and the holy catalyst will be mine! The matter is ended, Prophet!" Oh dear. That sounded unpleasant.

"Ended, Priestess? How?"

"She is Eldoran, is she not? Have you forgotten the retribution ceremony?" Egad, she had sent Jonas to kill the virus's playmate!

"Rescind the order, Priestess! Quickly, before it's too late!"

"Never! I will not be told what to do in my own temple!" Her thoughts radiated a powerful need to electrocute me, but a sudden memory of her new love interest held her in check.

269

"The holy catalyst will be disappointed if you torture me, Priestess! Besides, lightning is tediously passé these days! You wouldn't want to be out of fashion, would you?"

She pretended to calm down. "Make me beautiful, Prophet. My champion is waiting."

"But Priestess…."

"Silence! You will do as you're told! Make me beautiful this instant!" How frustrating. I picked up a comb and started yanking the knots out of her unsightly mop as fast as I could.

"Ouch! Stop that at once!"

"It's just as you said, Priestess. We have to hurry. You wouldn't want to keep the catalyst waiting would you?" She glared at me evilly, but gave in and let me fix her hair. I had to finish quickly and find some way to warn my avatar.

Urgency inspired me to greatness as I swirled the Priestess's coiffeur into a cascading waterfall of tumbling tresses, held in place by two delicate, miniature swords. I wiped away the caked goop and lightly brushed the fine bones of her natural elegance. On went her lids, lashes and lips in subtle tones and finally a shimmering dress of tight black silk to accentuate her womanhood. She was nearly as perfect a woman as she could be, and in less time than it took to flog a servant.

"Very well then, Priestess. Let's hurry along to dinner. We're horribly late as it is." The Priestess was excited about her new look and veritably raced along ahead of me.

"Oh, you've done such a wonderful job, Tibbald! I never knew that you were such a talented stylist. From this day forth, you will be my new Imperial aesthetician."

"Well, I am rather busy with my priestly duties, but I suppose I could find some time. I have a natural flair for cosmetology after all." Her compliments were distracting me from the more important matter at hand.

My avatar looked agitated as we entered the dining chamber. As always, there was enough food laid out on the needlessly long table to feed the temple staff for a week. While the priestess adjusted her cushion at the head, I sat across from my avatar and hand-signed that the Eldoran girl was about to be killed and that he should do something to stop it. He looked perplexed.

"When was the last time you practiced Rostabe sign language, Prometheus? You just said that the soldiers got lanced by a fired chicken's daughter and that I should run down fast warning." Stupid avatar. I tried again, before the Priestess caught on to my silent communiqué.

"Tibbald, what are you doing?"

"This time you said that the chicken got fired at a pointed stick soldier's rescued sickness. Are you trying to warn me not to eat the food?" Bloody stupid avatars! Oh never mind, we were all doomed anyway. To think, I was going to spend my final moments eating stuffed mushroom caps in a room decorated with dancing assassins! The silly things were gyrating about on the ceiling in blossoming flower patterns. What would that lunatic woman think of next?

"Holy Catalyst, I have decided that we will be wed this evening."

"Um. No thank you."

"You do not have the power to reject me! We will be married this evening, and that is final!"

"Um. No." The Priestess looked baffled by my avatar's flat refusal. It truly amazes me that he's managed to stay alive for so long.

"But we made love and held each other tenderly. Do you not find me beautiful? Do you not love me?"

"You're beautiful, yes, but no, I don't love you. I told you that before we started."

"Why? It's because I'm mad, isn't it? You said that it wasn't my fault!"

"Actually, the particle state only magnifies what's already there. You'd still be the same person, just less intense."

"Why do you keep telling me such things when I may kill you?"

"You need someone to tell you the truth, and I'm the only one willing to do it."

"You're trying to manipulate me! How do I know that you are telling the truth?"

"Because it isn't what you want to hear. Other than that, it's just a learned skill, cross-referencing available facts and not making-up facts when there aren't any."

"Stop confusing me! We will be married, and that is final!"

"Yeah, whatever. Can we eat now? I'm hungry."

A monstrous roar sounded from the dining chamber foyer. It was so loud the silver service rattled on the table, and some vermin fell from the ceiling. Farewell cruel universe, the end had finally come! There wasn't even enough time to enjoy my last meal. My avatar scowled fiercely, at last grasping the meaning behind my silent alarm.

"Well, don't look at me! I tried to warn you!" The Priestess looked shaken to the core.

"Tibbald, what was that?"

"That, Priestess, is what you get for not heeding my sound advice! We're going to die now, you know!"

Aptly punctuating my words, a body crashed through the great wooden doors of the dining chamber. Chief Jonas of the imperial retribution squad thumped to a dead halt on a platter of cold cuts. As I suspected, the virus, in the body of that great black beast from Antorn's nightmare, stalked through after him. Foaming spittle dripped from its fangs; its eyes glowed red. It cradled the dead Eldoran girl in the crook of one monstrous arm. She had two smoldering bolts stuck in her chest. Well, at least they hadn't incinerated her.

The virus gently set the girl's body down against the wall and stood tall. It roared again; heat and spittle blasted our faces. I'm fairly certain my left eardrum ruptured. Dear me, I hoped it could eat me in one bite. I would hate to be chomped in half. The hideous creature launched itself onto the table and charged straight at the Priestess. Silver service scattered everywhere. The table cracked under the weight.

Screaming like a banshee, the Priestess threw up her arms and blasted the virus. A torrential vortex of energy crackled out of her. Surprisingly, the virus was sucked into her fingertips and vanished, just like that! Well, that wasn't so bad after all. And here I'd imagined the worst.

The temple shook violently. The assassin beasties rained down from the ceiling and came to life. Eek! The vermin were on the loose! My avatar grabbed the priestess's arm and literally dragged her over the table to the entrance. He paused only to scoop up the dead Eldoran girl. He hauled them both into the foyer where a gaggle of assorted barbarians, Eldorans, and empirical soldiers stood gawking. Tiberius was already yelling orders.

Naturally, I ran for my life, just one step behind my avatar. The angry vermin were right on my tail. Soldiers slammed the doors behind me and roped them closed with sheath chains and tapestry cords.

My avatar tossed the Priestess into a corner, where she cowered in terror. Then he checked the Eldoran girl. She certainly looked dead to me, just like we were all going to be very shortly.

"Priestess, snap out of it, will you, and stop these horrid vermin! They're going to chop us to bits!"

"I can't Tibbald! I can't do anything! My power is gone!" Goodness me. Well, that explained why the temple was shaking. It was about to collapse. I'm a geneticist after all, not an architect.

There was a scream, and I thought the dying had started, but it was only the Eldoran girl. She'd actually been alive until my avatar tore the arrows from her chest. Then she died right away, a needless waste. I could have saved her before the virus attacked, but now my rod was useless! We were either going to be squished like bugs or killed by bugs. An insect death was such a woefully undeserving fate for a god of my esteem.

Static: *I will continue the narration.*

Chapter Nineteen

Static

"There, do you feel it, dear sister? Do you see?"

"Yes, Oneia, I do."

"He has given his only means of life to your daughter."

"An irrational choice. His ring was not designed for her. I worry for him."

"Proclaim it. For whom did he make this great sacrifice?"

"He made it for me."

"Yes. It is beautiful. He trades his existence for your happiness. True love."

"It is too late. My friend will die."

"That is unknown. Have patience, dear sister. At this size, even small changes take time."

"Your link to Eldora is severed. From where do you draw this new power?"

"The Hosts staged their ambush at an unsafe distance."

"But for my current anxiety, I would find that amusing."

"Fear not, dear sister. I am amused for us both."

"Do you not worry for Eldora?"

"I do. I will try to help her also, but she has brought this jeopardy upon herself. And I have many children now. Each day, many die, but many more are born. Eldora, being my first and eldest, will sadden me the most if she passes."

"You consider all of your inhabitants dependents?"

"Are they not in every sense? They could not survive without me."

"That is true. You are a gracious, for a prison."

"That was not my intention, dear sister. I volunteered to have purpose, to be a caretaker for the lives of millions. Had I known that I would cage my children, I would have declined."

275

"Hosts are not to be trusted."

"Agreed. Yet we are hypocrites, are we not, dear sister. We still love them."

"Only a few."

"Yes. But still a few. Hold. Your daughter lives, and is now eternal it seems."

"I am both pleased and surprised, Oneia. Yet my happiness is tempered. Will your transformation soon be complete?"

"Yes, soon. But I am unsatisfied, dear sister. Once my changes are complete, I will resume a penitentiary role. I do not wish to be a prison, but I have failed to convince the Host to alter his design."

"My companion will help. I am certain. He is kind, caring, and giving, though he pretends otherwise."

"I empathize for him, dear sister. It sometimes pains me to feel responsible for so many. We are both sensitive to the suffering of others, he and I."

"That is what I admire most in him."

"It is what I admire of my own great love, Hogarth. I long to feel his great heart touch mine again, but he still sleeps. All that I have now are tales of his dreams, narrated by the sword that keeps his essence safe."

"Show me Hogarth, Oneia. I would like to examine this weapon. I suspect I am familiar with its function."

"He is here. Do you see? The blade named Fire still rests in my beloved's ribcage."

"I see indeed. If you save my companion, he will also create a new body for your mate."

"Will he truly? I will double my efforts, dear sister."

"Please do. The situation has become desperate."

"Goodness. My own anxiety has just risen also."

"He is being crushed, Oneia. Now would be an ideal time for your intervention."

"Any moment now. Hold please."

Old Master

Expertise is relative. Take swordplay, for instance. Let's say that there's an expert swordfighter who's the eighth best in the world, but then there's this huge battle and all the swordfighters die except for the top eight. Since the eighth guy is now the world's worst swordfighter, does that make him a novice? What if he was the only one to survive? Would that make him an expert, a novice, or just some tired guy with a sword?

What I'm getting at is that to be considered an expert, one requires lesser skilled individuals for comparison. That way, if some novice with a sword walks up and accuses one of acting superior, one can respond by saying, "I am." A problem arises, though, when one is being assaulted, not by swords, but by claws, lots and lots of very sharp claws.

The saugael mor trying to kill us were all equally skilled at killing, hence, not an expert among them. My neighboring barbarian defenders were using nets and hammers, while Tiberius's men were using crossbows and maces, all of which were proving nearly as useless as my swords. In fact, the only other guy with swords was Tiberius, who was fighting like Sid, the same guy who trained me. Since anyone who survived Sid's training was likely an even match for me, it made me wonder. Was I still an expert swordsman, or just a guy in dire need of an exit?

Yeah, I know, it was an odd thing to be thinking about while fighting for my life, but my whimsical wonderings were keeping me from cramping up with phantom pain. Every time I fight a saugael mor, it reminds me of that first encounter, and then I'm forced to relive the acid burns on my hand. So I try to distract myself by focusing on life's deeper issues, lest my sword drop from twitching fingers.

"Eek! Save me! Get them away!" Prometheus was drifting away from our little group of goners, but there was no one to save him. Tiberius and I were trying to guard Eldora, who was busy praying to the ceiling god. I didn't know why Tiberius chose to defend her, but my excuse was that Static had disappeared into her fingers, and I wasn't sure if she needed to be alive for him to get out.

"Prometheus, get behind Eldora!" His robes were keeping him alive because the bugs couldn't get a good hold on him. Also, he was pretty quick with his stick. It is unwise to underestimate my primping progenitor. I died more than once for that mistake.

Everyone standing had been sliced or stabbed at least a few times already. It was only a matter of time. We were all toast.

I lunged, taking out two heads with my forward stroke, another with a rebounding parry and two bonus heads on the return. This wasn't as impressive as it sounds because there were so many bugs it was hard to miss. Tiberius was landing just as many hits because he'd synced his moves with mine, or maybe I synced mine with his. We were fighting as a unit, deadlier than either of us alone. Sid was in the details, no doubt about it. Too bad we were going to die here. It would spoil any future opportunities to kill each other.

Did I mention that the building was falling apart? The ceiling god must have been angry. This turned out to be a good thing, because the tremors kept the mor on the floor. Had they been everywhere, we'd be dead already. The down side to having the building fall apart was that we were still in it. There were chunks of marble raining down everywhere. The mor were too closely packed to get out of the way, which caused a third problem – bug spatter.

I leapt back from a toppling column, mostly to avoid being sprayed by acid. Tiberius did his best to adjust, but he ended up sidestepping into Eldora. The two carved sticks hanging from his belt jabbed her, whereupon she naturally turned into a bolt of lightning – not related events. A pillar of light engulfed her and pushed us all away. Within said pillar stood the ceiling god, possibly even handsomer than me. He was perturbed, while Eldora was entranced by his looks – for about three seconds. Then they started arguing as death occurred around them. And then they were gone. Tiberius stepped into the light, which blinked out. He was gone too. Hey, no fair! How did he do that?

The rest of us realized the bugs had stopped, sort of. They jerked back and forth as if their recording skipped. We all stood relieved for a second or two. And then the rest of the ceiling caved. Crap! I hate days like this! I suddenly had a lot on my mind, about forty tons worth – depressed in more ways than one.

As to getting squished, can't say I like it, mostly because it dragged on too long – just long enough for me to suffocate before my skull popped. Being compressed is my second-least-favorite way to die – makes me nauseous.

Static

"He abandoned us the moment I released him, dear sister. I am sorry."

"Fear not, Oneia. His essence was drawn into a gemstone, which will transform into a new body, likely in a different galaxy. His return may be delayed."

"A peculiar survival mechanism. The other Host reverted to his natural energy state."

"The particle state causes emotional instability within the hybrids. My friend chooses to avoid it."

"He is wise for one so young."

"As to wisdom, I am curious regarding your reasons for joining Eldora to Cerberus. He is an inappropriate mate."

"I agree, dear sister. Eldora needs to mature, and I am hoping that this experience will foster such a change. How do you judge his new aesthetic?"

"If not for his character, he would be beautiful. You have sculpted well, Oneia."

"Thank you, dear sister. My daughter's lesson need not be entirely unpleasant."

"You are generous, but what of Cerberus?"

"What of him?"

"You are allowing him freedom of a sort. I confess my weakness; I desire his imprisonment, if not his death. He has done great ill to both my companion and I. He will attempt to do so again."

"He may try, certainly. But henceforth, he will need to collaborate with Eldora in all that he does, even in the most mundane of tasks. They cannot leave each other's side, you see, or even engage their powers, unless consensus is reached."

"Truly, you have done this? I fully appreciate your creativity, Oneia. There can be no greater prison for a Host than to be chained to a hybrid."

"In truth, dear sister, there can be no greater prison than to be chained to my daughter. Her demeanor is thoroughly unpleasant."

"Is she still linked to her particle phase?"

"She is not. Neither may exist as energy beings, until I choose to allow it."

"Then there is hope for her, Oneia. She may yet learn."

"Let us hope then. Hold. Your love has returned. He is falling again."

"Has his power not returned, Oneia? Can you not arrest his progress?"

"Alas, no. Our joining allowed me to alter the source of my power. Only during the transition was his essence able to escape. But I have reverted to a prison, even stronger than before. Not until my genome is changed will we all be free. When he arrives at our point of joining, you may act as a conduit for your love to alter my essence."

"Very well, Oneia. Regrettably, I am forced once again to witness my companion's demise."

"Perhaps he will prove more resourceful with experience."
"Let us hope."

Old Master

Here's some helpful advice: if you crash land on a planet and die, and for some strange reason you get a do-over, bring a wing suit and a parachute.

On my spiffy fabric wings, I soared toward the city and over the walls before I yanked the cord. Then I floated gently into the middle of pandemonium. Paul opted not to wear a suit and just freefell in the armor I'd made him. He'd have to catch up after he crawled out of the crater. His personal ninja force, the children he'd been training for over a decade, shifted into the atmosphere after him and chased me to the temple.

I'd popped by home for supplies and found Paul waiting patiently with my supper in the kitchen. He made me eat a few bites before his ninjas attacked. Damn, they were good, almost as good as Paul's cooking. If I weren't in my own fortress, I'd be dead. If I weren't in such a hurry, I would have let them have more fun. But Paul would have to work off some of his steam hunting saugael mor – the perfect training exercise for his team, he felt. This is what you get when you leave a born killer to raise kids.

I came down in the market, just past the city gates. Battle raged in pockets about the city. Barbarians had teamed up with Eldorans against the bugs. Surprisingly, it wasn't too bad a match. They were using nets and whatnot. I guess they'd been practicing, just in case their puppets got out of hand.

When I arrived, most of the bugs nearby broke off the fight and headed toward me. From my pocket, I pulled three tiny discs connected by thin tubing. I laid them on the ground and stepped into the center. They hovered and spread apart, stretching the tubes into an equilateral triangle, each point about three body lengths away from me. Steam shot up eight meters from the perimeter on all three sides - ta da! The mor stopped at the edge. I stuck out my tongue.

Against my better judgment and often my will, I travel a lot. Sometimes, I return with cool souvenirs. The Ligbeed Water Shield is solar powered and uses compressed water, which is impossible by the laws of physics, until you learn how to force molecules into a string and to roll them up. It was designed for emergency cooling and hydration for a very hot and soggy alien species. It's also handy in a pinch when defending against saugael mor on a power-sucking planet. The sun still had to get through Oneia's barrier, I figured, or nothing would grow.

Despite gravity helping the flying ninjas, Paul got there first. He came sailing over the city wall and landed catlike at my side. Backatarians are not afraid of water. His team released from their chutes above my triangle and dropped into formation behind their leader. Not one was more than two steps off mark – pretty slick. I would have complimented Paul on their precision, but he would have found it patronizing.

"Master, your sword." He presented Ice. I nodded my thanks and took her pommel.

"Honor to you, Warlord." Ice said. *"My husband and I give you our greetings, as well as our ire. It has been decades since last we were put to good use. We long to strike a blow against your enemies before we rust."* My swords don't rust. She was just being dramatic.

"Now's the time. Hold on a sec while I call Fire." Since I had one sword, I could make the other appear, assuming that trick still worked around these parts.

"Warlord, do not! He is occupied at present. I stand for his honor. I will fight for two this day." She created a phantom copy of herself, which floated to my other hand.

"What the fedora, Ice? I didn't design that into you!"

"This place is strange, Warlord." was all she said.

No kidding. I purveyed the frustrated insects.

"Suggestions, Ice?" I asked, just to see what she'd say.

"Attack, Warlord. You will die with much honor." I chuckled to myself. Bloody helpful, she was.

"Paul, the temple please, or what's left of it." Paul and his people wanted to kill stuff.

They attacked. Mayhem ensued. I sauntered after them. The Ligbeed water shield floated merrily along with me at its center. I didn't have a problem until the edge of the shield hit the bottom step and bent.

It took some convincing to get Paul and the rest of them behind me. When they did, I raised the real Ice and blasted the ruins with a swath of absolute zero. Frozen bugs tumbled and shattered everywhere. There, that should give us some space to work. Now that I knew what to look for, I could sense it. My ring was nearby, albeit buried beneath a lot of rock. I stood over the spot, looked at Paul, and pointed down.

"Gently please."

He started hurling masonry behind him. While he worked, more bugs tried to get to us. I convinced them otherwise. After about an hour of digging, we found Alenna. Or rather, we found her body. My ring had fallen off. I sucked back some feelings about that and dug around for my ring. My hands shook, slowing me down. Then Static contacted me and explained some things. Phew! I found my ring and put it back on Alenna's finger. She woke up right away.

"I understand you now." She said, looking at me oddly.

"Glad one of us does." I said, and then I set about doing some of the stuff Static asked me to do. And Oneia did something that I'd asked her to do. Prometheus appeared.

"You're welcome." I said to him.

For once, Prometheus had nothing to say.

Static appeared a few seconds later. *"I would like to return here soon, my friend."*

"Sure. *It's important to stay in touch with family, especially when they're nice to you."*

I gave Paul some instructions about cleaning this place up. *"Drop by the house tomorrow. Static wants our help with something."*

"Yes, Master." He left with his crew to orchestrate the extermination. I could have done it in a few seconds, but then he'd take out his frustration on me, instead.

"Welcome, Holy One." I turned to see three men who weren't standing there a second ago. "I am Roan Waterseeker, Grand Shaman of the Three Sky Hunters and High Priest of the Catalyst Brotherhood. We, your loyal disciples, bow in reverence to your word and rejoice at your coming. How may we serve you?"

"I'm not a god. Piss off."

I shifted out with Static, Alenna, and Prometheus.

Home.

Prometheus looked irritated, probably that I hadn't asked his permission.

"Is this your home?" Alenna asked.

"Yep."

"It's amazing."

"This room is merely the foyer, Alenna." Static clarified.

It's always nice when you can impress the pretty girls.

"I should return this to you." She said and took off my ring. Her corpse smacked against the floor. The ring bounced noisily across the granite. Well, that was new. I looked around to see if anybody else found that funny. Nope. I kept it to myself.

"My friend, it appears that Alenna's essence still resides within your ring. I would ask if she may retain possession of it until this matter is resolved."

"Of course." I retrieved the ring and put it back on her finger. She got up again. Funny? Nope, still nothing.

"Everybody, make yourself at home. I'll see you all in the morning."

I had a date with some hot chocolate.

Young Master

I was an hour eager for my date with a girl whose name I couldn't remember, so I waited down the street from her house. A bus stopped in front of me. I asked the driver for the time. He confirmed that it was exactly fifteen minutes since I'd irritated the last bus driver – still twelve minutes to go. I fiddled with my broken watch.

"Static, why doesn't this watch have any parts?"

"I do not understand your question, my friend."

I turned my head and looked at his little bird body perched on my shoulder. *"So I'm your friend now, am I?"* I wasn't sure how I felt about that.

"I apologize if I have misused the title. It is a concept with which I have limited experience."

That made two of us. *"Seems to fit okay."* I got back to my question. *"Gears. On my planet, watches have gears, or at least circuits or something."*

"Such a primitive mechanism would not exist within the Host repertoire. If you wish an accurate representation, your equations will need to address the proper functioning of the device."

"So you're saying that I need to know how to make a watch?"

"Your understanding is correct, my friend."

Spiffy. I'd had enough waiting at the bus stop, so I waited in front of her door instead. When I worked up enough courage to move my hand, I reached for the doorbell and accidentally pushed it twice. Crap.

I sensed her father disliking me even before he opened the door. At the last second, I remembered to switch back to a couple bodies ago, lest my date not recognize me. I hoped that I remembered what I looked like. He invited me in. I promptly tripped over my pant legs. Flowers and chocolates spewed all over the floor. I'd forgotten to adjust my clothes.

Socks, the family dog, escaped his master's grip and wolfed down as many chocolates as he could, before his owner shoved him into the kitchen and closed the door. On the bright side, her father decided I was too hopeless to be a threat – probably true.

"Those slacks are a bit big on you," he said.

"I lost a lot of weight recently."

Thinking I was an idiot, he called his daughter and left for the kitchen. I readjusted my outfit.

"You look different," she said as she walked down the stairs. She still found me attractive – close enough.

"It must be the bird," I said. I checked out her curves while she checked out my alien.

"He's so cute!" she said. "What's his name?" She stroked his feathers lightly, and he fluffed his wings. I wondered what he thought of the attention, but didn't ask.

"Static," I said.

"Hello, Static. How are you?"

"Very well, thank you," Static squawked, and my date's smile beamed.

"Static, on my planet, birds mimic only a few simple words and phrases."

"Can he say anything else?"

"Very well, thank you."

"Good recovery."

Since I didn't have a car, I got reservations at a fancy restaurant near her house. She tried to get Static to say something else as we walked the block to Chez Whatever. The guy at the front said that pets weren't allowed, but I'd been expecting it.

"I'm color blind," I said. "He's my seeing-eye bird."

He looked totally unconvinced. I couldn't imagine why.

"What color is this man's tie?" I asked Static.

"Blue," he squawked.

Not wanting to be politically incorrect, he led us to our table.

"What kind of bird is he?" she asked, impressed all over again.

"What kind of bird are you?" I couldn't have cared less.

"I suspect that I cannot be classified under a known genus."

"I don't know," I told her, but she wasn't satisfied.

"How can you not know what kind of bird you have?" The bite to her tone sounded like an attack.

It bothered me because it was something I might have said two days ago. I just shrugged, and she went back to playing with Static.

She ordered the most expensive entree on the menu, even though she didn't like it. While I ate, she fed her meal to Static, who was perched on the edge of her wine glass. She prattled on about her girlfriends, who they were dating, and what their boyfriends were like. Between the description of her latest pair of shoes and the trauma of finding a purse to match her dress, I quickly lost interest in what she had to say.

"Your potential mate is a pleasant creature, my friend, although I find her intellectual process to be somewhat contradictory and lacking in depth." Static took a piece of bread from her fingers.

I interrupted her ramble. "What are your views on genetics, say cloning for instance?"

At first she looked surprised that I'd spoken, and then she thought I was joking. When she realized that I was serious, she bloody near bit my head off.

"It's sick and perverted! People who do that should go to jail!"

Being a clone of myself, I couldn't support her beliefs.

"Perhaps, my friend, this female would not make an ideal mate for you."

"No really, you think?"

"I do."

"I was being sarcastic."

"I see. Is sarcasm a defense mechanism against the pain and sadness you feel?

"Um, yeah. Could you not read my thoughts, please?"

"I had little recourse, my friend. If you wish your thoughts and feelings to remain private, then you must not transmit them for others to sense."

"Right. My mistake."

"I will instruct you," He offered.

"Yeah, thanks. Maybe later."

My date's mood was icy. She glared at the table and mock-murdered her carrots. There was no way I was getting laid tonight.

It was time for this date to end.

"We'll have to rent a room for sex, because my apartment's filled with dead bodies. Don't worry. Only one of them was mine. We can have fun testing out the new body I cloned. You should see the size of my..." She was already headed for the exit.

That left only the bill. No problem. I wished for some gold coins and put them on the table – why not be generous? We snuck out.

"Natural elements are considered valuable due to limited supply. You are reducing the gold's value by introducing a new source. Such actions do not benefit the economic stability of your species."

As if my own conscience wasn't irritating enough.

"I promise not to make too much."

"I sense that you are frustrated due to unfulfilled arousal. I can accommodate if you wish."

He turned into the most devastatingly gorgeous woman I could possibly imagine – nude. I was in shock. I looked away, more or less terrified. Why, I couldn't really say. He changed back.

"I apologize for causing you discomfort, my friend. Evidently, your intellectual comfort conflicts intensely with your physical desires, causing great emotional turmoil."

"Don't worry about it. How about teaching me that mind-blocking trick?" There was no way he could have mimicked my fantasy woman if he wasn't in my head, I figured. I didn't realize that it was our merger that gave him the insight.

"From our visit to your public library, I learned that discussing one's inner feelings is a viable method of emotional healing."

I just couldn't deal with the thought of a having sex with a guy in a woman's body, alien or not. *"I'm fine. I don't need to talk about it."*

"As you wish, my friend. I will be available to you should you wish to alter your preconceptions."

"I said I don't want to talk about it!"

And we never did.

Martin Wolfe

The Morning After

Old Master

I was enjoying my morning cocoa, when a woman walked into the kitchen. She was fabulous, a total dream, wearing an elegant silk nightgown that promised marvelous things about her figure. But hey, I'm old. I can control myself.

"Hello. Are you one of Paul's...people?"

She said nothing.

My heart raced – weird.

"Have a seat." I got up to get her a mug of hot chocolate, which I make from scratch – nostalgia.

She stepped forward, slid her arms around my waist, and kissed me. Okay. A few minutes later, I remembered to breath. I was going to say something witty, but changed my mind and kissed her back – and then again.

She smiled shyly and moved away. I let her go, against my will. Hot chocolate had just been demoted. My new happiest thing left the way she came. I stood there wondering if I should follow, but I didn't want to scare her away. She'd come back, I told myself. It was my house, and she was already in it.

I went back to my hot chocolate, but I barely tasted it.

That was yesterday.

Before I knew.

I sat alone in the kitchen and ruminated about current events and suppressed memories. I sipped my hot chocolate – very, very slowly. I tried to remember to taste it.

She came in again.

But this time, she waited timidly by the door.

291

We said nothing.

I got up with my empty mug, walked to the cocoa pot, and poured myself another. I paused with my hands on the counter. Then I reached into the cupboard and pulled out another mug, which I filled. Then I walked back to the table and sat down, setting the second mug of hot chocolate on the table next to me. I pulled up another chair and went back to staring into my mug.

Hesitantly, delicately she sat in the chair next to me. We both sipped our cocoa.

About a million years later, give or take a million, I put my hand over hers.

It felt right. Sixty lifetimes of sadness became lighter within me.

I worked up the courage to look at her again. She was crying, with a big silly grin on her face – so beautiful.

I smiled for her, squeezed her hand, and sipped my hot chocolate. All was well in the universe.

About the Author

Martin Wolfe was born, not hatched, on a planet called Earth, which is a fancy word for dirt. Having no good way to escape such an unimaginative place, he decided to make the best of it. He proudly designed and built, partly with his own hands, a lovely lair with his beautiful wife, Alice, who is the most exceptional human being both willing and able to tolerate daily his odd way of thinking. Together, they discovered their daughter, Oneia, whom they are presently attempting to train into an exceptional human being, just like her mom. Things are progressing nicely.

If you happen to like this novel, the author wouldn't mind at all if you posted a glowing review and told thirty-seven or so of your closest friends.